TEACHING THE POSTSECONDARY MUSIC STUDENT

WITH DISABILITIES

Teaching the Postsecondary Music

Student with Disabilities

Kimberly A. McCord

OXFORD
UNIVERSITY PRESS

Oxford University Press is a department of the University of Oxford. It furthers
the University's objective of excellence in research, scholarship, and education
by publishing worldwide. Oxford is a registered trade mark of Oxford University
Press in the UK and certain other countries.

Published in the United States of America by Oxford University Press
198 Madison Avenue, New York, NY 10016, United States of America.

Library of Congress Cataloging-in-Publication Data
Names: McCord, Kimberly, author.
Title: Teaching the postsecondary music student with disabilities /
by Kimberly A. McCord.
Description: New York : Oxford University Press, 2016.
Identifiers: LCCN 2016018911 | ISBN 978–0–19–046776–0 (cloth : alk. paper) |
ISBN 978–0–19–046777–7 (pbk. : alk. paper) | ISBN 978–0–19–046780–7 (online content)
Subjects: LCSH: Music in universities and colleges. | Musicians with disabilities. |
Music—Instruction and study.
Classification: LCC MT18 .M16 2016 | DDC 780.71/1—dc23
LC record available at https://lccn.loc.gov/2016018911

9 8 7 6 5 4 3 2 1

Paperback printed by Webcom Inc., Canada
Hardback printed by Bridgeport National Bindery, Inc., United States of America

For Johanna, thanks for your support and patience, and Betty Atterbury, my early mentor. Dr. Atterbury was one of the first special music educators and an inspiration to all of us who came after her.

Contents

Acknowledgments

HEARTFELT THANKS TO my friends and colleagues who answered my questions that are specific to their expertise, including Elaine Bernstorf, Mary Adamek, Alice-Ann Darrow, Jennifer Wetzel-Thomas, Lyn Schrarer-Joiner, Markku Kaikkonen, Nancy O'Neill, Leah Crews, Sandy Colbs, Johanna Rayman, Lisa Tabaka, Nancy Harr, Stacey Jones-Bock, and Donna Zawatski. Thanks also to Illinois State University oboe professor, Judith Dicker and her former student, Jenna Blayney who share the cover of this book. I am humbled by my many former and current students who have disclosed their disabilities and explained their experiences of navigating schools of music with a disability. I appreciate Tristan Burgmann's willingness to talk openly about living with Crohn's Disease and deaf education students, Kaity Bricker and Molly Lesnik for modeling American Sign Langauge words in Chapter 10.

A special thanks to my friend and past co-editor, Deborah Blair Vanderlinde, for reading through everything and doing light editing for each chapter. Deb, your ability to catch even the smallest errors never ceases to amaze me! Finally a big thanks to Judith Jellison who suggested the topic; you are so very wise and I appreciate your support more than you will ever know.

About the Companion Website

www.oup.com/us/teachingthepostsecondarymusicstudentwithdisabilities

Oxford has created a website to accompany *Teaching the Postsecondary Music Student with Disabilities*. This site includes supplemental content such as videos and features that highlight principles throughout the book. Readers are encouraged to explore the site's additional content in conjunction with the content of this book.

TEACHING THE POSTSECONDARY MUSIC STUDENT

WITH DISABILITIES

1

DISABILITY-FRIENDLY SCHOOLS OF MUSIC

Helen is blind and uses a guide dog. She is a cellist and has been searching for an undergraduate program with a cello teacher who is experienced in teaching musicians with vision loss. Doing a Google search on her computer, she found one teacher at a midwestern university who is blind. The university is in another part of the country and Helen was hoping to live closer to home. She is planning to audition at several schools in her area in addition to the midwestern school with the cello professor with vision loss. She will also carefully interview the cello teachers at her local universities when she auditions to determine whether the teachers will be comfortable accommodating her lack of vision.

When she receives audition information, she is disappointed. For most schools, the information says nothing about accommodations for students with disabilities, and some say sight-reading may be required. She wonders whether the audition committee will allow her dog to accompany her and if she will be asked to sight-read. Sight-reading scores would need to be put into Braille music ahead of time. However, Helen prefers not to use Braille music because she cannot play the cello at the same time she reads the Braille score. She must first memorize short chunks of the music and play part of the music before continuing. Sight-reading puts her at a disadvantage when compared to typical cellists.

She begins by eliminating all schools that mention sight-reading in the audition information and she decides also to eliminate all schools that do not mention accommodations for students who require them. Helen believes schools that do not naturally think of being inclusive to students with disabilities will likely present too many challenges for her to be successful. She is accepted at the midwestern school after a wonderful audition and finding a welcoming atmosphere toward accommodating disability.

DISABILITY-FRIENDLY SCHOOLS OF MUSIC

Disability-friendly means anticipating the needs of all possible students with disabilities who might attend the school and setting supports in place that can be accessed if needed. Disability-friendly also refers to images on the university and school of music website and in printed materials. Buildings and the campus are accessible in disability-friendly universities, and someone has put thought into arranging students' schedules and providing accessible transportation and housing.

Many times, schools of music continue to operate the way they have always done in the past without thinking about the need to change. Some professors and administrators find it difficult to adjust the way they teach music students or they may be unaware of how to change. Schools have to be willing to challenge set-in-stone philosophies about what makes a great school of music and what music students should know and be able to do in one. Further, in regard to students knowing and being able to do something, *how* they do it seems to be just as important. For example, it is embarrassing to be required to wear a sleeveless concert dress if a student has had an arm amputation. Students who have difficulty if they are forced to learn through Braille music notation may learn extremely well when they can hear music on recordings or listen to their professor playing it.

Is it really essential that schools of music require sight-reading? If the student shows talent and promise in an audition, what more can a sight-reading requirement add to that? Some very talented and motivated students with disabilities are unable to sight-read in the traditional way, or they are exceptionally slow when reading music notation for the first time because of slower cognitive processing.

If a student with a physical disability plays his tuba using an adaptive device to press the valves of the instrument, is that acceptable? What if the device cannot be programmed to play alternative fingerings? If a percussionist develops muscular dystrophy while he is earning an undergraduate degree, can he perform his senior recital playing a virtual snare drum on his iPad? Physically, he can play with better accuracy and with less fatigue on his iPad.

MAKING YOUR SCHOOL OF MUSIC DISABILITY-FRIENDLY

Today's music students are less traditional than many of their professors. They are able to access apps and software programs to identify parallel octaves and fifths in their music theory assignments, they can use technology to help them identify pitches they tend to sing flat, and some can print a saxophone thumb rest on a 3-D printer if their original one breaks off.

Many students have invisible disabilities such as specified learning disabilities that will likely impact their ability to read music fluently. Others may have chronic mental health disorders that may impact their abilities in day-to-day situations. Students with anxiety disorders may experience an increase in symptoms as their student recitals, juries, and auditions approach, and students with stuttering disorders may struggle with communication or avoid verbal communication altogether.

In some ways it is easier to accommodate a disability that can be easily seen; however, invisible disabilities are high-incidence disabilities and are often the ones that professors discount or, in some cases, do not believe exist. High-incidence disabilities are more frequently occurring in the population than low-incidence disabilities. Many students choose not to disclose their disability to professors and sometimes to the university. If a professor notices students significantly struggling in a way that seems very different from most typical students, she might tell them that reading music seems difficult because she has noticed they make mistakes in sight-reading that don't seem comparable with their talent. If a professor approaches this sensitive situation in a kind and supportive manner, the student may feel safe enough to disclose the disability. If the student chooses not to disclose, the professor should not continue talking about it but perhaps approach it again at a later time when a similar issue emerges.

If your teaching is flexible and student-centered, you will likely be able to accommodate all students. Lessons can include some playing by ear as well as reading music. Imagine a certain period vocal style that can be taught through an excellent recorded model. Ask the student to prepare for his or her next lesson by listening to the recording and come to the lesson ready to sing in the style. The student and professor could then discuss how the vocal technique is performed and if the student produced it correctly. In jazz, musicians often learn by transcribing recordings by ear to figure out a particular musician's performance techniques or a composer's harmonizing methods. Experiencing music through listening and figuring music out by ear is becoming a lost art due to a heavy emphasis on notation reading skills. Including learning by ear helps to create some balance for students who are challenged with reading music.

Students who need to move or stand up should be encouraged to do this. For a musician with ADHD (attention deficit/hyperactivity disorder), this helps the student focus well. For a student with hearing loss, standing in stocking feet on a wood floor helps them to experience sound more clearly from other instruments. Using an iPad music reader system helps musicians with vision loss to customize the appearance of the music. These are a few examples of learning strategies that are different from the traditional ways a performer learns.

Students with disabilities should always be asked, "What would help you to approach this piece and learn it better? What can I do to help you?" This shows your own flexibility and willingness to support the student in overcoming barriers to learning music.

AUDITIONS

Auditions are stressful for everyone. If you are a musician with a disability, auditions can be disabling. Students with anxiety, students who are unable to sight-read, students who have physical disabilities that make them self-conscious about their appearance, or students with social issues such as autism all experience auditions as highly stressful.

At the minimum, schools of music should ask students in every application form if they need accommodations for a disability; even better would be a separate form that lists possible audition accommodations, such as the one in Figure 1.1.

Schools should include this page of the audition application along with a map showing accessible entries to the building where the audition will be held, including where elevators can be found, for all applicants. They should not wait for the student to request it. This demonstrates that the school of music believes accessibility is not an afterthought and encourages prospective students to feel comfortable disclosing their disability. If there is a quiet space away from others where a student can warm up and be undisturbed while waiting for the audition, it will help those with autism and some mental health issues. Label that place on the map as well. Accessible parking should also be shown. Think of a student who uses a walker trying to carry an instrument and move on possibly icy or snowy walkways. When a university considers how a student with a disability accesses a building and provides him or her with directions in advance, it is being disability-friendly.

For a student with vision loss, allow music to be enlarged in size, accessed as a PDF on a tablet reading device, or be available as an audio file that the student can listen to and then play sections from memory. Many musicians with vision loss have exceptional memory for sound and an excellent sense of pitch.

AUDITION APPLICATION

Thank you for your interest in _____ School of Music.

We take pride in offering inclusive auditions for everyone. If you have a documented disability that requires accommodations for your audition, please indicate which accommodations are needed and we will work with you to ensure a fair audition.

☐ I have a documented learning disability that impacts my ability to sight-read fluently. I would like to be excused from sight-reading on this audition.

☐ I have vision loss and am unable to read music. I will need sight-reading prepared in Braille.

☐ I have vision loss and am unable to read music. I would like to be excused from sight-reading on this audition.

☐ I have anxiety and would prefer to audition in a studio with a minimum amount of professors present.

☐ I have hearing loss and prefer to audition on a wood floor. I also need an ASL interpreter.

☐ I have a physical disability and need my audition to be in a wheel-chair accessible space.

☐ I have autism spectrum disorder or a communication disorder and would prefer communication skills not be considered as a part of my audition.

☐ I have a need not listed here, it is:

FIGURE 1.1 Audition Form

Consider using small studios with wood or tile floors with a minimum number of people in the room. Lighting should be very strong from a source other than fluorescent bulbs. The student should be allowed to either sit or stand. For some students with anxiety, sitting with their feet solidly on the floor helps to reduce anxiety. Welcome the student by offering your hand. However, if the student prefers not to shake hands, do not be insulted; some are not comfortable touching. Eye contact may be uncomfortable for some students. Try to limit your impressions of the student specifically to his or her musical skills.

Students with disabilities look carefully for signs of inclusive policies at universities and schools of music. Websites typically highlight student musicians who do not appear to have disabilities. If the school decides to not represent diversity in printed and online materials, it should at least make sure to include welcoming information for those with disabilities in text format (see Figure 1.2).

A review of the most frequently mentioned disability-friendly universities and music schools provides very few web pages that are inclusive or welcoming to students with disabilities. The Berklee College of Music is an exception. Their website has specific resources for music students with disabilities. The most impressive of resources is a course, PM-111, Essentials for Success: Opportunities for Academic

---

How Accessible Is a School of Music?

☐ A nondiscrimination statement appears on the website and in all printed materials.

☐ School of music material shows images of music students with disabilities.

☐ Website is accessible to those with vision and hearing loss.

☐ Audition forms ask if students need accommodations.

☐ Assistive technology and software is compatible for students with various disabilities.

☐ Written and verbal communications use person-first language.

☐ Music building(s) are accessible.

☐ Furniture is accessible. Persons who use wheelchairs are not relegated to the back of large classrooms and are able to sit in different places in the classroom. Tables are adjustable for students of different sizes and users of wheelchairs.

☐ Scholarships are fairly distributed; in other words, if a person has a disability that impacts sight-reading he or she is not denied a scholarship.

FIGURE 1.2 Checklist for Creating an Accessible School of Music

Success with Individualized and Small Group Support. This course is specifically designed to help students make a smooth transition to college life. Included in the course are opportunities for students to develop skills, behaviors, and attitudes necessary for academic and personal success in college (Mulvey, 2015).

In addition, there is a detailed web page titled Disability Services for Students that clearly explains the process of becoming a documented student with a disability at Berklee. In the most inclusive statement I found on various schools of music websites from universities reported to be disability-friendly, Berklee is the only one with welcoming language to students with disabilities: "The Disability Service staff in the Counseling and Advising Center offer students with physical, learning, health, and psychiatric disorders a wide array of supports to foster participation in, and enjoyment of, musical and educational opportunities, develop and maintain independence, and facilitate equal educational opportunities. These supports include access to classrooms, services, programs, and events at Berklee" (Berklee College of Music, 2015).

RECRUITMENT

It is unclear whether any schools of music specifically recruit or allocate special scholarships for students with disabilities. Haller (2006) investigated how prospective students with disabilities were recruited by universities. She found that other than occasional images of students with disabilities in recruitment literature, there appeared to be no specific efforts, such as cover letters targeted for students with disabilities explaining resources and policies. Less than half of universities surveyed mentioned disability services in recruitment literature and only 39% of schools that sent any general materials included information on how to register with the school's Disabled Student Services.

Under Section 504 of the Rehabilitation Act of 1973, postsecondary institutions that receive federal funds must reasonably accommodate individuals with disabilities and not discriminate against them. Discrimination would include limiting admission of qualified students with disabilities. The university is required once students are admitted, to provide reasonable accommodations, including allowing students to participate fully in required activities. Consider the following: a student with a physical disability is a saxophone student and the saxophone professor's studio is on the fourth floor of the music building that has no elevator. That student is denied reasonable accommodations and is also unable to participate fully in a required activity (studio lessons and saxophone quartet rehearsals).

Parking is another area that can cause inaccessibility for students with medical and physical disabilities. Often students cite the lack of enough accessible parking spaces close to buildings. Finding available routes to campus buildings, including accessible doors can be a nightmare for students with physical disabilities. Elevators that do not work cause students with some types of physical disabilities to miss class completely.

Kennedy (2000, p. 17) explains that campus attitudes can be larger barriers than architectural barriers. "They might put a ramp to the stage of the theater, but their policy doesn't allow students with disabilities to audition for the play." This could apply to music as well.

Another barrier that is often reported by students is poor faculty attitudes toward students with disabilities. Students with disabilities stated that faculty attitudes, including full cooperation and support of accommodations, are the most important factors in student success (Nelson, Dodd, & Smith, 1990). Not only was the faculty at times unsupportive, but many lack training about how to effectively include students with disabilities (Wilson, Getzel, & Brown, 2000).

Individuals with disabilities continue to lack access to higher education. Young people without degrees in higher education have higher unemployment rates and poverty levels. Stodden (1998) reported poverty levels for people with disabilities who are college educated at 15%, while poverty levels among people without college educations are 50%. Access to a college education is critical for success in life.

Campus mental health centers and disability services offices are often overwhelmed and underfunded. There are not enough experts on staff in the disability services offices who are knowledgeable about how to accommodate students' diverse needs (Thomas, 2000).

Once students are on campus, are there easy-to-find resources for obtaining help? In a recent survey of college students by Gruttadaro and Crudo (2012), 64% of students reported there was either no useful information, or students didn't know whether there was helpful information on mental health on the university website. College students expressed ways that websites were helpful for students with mental health concerns:

1. The website provides information about resources available on and off campus.
2. The website allows students to make appointments online.
3. The website has an online mental health screening tool for students that links them to help when needed.
4. The website includes frequently asked questions about mental health.
5. The website shares information on where and how to access accommodations and free mental health services and supports (Gruttadaro & Crudo, 2012).

University websites are often not user-friendly or did not meet content accessibility standards (Flowers, Bray, & Algozzine, 2001). Students with disabilities are underrepresented in images shown in printed materials and on websites compared to depictions of racial diversity, yet people with disabilities are the largest minority group in the United States with more than 56.7 million people reporting a legally defined disability (US Census, 2012). Images of students with disabilities in printed materials and websites were not diverse in regard to disability. Haller (2006, 1995) found that students in wheelchairs were depicted most frequently (54%), followed by students with hearing loss (images with hearing aids or cochlear implants) (9.9%), vision loss (8.8%), and cerebral palsy (7%). All of these are low-incidence disabilities. Do students with disabilities looking at recruitment materials and websites see themselves in these images? Probably not.

POSTSECONDARY MUSIC STUDENTS WITH DISABILITIES

Once students are accepted and enrolled, new challenges emerge, and access to education remains a barrier. The student must prove that he or she has a documented disability and advocate for the types of accommodations needed (Stodden et al., 2001). This becomes a problem for music students who might need specific music-related assistive technology that staff in the disability services office do not understand. For example, students with vision loss who need software to complete their music theory assignments will require very specific types of computers, voice-activated software, and music notation software that works with voice-activated programs. There is no other way to complete assignments unless the student with vision loss relies on another student to dictate assignments, and then the student with vision loss has no way to check the assignment for accuracy. Music technology enables the student with vision loss to hear assignments played back through the computer or MIDI (musical instrument digital interface) device. Schools of music should be proactive when interventions are needed in order to make sure music students with disabilities have accommodations, and in particular, unusual music-related accommodations that disability services staff have no experience with.

There are many opportunities for students to be overlooked once they enter college. In high school, the student's special educator and his or her parents were likely looking out for him or her, but in college, students have to be very strong self-advocates to make sure all aspects of their educational and living needs are met. At Berklee, students with disabilities receive some support and direction from their advisors. The advisor is a good person to look out for music students with disabilities, but it is essential that these professionals be trained on how to direct students to the proper resource. Some may be unsure if the student has a disability. Students with disabilities get the best support when they disclose their disability to everyone who has an impact on their education.

Schools of music can help by establishing a culture of acceptance for all students. Instead of expecting students to function in an environment that requires everyone to think, test, and make music the same way, schools of music can become more inclusive and accessible for all by using principles of universal design that allow for greater flexibility.

An excellent resource that many students and their families refer to when considering where to attend college is the *K & W Guide to Colleges for Students with Learning Differences*. In its 12th edition, the book reviews more than 350 schools focusing on admission policies, accommodations offered, graduation requirements, and disability services available. Although there is no specific information on music programs, many prospective students and their families use the guide to identify universities that have disability-friendly policies in place. Size of university and overall ratings of universities in the annual US News and World Report ratings of the top schools in the United States give little indication of whether a school is disability-friendly. Many well-known universities with high rankings score low in disability-friendly ratings.

Currently, the most disability-friendly music degree-granting school is the Berklee College of Music. As a college founded on diversity, it naturally leans toward inclusivity of students in curriculum, in assessment, and in universal design of facilities—no small feat for a school retrofitted into former hotels in an older neighborhood in Boston. Berklee has been on the cutting edge of accepting students with disabilities, including Tony DeBlois, a musician with autism. The story of Tony's growth as a musician during his years at Berklee was made into a movie in 1997 called *Journey to the Heart*.

SUMMARY

This chapter has helped to identify simple strategies to making auditions, websites, printed materials, and faculty and staff more welcoming to musicians with disabilities.

- Using images and text in promotional materials and websites that demonstrate inclusion and valuing neurodiversity.
- Designing flexible audition policy that ensures the best possible setting for the auditioning student to experience success.
- Ensuring that faculty and staff are trained or know where to go for help with inclusion strategies.
- Having a trained staff or faculty member who is aware of various types of assistive technology needed specifically for musicians.
- Employing universally designed curriculum, classrooms, and websites.

Disability-friendly schools of music are a relatively new concept. Many universities are disability-friendly overall, but the supports and inclusive practices do not always trickle down into schools of music.

Schools of music can easily make some simple changes in recruitment, auditions, and supports during the degree program along with effective training of faculty and staff. When purchasing furniture and designing classrooms, rehearsal, and concert spaces, universal design principles should be incorporated to create a more welcoming music learning environment for all.

2

TRANSITION TO POSTSECONDARY MUSIC EDUCATION

Kerry is a 16-year-old-high school student with Down syndrome. She is passionate about music and her favorite rock star, Katy Perry. Kerry has been playing guitar in a community-based rock band for adults and high school students with intellectual disabilities. She can sing and play guitar at the same time and reads adapted music notation.

Kerry has a transition plan developed by her Individual Education Program (IEP) Team at her high school. The plan was developed with Kerry and is based on her interests and goals as an adult. Kerry would like to be a musician and she also enjoys very young children. She can teach music in pre-schools as an adult. She is able to play simple songs on her guitar and lead activities with young children if another adult teacher is present. She would also like to continue to play with peers in rock bands and earn college ensemble credit for her participation.

Her local university is developing a transition program for high school students with disabilities who want to enter two- or four-year degree programs. The program brings high school students to the college campus twice a week for courses that they take with typical peers. Special education students take a transition skills course with the transition high school students, and a number of activities are embedded in the course that prepare them for independent functioning in higher education. Kerry's IEP team has inquired about the possibility of an Advanced Placement course in music that would allow Kerry to play in a rock band with music education majors and earn college credit. Playing with the rock band would work similarly to the transition course; Kerry would study with typical peers focusing on skills to help prepare her for music courses and ensembles in college.

WHAT IS TRANSITION TO POSTSECONDARY EDUCATION?

Young people with disabilities need to be able to learn skills that will allow them to secure employment, pursue postsecondary education opportunities, participate in the community, live independently, and engage in social/recreational activities (Gargiulo, 2012). Youth without disabilities, for the most part, do not need formal support to make the transition to adulthood. Transition to adulthood is an important goal that for most individuals with disabilities remains unattainable. Consider these statistics from various national surveys:

- Only one-third (32%) of working-age people with disabilities were employed on average in the 2010–2012 period, compared to more than two-thirds (72.7%) of people without disabilities (Kruse, Schur, & Ali, 2010, pp. 31–78).
- Completion of high school by students with disabilities is improving (61%) but still lags behind the graduation rate of students without disabilities (80%) according to the most recent statistics based on the 2011–2012 school year. However, those statistics range from a low of 24% in Nevada to 79% in Arkansas (Stetser & Stillwell, 2014).
- Employment rates for youth with disabilities (ages 20 to 24) in the most recent report from the US Department of Labor for August 2014 are 31.6% as compared to 65% for youth without disabilities (2015).
- In 2013, the employment rate for working-age people (ages 21 to 64) with disabilities working part-time or full-time was 34.5% and the percentage of people with disabilities working full-time/full-year was 21.5% (Erickson, Lee, & von Schrader, 2014).
- In 2013, the poverty rate for individuals with disabilities (18 to 64) living in US communities (non-institutionalized) was 28.7%, while the poverty rate of individuals without disabilities (18 to 64) living in the community was 13.6%—a poverty gap of 15.1%. (US Census Bureau, 2014).
- Cornell University reports that an estimated 32.1% of civilian, non-institutionalized men and women with a work limitation, aged 21 to 64 in the United States, lived in families with incomes below the poverty line (vonSchrader & Lee, 2015).

- The highest poverty rate is among individuals with cognitive disabilities. In 2013, that figure was 34.6%, while the lowest rate was among people with hearing loss at 20.6% (Erickson, Lee, & von Schrader, 2014).
- The median household income for families of working-age people with disabilities in 2013 was $39,400; in comparison, the household income for families without disabilities was $62,000 (Erickson, Lee, & von Schrader, 2014).
- The percentage of individuals ages 21 to 64 with disabilities who had a bachelor's degree or more in the United States was 13.5%; for individuals without disabilities (21 to 64) the percentage was 32.1% (Erickson, Lee, & von Schrader, 2014).
- For individuals with disabilities who achieved a bachelor's degree or more in 2013, the highest rate was for individuals with hearing loss (17.1), followed by individuals with vision loss (13.7), physical disabilities that impact movement (11.5), those unable to manage basic grooming, toileting, or feeding (10.8), people with cognitive disabilities (10.1) and those unable to live independently without support from another adult (10.0) according to Cornell University (Erickson, Lee, & von Schrader, 2014).
- About one in three adults with disabilities is very satisfied with life in general compared to 61% of adults without disabilities (Harris & Associates, 2004).

This is a particularly bleak prospect for many with disabilities and as a society it is unacceptable. Individuals with disabilities who are fortunate enough to have postsecondary certificates or degrees have the highest possibilities of gainful employment and happiness in their adult lives. We are in the midst of a slow movement toward ensuring better opportunities for young people with disabilities by guaranteeing them equal access to education and employment training after completion of high school. This is the central focus of transition planning that begins at age 16 and annually thereafter for all students in high school with IEPs.

The current federal law, PL 108-446 (IDEA, or Individuals with Disabilities Education Improvement Act, 2004), stipulates that each student with a disability is to receive transition services, which are defined as a coordinated set of activities for a student with a disability that

A. Is designed within a results-oriented process, focused on improving the academic and functional achievement of the child with a disability to facilitate the child's movement from school to post-school activities, including post-secondary education, vocational training, integrated employment (including supported employment), continuing and adult education, adult services, independent living, or community participation;

B. Is based upon the child's needs, taking into account the child's strengths, preferences, and interests; and

C. Includes instruction, related services, community experiences, the development of employment and other post-school adult living objectives, and when appropriate, acquisition of daily living skills and functional vocational evaluation. [20 U.S.C. § 1401 (34)]

Gargiulo (2012) recognizes that students need experiences beyond the high school curriculum to prepare them for an independent and satisfying adult life. Many students with more involved disabilities have the opportunity to continue high school until their 22nd birthday; however, schools lose their relevance after four years because typical students and students with mild disabilities graduate and leave school at 18 (Hall, Kleinert, & Kearns, 2000; Moon, Grigal, & Neubert, 2001). Students who learn in an authentic, integrated environment are more likely to secure employment and live in their communities rather than transitioning to institutional living settings. Recreation, transportation and mobility, social, and other skills for adulthood are emphasized in these authentic communities (Neubert, Moon, & Grigal, 2002). Other researchers recommend that the time between ages 18 and 21 be used to engage in seamless transitioning and services between families, schools, and adult services and natural supports to ensure success for individuals with disabilities (Hart, Zimbrich, & Ghiloni, 2001).

A 10-year longitudinal study sampling more than 11,000 students in special education who were 13 to 16 years old on December 1, 2000, followed these students as they moved out of secondary school and into adult roles (Wagner et al., 2005). Attending college and postsecondary vocational programs greatly increases the likelihood that individuals will obtain employment and experience happiness and success as an adult. The National Longitudinal Transition Study-2 (NLTS-2) reported that students who did not have transition plans that stipulated postsecondary education often did not receive any formal training after high school. Only 31% of out-of-school young people with disabilities who had no transition plan goals of seeking postsecondary education were enrolled in postsecondary school in the two years since leaving high school. This is much lower than the 77% of students who had transition plans that included attending postsecondary education as part of their education goals written into their transition high school plans (Wagner et al., 2005).

A college degree is not a guarantee of employment, but it does greatly improve the possibilities of a job with increased earning and satisfaction in the chosen career. Individuals with disabilities who obtain a postsecondary certificate or degree can expect to have better health, greater self-confidence, increased career options, higher-level problem-solving skills, improved interpersonal relationships, and a higher level of open-mindedness as well as increased involvement in their communities, recreation, and other interests adults enjoy (Madaus, 2006). It is also known that individuals with postsecondary education become less dependent on their parents and government benefits than will their peers who do not pursue postsecondary education (Turnbull et al., 2003).

Denying opportunities to postsecondary education for individuals with disabilities has become a critical injustice that our society can no longer ignore. It should not be acceptable that literally millions of people leave high school with little preparation for postsecondary education. Higher education can blame high school special educators and administrators, while possibly many colleges quietly hope that the low demand for education by populations of students with disabilities remains that way in order to save dwindling university financial resources. Perhaps parents worry that sending their child away from home or into an environment that lacks the consistent support systems of high school opens up possibilities for bullying, sexual abuse, and other dangers. These are all realities of life for many youth with disabilities. However, there are universities and programs that can serve as exemplars for other institutions.

TRANSITIONING YOUNG ADULTS WITH DISABILITIES TO POSTSECONDARY EDUCATION

Often transition programs are launched by a small group of individuals or even just one person who introduces the idea of expanding opportunities for students with disabilities at two- or four-year colleges. There are very successful programs that have increased graduation rates among students with specified learning disabilities, ADHD, and mild autism disorders as well as more specific programs for students with intellectual disabilities, severe physical disabilities, and chronic medical conditions. Schools of music are often exceptions to these programs. If they do offer classes, these are likely to be music appreciation-type programs, with actual music-making opportunities lacking for those who would like to participate.

Adamek and Darrow (2012) pointed out that involvement as an active music maker in the school curriculum develops important transition skills in self-determination, flexibility, self-esteem, and socialization. Jellison (1999) states, "We need to develop teaching goals and research questions about transitions across 'real-world' music environments—transitions across a variety of school and non-school music environments throughout childhood and adulthood." I am not sure all transition teams think about music being included in transition plans alongside skills in cooking and learning to ride the bus.

HIGH-INCIDENCE DISABILITIES

For students with high-incidence disabilities (learning disabilities, ADHD, and chronic mental illness), the NLTS2 study found that these groups are often lacking in skills in creating positive social networks that help them to strengthen their opportunities for employment, community involvement, and leadership. The study also showed positive indications of social involvement: 64% of individuals with disabilities were registered to vote, and 46% volunteered or engaged in community activities. Negative factors included high levels of involvement in the criminal-justice system: 35% of males with disabilities and 19% of females reported having been arrested; 20% of these men and 8% of these women had spent a night in police custody (Wagner et al., 2005).

Adolescents with high-incidence disabilities often experience perceptual, sensory, and other process-oriented developmental differences that impact the development of interpersonal relationships important for success in career and life (Trainor et al., 2013). The social stigma of having a disability often leads to social rejection, which in turn leads to diminished social opportunities for young adults with high-incidence disabilities. High-incidence disabilities occur in over half of all youth who receive special education services while in high school; it is critical that addressing social skills and working on issues of self-esteem and self-determination be included in their transition training goals (Durlak, Rose, & Bursuck, 1994). NLTS2 found that 87% of high school students with learning disabilities received some kind of support, but once they entered college only 19% continued to receive support (Wagner et al., 2005). In addition, for all students with disabilities, most will experience greater acceptance by professors and peers if they are able to develop the confidence to talk about their disability with others (Ashmore, 2010).

It is very common for high-incidence students to be enrolled in schools of music. Some may be considered twice exceptional, as they are talented in music or other areas but have a disability such as dyslexia that impacts their music and academic learning. If the student has learned to hide the disability by dazzling others with his or her talent as a musician, teachers may have overlooked it, and special educators may have been able to help the student acquire strategies for learning with that particular disability during the K-12 years. Or a student with anxiety, who needed no treatment during high school because his or her school environment was relatively low stress, may experience debilitating anxiety when he or she first is expected to perform solo for other peers in a studio master class or, for a music education student, it may appear the first time he or she stands in front of a class of children. Because of the negative experience of the master class or possibly a studio professor's lack of empathy, the student may develop an intense fear of performing.

Music school is very different from high school music programs. Students are less able to hide their disabilities, and their lack of social awareness may not be tolerated by the dozens of professors they encounter during their four years in college. Moreover, before college, students had parents who learned to step in and rescue children by propping up their bruised egos; now the students often experience a lack of emotional support when they are suddenly without that understanding network of help. Students who feel inadequate may begin to sink into depression for the first time in their lives or, if they are defensive about their disability and unwilling to disclose it to others, it is likely they will resist seeking help for depression.

Ultimately, it is the student's responsibility to learn to seek help including disclosing to others when they need that help, but the reality is that very few actually are able to take steps to resolve their difficulties (Sparks, 2015). Professors and music administrators often see signs of music students crashing. In my teaching experience, I might have had one student a year fail or withdraw from music education; in one recent semester alone, I had three fail and one student on the edge of failing due to a serious depression that set in at mid-term. This was in a class of just 17 students.The increase in numbers of students with mental health disorders is partly due to this change, but in recent years of declining enrollments in postsecondary education, schools of music that might not have accepted students who demonstrated unusual social skills, anxiety or other behaviors that may have kept them from being accepted over a similar student with a more engaging personality.

Students with learning disabilities and attention disorders often get to the end of their first semester on music theory and find they are failing. In truth, many were behind in assignments or were simply unable to complete exams before the class ended. They could have received accommodations, but large numbers of students with high-incidence disabilities do not disclose their disabilities to the disability services office or to music professors. When they get to the end of semester and find they are failing, they do not have the social skills or confidence to ask for help and instead continue to hide their disability only to hurt themselves in the end. This could be addressed better through one of the many models for transition to postsecondary education and transition support programs once the student enters college.

Berklee College of Music has a course for students with disabilities that acts as a sort of transition to a music school in a very highly competitive program in the heart of a busy city. The course, Essentials for Success, is described as an opportunity for students to develop skills, behaviors, and attitudes necessary for academic and personal success in college. Skills that are addressed include time management, study methods, learning style, faculty relationships, critical campus resources, test-taking strategies, learning the important people and places on campus including who to ask for help, and academic policies and procedures. The course is taught in small classes in a discussion format to support the formation of peer relationships and study groups (Mulvey, 2015).

I imagine that students who take advantage of this course experience a much easier transition to music school and for the most part are able to feel that they can ask for help should they begin to struggle academically or personally. Berklee benefits when students stay in school, achieve musically and socially, and continue on to productive careers in music. Although there are no published statistics on the success of this class, it seems like a relatively easy step that all schools of music could implement to ease the transition of students who are at risk for failure in school.

LOW-INCIDENCE DISABILITIES

Many individuals with intellectual disabilities, vision loss, hearing loss, physical and chronic medical disabilities, and those on the autism spectrum have aspirations of becoming musicians, music teachers, music therapists, or other music professionals. It is critical that their high school IEP teams prepare them for college; doing so is also a challenge, and for students with high-incidence disabilities and especially autism and intellectual disabilities, it is also difficult. Again, many universities and programs have found highly effective ways not only to support these students' transition to postsecondary education, but also have increased opportunities for typical students to interact with them in courses, clubs, sports, and other university activities.

Students with intellectual disabilities often attend community college or four-year universities. Most do not complete degrees but instead attain certificates that involve college courses (either separate courses or inclusive courses they take with typical peers), and courses designed to prepare them for jobs, independent living, and other essential skills for success in the adult world. Many are dually enrolled in high school and college as part of their transition plans. Dual enrollment is particularly effective as part of a transition plan if a university or community college is available in the same community as the student's high school.

When dually enrolled, the student attends the high school for part of the day or every other day and the college for the other time. Many students are also employed at the university—another important transition goal. Employment of students with intellectual disabilities (either dually enrolled or those attending postsecondary education after high school) has been increasing on college campuses, from 30% in the 2010–2011 school year to 39% in the 2013–2015 academic year (Diament, 2015).

When students with intellectual, physical, chronic medical disabilities, and autism reach age 22, they officially age-out of high school, and they need help making the transition to the adult world. High schools that collaborate with local postsecondary institutions on transition plans for these students offer important experiences that give them better preparation for the outside world than can be achieved in the self-contained classrooms in the high school. Self-contained special education transition classrooms train young adults for isolation in segregated work and day programs, or to stay at home, despite decades of evidence that people with intellectual, communication, and physical disabilities can work and learn in integrated settings (Rogan & Rinne, 2011). Students need to learn in authentic environments with typical same-age college peers in order to experience college in the actual setting.

Community-based instruction for job preparation has been successfully used for decades as part of transition planning services. However, college-based instruction is relatively new (Grigal, Neubert, & Moon, 2001; Hart, Zimbrich, & Parker, 2005; Stodden & Whelley, 2004), inspired by the federal Higher Education Opportunity Act (HEOA) (PL 110-315) of 2008. HEOA contains provisions that improve access to postsecondary education for students with intellectual disabilities and to the Think College initiative (Rogan et al., 2014).

The transition language in IDEA (2004) specifically states that the student's strengths, preferences, and interests should be part of the goals considered when the transition plan is developed. If a student desires to teach in a pre-school, where will he or she best learn how to do this? Probably by taking course work and learning to teach actual pre-school children under supervision, just as other college students do. And their chances of becoming a good teacher of pre-school children increase if they learn alongside other typical same-age college students.

Transition plans of students with intellectual disabilities that identify their positive strengths and traits and develop ways for them to use these strengths with others increase the possibilities for these young adults to have meaningful careers and happiness in adulthood (Carter et al., 2015; Dykens, 2006; Shogren et al., 2006). Society has long segregated and relegated individuals with intellectual disabilities to factory assembly jobs, such as washing dishes in restaurants, and other jobs that may not tap their interests or abilities. Reinders (2011) cautions that it can be difficult to collaborate with community connections and colleges when individuals with disabilities are described by their deficits alone. All people, including those with significant disabilities, have strengths that they can share with others.

Young people with autism are often described by their deficits: difficulties in social communication; restricted, repetitive patterns of behavior and interests; trouble with transitions and change; and anxiety (Smith et al., 2012; Wehmeyer et al., 2010; White et al., 2009). Individuals with autism can also be described as exceptionally good problem solvers, experts on subjects or activities that interest them, and quick to learn when information is presented visually. If a person with autism was interested in musical instruments and in particular, how they work, the individual might attend college and take instrumental methods courses alongside music education majors learning how to play different instruments to help prepare for a career as an instrument repairperson. The student might work part-time with the university instrument repairperson who keeps school-owned instruments working for various ensembles and the music methods courses.

A list of universities that provide training and certified programs, including individualized and group support services for students with autism spectrum disorders, can be found at www.CollegeAutismSpectrum.com. The schools are listed by state, with an additional list of universities that offer summer programs specifically designed for students with autism entering college.

Students with physical disabilities or chronic health disorders have additional transition considerations that include personal assistance services and assistive technology (Targett et al., 2013). Personal assistance services help the individual maintain well-being, comfort, safety, personal appearance, and interactions within the community and society as a whole (Holt, Chambless, & Hammond, 2006). Personal assistants allow the person to participate more fully in community settings and activities, including employment. During childhood and adolescence, the personal assistant tasks are typically carried out by parents and other caregivers. In school, teachers, aides, or occasionally other students perform personal assistance. However, essential to transition goals, personal assistance needs to relate to employment, college, and other community-based environments (Turner, 2007).

Assistive technology (AT) equipment and procedures help individuals to gain more control, independence, and efficiency in day-to-day activities. AT is also important to help them with communication and to access devices that increase interaction with others so they can participate more fully in employment, postsecondary education, and social activities. Many devices that are often thought of as music technology can actually be music assistive technology. For example, one popular improvisation and composing program, Band-in-a-Box, now works with voice commands so that individuals with limited mobility or vision loss can use the software when coupled with certain types of hardware. A vocalist with cerebral palsy may be able to practice vocal warm-ups with Band-in-a-Box supplying the piano accompaniment. Music students with physical or medical disabilities need time to learn complex software and other AT devices. Transitions allow the student to come to the school of music during high school and learn to use the devices and software in the music technology lab alongside college students who are also in the lab using music technology. This is also a valuable opportunity for social interactions and to receive peer teaching of music software by others who use it themselves.

Transition planning is important in identifying universities that are equipped to house and transport students with severe physical disabilities, and to accommodate their specific needs (Targett et al., 2013). For more information, read about the University of Illinois, a disability-friendly university with exceptional supports for students with physical and medical disabilities (see www.oup.com/us/teachingthepostsecondarymusicstudentwithdisabilities).

TRANSITION EXEMPLARS

Programs sponsored by universities and others to prepare students for transition are occurring in the summer as a type of summer camp experience. Landmark College and Winston Preparatory School offer a nine-day non-residential program for college-bound high school graduates and rising seniors at Winston Preparatory School in New York City. Students enrolled in the program prepare for challenges they will encounter in the college setting and have mock college application reviews with college admission representatives. Parents are also offered sessions on how to support their child in the transition to college. In addition, Landmark College offers a residential summer program at the campus in Putney, Vermont. Skills that are targeted during the transition program include these:

- Learning to articulate individual learning issues that need attention
- Learning how to identify the specific supports and accommodations students will need in college and how to access the supports
- Practice enrolling in a freshman lecture class and other courses freshmen usually take
- Using self-advocacy skills students need to navigate the freshman year
- Learning to apply organizational skills, helpful habits, and useful behaviors students need to succeed at college, and how to identify problem habits and behaviors that might surface during their first year (Landmark College, 2015)

McDaniel College in Maryland offers a five-day, early move-in transition program for incoming freshmen. The program, McDaniel Step Ahead, gives students with disabilities the chance to acclimate to college before the other students move in for the fall semester. The program focuses on equipping students with the academic, independent living, and social skills required for being in residence at college. During the five days, students take workshops on classroom etiquette, time management, study and test-taking skills, and organization. Different learning styles are also addressed along with accommodations and assistive technology to help students manage through their college career. Peer mentors are provided and attend the five-day program with their mentees.

Tips for creating a bridge program similar to the McDaniel College model can be found at http://www.disabilitycomplianceforhighereducation.com/m-article-detail/5-day-program-helps-students-with-disabilities-transition-to-college-more-smoothly.aspx for postsecondary institutions interested in providing short programs to acclimate students with disabilities to campus (Gomez, 2015).

SITE at Indiana University-Purdue University Indianapolis (IUPUI) is another outstanding postsecondary program for students with intellectual disabilities. The program is in partnership with the Indianapolis Public Schools and provides a one- to two-year postsecondary program for students. SITE stands for Skills for Independence, Transition and Employment. SITE students are not working toward a college degree but are participating in an innovative non-school (community-based) transition service option for young adults ages 18 to 21. Students who complete the program earn a Certificate of Completion from the Indianapolis Public Schools.

SITE students do audit college classes based on interest but do not receive a grade. SITE students can audit a number of classes, including music classes like the History of Rock and Roll and Survey of Urban African-American Music. One of the outcomes for SITE students is employment. SITE is free to students and their families. A teacher, an instructional assistant, and a part-time job coach from the school district work with approximately eight students (Rogan, Updike, Chesterfield, & Savage, 2014).

Many schools of music offer camps for high school students in the summer and are, therefore, comfortable with summer programs for high school students. If the disability services office collaborated with the school of music on designing and implementing a program, then a similar program geared toward music students with disabilities could be offered. Schools of music would need to identify students in the audition process and follow-up with all students who disclose a disability. Using strategies from the Berklee course mentioned earlier in this chapter and skills Landmark College teaches in their summer course, a short residential program could be offered to introduce music students with disabilities to various skills and procedures they need to know to be successful in their first year of college. Suggested topics to be covered include these:

- Audition procedures for ensembles
- Expectations of studio professors
- Recitals and preparing for recitals
- Concert attire
- Where to practice and how to schedule practice time
- Finding and using the music library
- Degree requirements and the importance of regularly seeing the advisor
- Organizational skills
- Finding tutors for music theory and other subjects
- The disability services center and accommodations
- The student counseling center and the student health center
- Concert etiquette and concert facilities

Universities that have created postsecondary programs for students with intellectual and developmental disabilities, including autism, are becoming more common each year. Universities that find ways to accept students with diverse learning needs demonstrate that higher learning is really more concerned with whom they accept rather than whom they do not accept.

The George Mason University LIFE (Learning into Future Environments) Program is described as a supportive academic university experience offering a four-year curriculum of study to postsecondary students 18 to 23 years old with intellectual and developmental disabilities (George Mason University, 2015). This program is an excellent example of full integration into special topics or courses offered at the university. The special topics classes permit faculty to adapt and modify class assignments and exams as needed. Inclusive course offerings listed in the LIFE brochure include Public Speaking, Debate, Visual Arts, Japanese, Judo, Karate, Dance, Golf, Astronomy, Social Work, Newspaper Workshop, Technical Theater, Acting, Classical Music, Drawing, Piano, and World Religion. Second- through fourth-year students have job experiences in the campus libraries, mail services, the child development center, and the aquatic and fitness center. A residential component encourages development of independent living.

Temple University in Philadelphia offers a four-semester certificate program providing individuals with intellectual disabilities an authentic college experience while developing vocational skills and career aspirations. The Academy for Adult Learning offers academic courses in addition to a weekly seminar exploring college life and career options based on individual students' interests and goals. Each Academy student is matched with a mentor who is a Temple student, and together mentors and mentees participate in a wide variety of activities, events, and organizations within Temple University. Students enrolled in the Academy must have the ability to pay for classes through service funds or privately and have transportation to Temple. Students are expected to participate in extracurricular activities for a minimum of 10 hours a week. Students also complete a semester-long, three-hour-weekly internship that provides them with work experience and support on maintaining basic employment skills such as attendance, punctuality, following directions, and co-worker relationships. All internships take place on the Temple University campus. Students are placed according to their career interests. The basic principles of the Academy for Adult Learning are these:

- The program is an authentic learning experience.
- Academy students determine and direct the support they need.
- Academy students select their own course load according to interest.
- In addition to their academic courses, Academy students are enrolled in a weekly seminar focusing on building success in college and in the workplace.
- Academy students complete a one-semester, weekly internship located on the Temple campus.
- Academy students develop relationships with other Temple students to gain support and guidance in reaching positive academic, career, and personal goals.

Temple has an extensive application that is available online at http://disabilities.temple.edu/programs/inclusive/aal.shtml that would be helpful for universities considering similar programs (Miller, 2015).

The Virginia Commonwealth University ACE-IT in College program began in 2001 for students with learning disabilities. Since then VCU has expanded the program to include students with traumatic brain injuries, intellectual disabilities, autism, and more recently, veterans with traumatic brain injuries, spinal cord injuries, or post-traumatic stress disorder. The university just completed a five-year demonstration grant funded by the US Department of Education, Office of Postsecondary Education, to further develop their inclusive postsecondary education experience and career development.

Students with intellectual disabilities, traumatic brain injuries, autism spectrum disorder, or multiple disabilities commit to a 30-month college and work experience. Students pay their own tuition and fees and provide their own transportation. All students accepted into the program have graduated with a modified standard or special diploma and have a strong interest in attending college. The ACE-IT brochure lists what students can in return expect from their VCU college experience:

- A person-centered plan to discover student career goals and course selection
- An individualized program, up to six credits per semester, with core courses and electives from the VCU class schedule
- Service-learning courses that blend campus and community life
- Work experience opportunities
- Education and job coaches for on-campus support
- Access to campus social activities and student clubs (Virginia Commonwealth University, 2015)

One of the first inclusive university programs is DO-IT at the University of Washington. The DO-IT Scholars program begins for most students in the sophomore year of high school. Assistive technology is an important component of DO-IT, providing students with computer equipment, assistive devices, and Internet access in their homes. AT includes sophisticated devices for individuals who are blind, those with disabilities that impact the ability to read, alternative keyboards for individuals who lack the use of their hands, and communication devices that enable students to develop social relationships. Mentoring and peer support are provided to each scholar. Sessions are held each summer for the scholars at the university to help students learn to maneuver around campus, request disability services and accommodations, and learn to live with roommates and succeed in college courses (Burgstahler, 2007).

The University of Iowa's REACH program is a residence program that offers a certificate for completion of a two-year program designed for individuals with intellectual disabilities and autism. REACH has a strong music component; music therapy students and professors offer drumming sessions to help relieve stress in students and to develop community among the REACH students.

DePaul University in Chicago has the PLuS program, which stands for The Productive Learning Strategies Program that is designed to assist students with learning disabilities, ADHD, Asperger syndrome, obsessive-compulsive disorder, and bipolar disorder. This is the only program that specifically reaches out to students with mental illness.

Finally, SUCCEED at the University of Missouri St. Louis is a certificate program that received the Governor's Council on Disability Annual Inclusion Award in 2013. The program is for students with intellectual and developmental disabilities. The

SUCCEED website points out that the purpose is to encourage and develop pathways toward student independence through three program pillars: academics, vocational experiences, and residential and student life (University of Missouri St. Louis, 2015) and offers scholarships to prospective students. The Department of Music is a sponsor with courses, lessons, and work opportunities available through the UMSL Department of Music. To my knowledge at the time of publication, it is the only exemplary program that has a strong link to the university music program. More information on SUCCEED is available at their website, http://www.umsl.edu/~pcs/succeed.

CAUTIONS FROM STUDENTS WHO ENTERED COLLEGE

Many students with disabilities are not told of certain problems that may occur if they choose an accommodation. For example, an asterisk appears next to all SAT scores that were taken with an extra time accommodation. How will prospective universities perceive that?

Disclosure is a choice, but it is also essential for students to be successful in college. Enclosing disability documentation with admissions applications may negatively impact the school's decision to accept the student; instead the student should turn in documentation directly to the disability services office.

Students with disabilities probably should ask professors not to mention their disability in letters of recommendation. Again, this could negatively impact employment prospects if the potential employer sees the disability as a potential problem. For example, someone with cystic fibrosis applying to be a music teacher may not get an interview if the school district worries that the person would be absent frequently because of illness or even die. The applicant might actually have a mild case of cystic fibrosis that is very well managed.

GETTING WITH THE PROGRAM

If your university isn't mentioned here or listed in the 20 incredible colleges for students with special needs at http://www.bestcollegesonline.com/blog/2011/09/21/20-incredible-colleges-for-special-needs-students/, it might be time to encourage reaching out to high schools in the area to create a university collaboration for high school students transitioning to college and to begin developing a university program for students with disabilities. Grigal and Hart (2010) in *Think College!* provide a guide to developing programs for students with intellectual disabilities. The work of *Think College!* has been the model for all programs that wish to add a certificate program or dual enrollment programs for students with intellectual disabilities.

Diversity is at the top of the list of most postsecondary schools today, but I sometimes wonder if schools that promote the term "diversity" consider neurodiversity and disability. Disability rights seem to be the last hurdle of the civil rights movement. As long as society continues to consider it tolerable to ignore and exclude those we have long determined to be not good enough composers, singers, and players, then what does that say about our universities as the pillars of openness and forward thinking?

If we believe that all people have the right to experience music and to be musical, we need to move forward with more inclusive higher education environments. I will offer in this book many ways that schools of music can begin to reach out to those in the community who are left out of music opportunities and events in the community and within the local school of music. Sensory-friendly concerts are the easiest way to begin, and full inclusion with supports for students with disabilities is the ideal solution to work toward.

This may require some deep discussions with your university and faculty. It means shifting from being a culture of auditions and competitive chairs in ensembles that is centered on exclusion to one that is universally designed to create seamless inclusion for all.

SUMMARY

In this chapter, these strategies were discussed:

- Ways to help students in high school to prepare for college through dual-enrollment courses, summer transition courses, and workshops; encouraging high school special educators to collaborate with local community colleges and four-year institutions
- Simple programs for entering freshmen with disabilities that help to acclimate them to multiple changes and requirements they will experience in their first semester
- Examples of programs offered by postsecondary institutions

Universities and schools of music that are interested in inclusive opportunities for diverse learners can explore transition programs as one way to support music majors with disabilities and transition programs for individuals with more significant disabilities who are interested in pursuing music as a career or taking courses or ensembles as electives.

Programs are available for support of both high-incidence disabilities such as learning disabilities, ADHD, and mental illness, and low-incidence disabilities such as intellectual, physical, medical disabilities, and those in the autism spectrum. There are many exemplary models across the country but few specifically integrate music studies in a major way. I don't believe this is because individuals with disabilities are not interested in music; rather, schools of music do not seem to be interested in including individuals with disabilities. There are many ways that students with disabilities can function well in music courses, lessons, and ensembles, and this participation helps prepare them to be employable and enjoy a rich adult life.

Music ensembles are communities and are excellent vehicles for promoting social skills and inclusion.They offer perfect opportunities for developing confidence and self-advocacy skills. Students who can tell the professor they need their music modified in order to understand it better are more able to tell another adult, "I do not want to pay for an extended warranty on my new television!" A young person who discovers Bach in a music history course and becomes obsessed with his music may have autism, but it is nonetheless thrilling for you to know you have introduced that student to a composer he or she will enjoy forever. Knowing students on the autism spectrum, you will also likely learn more things about Bach and his music than you might if you had written a dissertation on Bach. People with disabilities all have positive traits they can share with us, even if it is only a big smile when they hear a great jazz band swinging.

3

POSTSECONDARY MUSIC EDUCATION AND APPLICABLE LAW

Barry just auditioned for the jazz studies undergraduate program. He played a very impressive audition on piano and drum set. He is able to play more than 500 standard tunes in any key and improvises very sophisticated solos. He also accompanied a singer very sensitively and listens well to the other members of the rhythm section. The singer performed a composition of his that could have been written by jazz great Bill Evans. Barry's audition was the best the jazz faculty has heard all day. Barry happens to be blind.

EDUCATION IS PROBABLY the most valuable asset a person can have regardless of abilities. According to the National Center for Education Statistics, during the 12-month 2008–2009 academic year, 88% of two-year and four-year Title IV degree-granting postsecondary institutions reported enrolling students with disabilities. In a more recent study, almost all public two-year and four-year institutions (99%) and medium and large institutions (100%) reported enrolling students with disabilities (Raue & Lewis, 2011). Universities that used to be the domain of young, able-bodied Caucasian males are becoming more diverse (Burgstahler, 2008). Indeed, estimates are that somewhere around 6% or more of the university student population will identify as having one or more disabilities (Horn & Nevill, 2006; Lewis & Farris, 1999; Raue & Lewis, 2011). It is likely that students like Barry have auditioned for your music program or will be auditioning in the coming years as more students with disabilities elect to study music in postsecondary institutions.

The audition committee probably had a discussion about how the program would accommodate Barry: "How will Barry read assigned books and articles and complete theory assignments?" "How can he find his way in our confusing maze of a campus?" "With new university writing standards, how will he complete the required assignments?" It is possible that one or more professors may confess, "I am uncomfortable with a student like Barry. I don't even know any blind people. I'm afraid I wouldn't know the first thing about teaching someone who can't see what I write up on the board."

These are important questions to ask and consider but should not affect the decision of whether to accept Barry as a jazz studies major. Barry is obviously qualified and he has demonstrated that he might be one of the more outstanding musicians in the program.

AMERICANS WITH DISABILITY ACT AND SECTION 504

Universities have a legal obligation to avoid acting in a discriminatory manner in rejecting a student like Barry based on concerns such as those voiced by the imaginary audition committee. Legally, both the Americans with Disabilities Act (ADA) and section 504 of the Rehabilitation Action of 1973 protect students with disabilities seeking postsecondary education. Specifically, the ADA prohibits actions that

- Deny qualified students with disabilities an equal opportunity to participate in programs or activities;
- Provide aids and services that are not "equal to" or as "effective as" those provided to others;
- Provide different or separate aids, services, or benefits than those necessary for providing meaningful access;
- Provide significant assistance to third parties that discriminate against qualified individuals with disabilities;
- Use methods of administration that result in discrimination;
- Use eligibility criteria that tend to screen out individuals with disabilities;
- Fail to provide reasonable accommodations. (Simon, 2011)

In addition, the US Supreme Court has advised that institutions must not only avoid discriminating against students with disabilities, but they must also make "reasonable accommodation" to best ensure "meaningful access" (*Alexander v. Choate* 1985, p. 301). Students who have a physical or mental impairment that substantially limits a major life activity or have a record indicating impairment are protected under federal laws. Major life activities are activities that a typical person can perform with little difficulty. In 2008 Congress altered the language in the ADA to clarify what is meant by major life activities. These now include "sitting and standing, lifting, thinking, reading, concentrating, communicating with others, sleeping, and major bodily functions." This list is not exhaustive because in 1998, test taking (*Bartlett v. New York State Board of Law Examiners, 1998*) was considered a major life activity (Simon, 2011). Major bodily functions now include functions of the immune system. For example, a student with HIV no longer has to prove that the condition substantially interferes with his or her ability to procreate. The fact that the infection limits healthy functioning of the immune system is proof enough (Grossman, 2014). The Equal Employment Opportunity Commission (EEOC) has expanded the list of physical, psychological, and medical impairments that now meet the definition of disability covered by the ADA and Section 504.

Congress also made sure that those amendments clarify the following:

- When to shift attention from whether the individual's impairment qualified as a disability to whether discrimination had occurred;
- Confirmed that individuals with episodic conditions such as recurrent depression or multiple sclerosis were protected;
- Do not require a student to be severely impaired in order to be protected;
- Rejected the assumption that an academically high-performing student cannot be substantially limited in activities such as learning or reading;
- Confirmed that it supported the decision in *Bartlett v. New York State of Law Examiners* that stated students with learning disabilities would be considered disabled under the law even if they managed their own adaptive strategies or received informal or undocumented accommodations that lessened the deleterious effects of their disability (*Federal Register,* 2008, p. H8291);

Changes made to Titles II and III of the ADA in September 2010 include provisions for the need to document a disability and to define a "service animal" and "qualified interpreters" (Grossman, 2014). Included in the nine new rules implemented in 2011 by the EEOC is language that states "the determination of whether an impairment substantially limits a major life activity shall be made without regard to the ameliorative effects of mitigating measures" such as medication or hearing aids so that a student with attention deficit/hyperactivity disorder (ADHD) or a psychological condition may no longer be excluded from the protections of the ADA or Section 504 on the grounds that, with medication, the impairment does not substantially limit a major life activity (Grossman, 2014). Grossman explains that students with impairments that are episodic or in remission such as bipolar disorder or cancer still are covered by the ADA and Section 504.

ADA, SECTION 504, AND AUDITIONS

As discussed in Chapter 4, specific learning disabilities often impact learning and reading, including learning and reading written music notation. It is customary to require sight-reading of music at auditions and in lessons and ensembles. I believe requiring students with documented learning disabilities that negatively impact their ability to fluently read and process music notation creates a discriminatory practice when grades, audition placement, and entry into music programs hinge on excellence in this ability. Students with psychiatric disorders such as anxiety disorder may also freeze up during sight-reading. For these students and others without disabilities the question must be asked, is it really essential that students demonstrate the ability to fluently sight-read to be successful as musicians? If so, can it be assessed in a less threatening situation? Performing for a jury of professors can make typical students nervous, but students who struggle with efficient processing of abstract symbols experience heightened problems when they are in stressful situations. In other words, students who will not do well in a high-stakes situation may be more successful if their studio professor routinely records them sight-reading in their weekly lessons and saves these recordings, making note of the better sight-reading episodes. These can later be shared with faculty juries and would be more representative of their abilities under a less stressful environment.

THE STUDENT'S RESPONSIBILITY

Essentially, students must take responsibility for officially registering with the campus disability services office and meeting with professors to make them aware of their disability. At the time of the meeting, it is common that students will share a letter from the disability services office that indicates the student has a documented disability and includes a list of recommended accommodations. It is not necessary for the professor to know the specific disability but he or she needs to know that there is a disability and that the student requires accommodations to be successful in class.

TRANSITION FROM HIGH SCHOOL TO COLLEGE

It is not uncommon that students decide once they enter college to try to function without revealing their disability to the student disability office or to their professors. Students who received support during their K–12 education may have experienced embarrassment from being identified as a student with a disability and the student might prefer to start college with a clean slate where no one knows about the disability. Of course, this is possible only if the student has what are often referred to as *invisible disabilities*, that is, specified learning disabilities, speech and language disabilities, psychiatric disorders, or Asperger syndrome.

Another common issue that new students to college may experience is a shift from an education environment that has a team of professionals advocating for and providing needed supports for the student. In K–12 schools, the Individuals with Disabilities Education Act (IDEA) provides a range of services for qualified students. A team of professionals evaluated the student and prepared an Individual Education Program (IEP) that documented his or her abilities and challenges. The team led by a special educator decided what was needed and arranged for adaptations and accommodations. The parent and student (once the student is old enough to understand and participate in the process) were also members of the IEP team. Even though the current best special education practice is to teach skills of *self-determination*, or learning to ask for needed adaptations, many students become used to someone else taking care of their needs, including advocating for them when necessary. The IEP is a legal document that describes the abilities and disabilities of the student, lists goals and objectives for teachers to address, and specific adaptations and accommodations needed to achieve the goals and objectives. At the postsecondary level, there is no longer an IEP team to do this for the student.

Results of a 2012 survey by the National Alliance on Mental Illness (NAMI) found that 64% of students no longer in college indicated that they left school for mental health reasons (Gruttadaro & Crudo, 2012). Without a support system, many students find themselves struggling to make it to class on time, to complete assignments, to make friends, or to assimilate into college life in general. In Chapter 7 psychiatric disorders are discussed more fully.

LAW AND EDUCATIONAL ACCESS

Access has been described as both physical access and communications access to programs and accommodations. To be in compliance with ADA and section

504, universities need to make sure that the following areas are accessible for all students:

- *Physical access on and off campus.* Students should be able to enter buildings, classrooms, rehearsal spaces, and faculty offices. Restroom facilities, student lounges, and libraries should be equally accessible. If buildings off-campus are used, for example, as alternative spaces for recitals or music club meetings, those need to be accessible as well.
- *Program access.* For example, if a student in a wheelchair sings in a university choral group and that choral group sometimes sings from the choir loft in the concert hall, is that choir loft accessible by wheelchair? If the choir is singing on stage on risers how is the student in a wheelchair positioned so he or she is seamlessly included rather than sitting off to the side of the choir?
- *Key accommodation provisions.* Students must provide adequate notice of disability and once the student provides notice of a disability it then is the responsibility of the university to reasonably accommodate the student's disability (*Concepcion v. Puerto Rico*, 2010; Wichita State University, 1991). The laws protect only students with disabilities who are "qualified" or able to meet technical and academic qualifications for entry into the school or program of study (*Wong v. Regents of the University of California* 1999; *Wynne v. Tufts University School of Medicine*, 1991).

Auxiliary Aids and Services are key accommodations that include qualified sign language interpreters, video relay interpreting (including real-time captioning, voice, text, and video-based telecommunications products and systems), note-takers, qualified readers, Braille and large-print materials, screen reader software, magnification software, optical readers, secondary auditory programs, and adaptive equipment and software.

Academic adjustments are also important accommodations. These might include extended time for tests, completion of course work, or graduation; audio recording of classes; course substitution to meet degree requirements; and modification evaluation so as not to discriminate except where such skills are specifically being measured. Students need to take responsibility for asking the professor to identify a student in the class, for example, to take notes. However, if this is not successful it then becomes the institution's responsibility to find someone to take notes. The student is required to report to disability services office if the process was not successful so the institution knows to help with finding a note-taker (Solano Community College, 1995). If students have difficulty articulating why they need accommodations due to their disorder or disability, institutions and faculty should be aware that it is their legal obligation to assist with securing accommodations. For example, if a student with autism has difficulty approaching a fellow student to ask for help with note-taking because of social challenges, the university (or professor) has a responsibility to step in and help facilitate the process.

Technology access is essential for all students in college, and technology should be accessible to students with disabilities. If music technology is used in the curriculum and a student with a physical disability has difficulty playing a piano keyboard to enter notation for a music theory assignment, there should be alternative ways to use technology so the student is still able to participate equally and learn from the curriculum. Alternative electronic controllers that work with an electronic keyboard are available that can accommodate a variety of abilities. Music notation can be achieved for students with physical or vision disabilities through spoken commands. Assistive technology is discussed more fully in Chapter 17.

Recent Supreme Court decisions (*Sutton v. United Airlines*, 1999; *Toyota Motor Manufacturing v. Williams*, 2002) now require students to provide appropriate evidence to the institution's disability services office demonstrating a documented disability or disabilities. Students with invisible disabilities including specified learning disabilities, attention deficit/hyperactivity disorder, and psychological disorders are finding this to be especially true (*Price v. National Board of Medical Examiners*, 1997; *Gonzales v. National Board of Medical Examiners*, 2000; *Wong v. Regents of the University of California*, 2004). Invisible disabilities are those that are not physically apparent when you look at a student. Even students with hearing loss often use hearing aids or cochlear implants, often not apparent. It is difficult for professors to sometimes believe that an otherwise talented music student struggles with certain aspects of learning if the professor cannot see a disability.

Documentation from prior recent IEP documents or section 504 documentation that shows recent testing and evaluations that help to document needs for accommodations are most commonly used when the university disability services team evaluates a student for accommodations. However, institutions "may not establish unduly burdensome documentation criteria or establish criteria that are inconsistent with accepted practice, especially where accepted practice requires clinical judgment" (Bartlett, 1998).

- *Access to print or alternative text* should be offered at a minimum at the beginning of the semester or when the first reading assignment is due. Handouts should be accessible to all students. For example, if print copies are given to students, a student who is blind will need an electronic copy that can be read by his or her screen reader. PDF files generally do not work well with screen readers.

- College military veterans are entering college in record numbers, some with disabilities. Simon (2011) cautions that many students are less likely than non-veterans to ask for accommodations. Recent mental health disorders as a result of battle are sometimes seen as a weakness with many veterans choosing not to disclose their disability.

Faculty and administrators in music schools and departments have a responsibility to adapt and include students who wish to major in music or participate in ensembles or classes. It is no longer permissible to reject students based on disability; that being said, students in postsecondary education have the responsibility to register with their disability services office and to disclose their needs and accommodations to professors and programs. Students who do not wish to personally disclose their disability to professors only need to provide a letter from the disability services office documenting that a disability is present and the required accommodations; the letter does not have to mention the type of disability.

It is not unusual to see individuals with disabilities, mild and severe participating, as music performers, composers, and teachers in popular media. For young musicians with disabilities, this has been a major motivating factor to become musicians themselves. Before we reject or place unduly difficult tasks on someone, it is important to consider alternative ways that the individual can demonstrate learning and musicianship.

HOW TO TALK TO A STUDENT WHO YOU THINK MAY HAVE A DISABILITY

Even though we care about our students and want to help, most of us are not qualified to make a diagnosis of a disability. Special educators do not make a diagnosis in public schools; a team of professionals determines a label. What we can do is provide support and validation. For example, you might comment this way if you notice a student struggling with particular issues; "I observe toward the end of the lesson that you make more reading errors than you do at the beginning, have you noticed that?" "Does it help to stand and play instead of sitting? I know some students play better when they can stand and move." "I had an email from your music theory professor, and he says you haven't been to class for over a week, yet I notice you never miss choir; I'm concerned about you. How can I help?"

It is important for you to listen without interrupting and maintain eye contact. Summarize what you hear the student saying and ask, "Do I have that right?"

Follow this with, "How can I help you?" This is a very critical but difficult moment for many students, especially if they are not comfortable with disclosing their disability. For music students there can be worry about losing a scholarship, principal chair, lead in the musical, position as drum major. Assure the student that if he or she does not want you to disclose the disability to others, you will respect that.

When a student discloses a disability to you, try to react in a positive manner. Being positive and supportive is very important to establishing a trusting relationship. In interviews with students, many say they will research a postsecondary music program by having a lesson with the studio professor to see if the professor is able to teach them and if the students can learn from and feel comfortable with the studio professor. Professors who respond negatively to a disclosure will likely lose the student to another school. For example, a student interested in pursuing a doctorate in music education disclosed to his advisor that he knew statistics would be very difficult due to his learning disability. The professor replied, "Maybe it isn't the best idea to pursue a doctorate then." A better response would be "Our university has a disabled student services office, and you should register with them as soon as possible in order to determine if you can secure accommodations to help you with statistics." The professor should not be the person to decide whether the student's disability will prohibit the student from successfully completing a degree.

SUMMARY

Although there are fewer laws and regulations in higher education than there are in K–12 education, music professors and administrators are bound by two important legal obligations: the Americans with Disabilities Act and Section 504. The most important points to remember are these:

- We CAN'T deny qualified students with disabilities an equal opportunity to participate in programs or activities.
- We CAN'T use methods of administration that result in discrimination.
- We CAN'T use eligibility criteria that tend to screen out individuals with disabilities.
- We CAN'T fail to provide reasonable accommodations.

Reasonable accommodation is determined by the disability services office often in collaboration with the school of music. Professors are not qualified to decide what is a reasonable accommodation. It is the students' responsibility to register with the disability office; if students are not registered, then no accommodations are legally required. However, nothing stops a caring professor from setting up the rehearsal room so the student who is temporarily in a wheelchair can easily navigate to his or her spot.

When considering access to education, section 504 advises that the following be considered:

- Physical access on and off campus
- Access to activities and programs
- Knowing that the law protects only those who register with the disability services office
- Auxiliary aids and services
- Adjustments to the way the professor traditionally teaches or assesses
- Access to technology
- Access to print or alternative text

4

STRATEGIES FOR CREATING INCLUSIVE MUSIC CLASSES, ENSEMBLES, AND LESSONS

Sarah is a music education major with a specific learning disability. She is struggling with reading and writing in school and has dyslexia. She received special education services for her learning disability from kindergarten through high school. She hates to read, and her writing is riddled with misspellings and grammar problems. Her SAT scores were borderline for admission to the school of music, but she plays bassoon well and is needed by the instrumental music ensembles.

Her audition was very good except for the sight-reading portion. The professors chalked it up to nerves but later her bassoon professor realized that her sight-reading was no better in her lessons. She had the most trouble with rhythms but also would sometimes mix up space notes (i.e., read A as C), and she often forgot to look at the key signature, time signature, and other markings.

In music theory classes, her written notation was difficult to read and grade, and by the end of the semester, she consistently failed every assignment. She never asked for help or asked for an appointment with the professor. Ten weeks into the semester the professor caught her as everyone was leaving class and asked if she wanted to meet about the course and her grades on her assignments; Sarah agreed and made an appointment.

In the meeting, Dr. Adams, her professor, explained that she thought Sarah was not going to pass the first semester of music theory. She asked Sarah why she hadn't come for help and if she realized she had to pass music theory to continue in the music program. Sarah burst into tears and said she spent hours every night trying to understand and do her assignments right but never seemed to improve. Sarah explained that she knew she needed to pass music theory but had no idea how anyone could help her. She confessed that she loved everything else about being a music education major but she had grown to hate music theory.

Dr. Adams spoke to Professor Schmidt, Sarah's bassoon teacher, and found out about the struggles Sarah was experiencing with reading music. They decided since Professor Schmidt had developed trust and a good relationship with Sarah that she would talk to her during her next lesson about the trouble the two professors were seeing.

Professor Schmidt confided in Sarah that Dr. Adams spoke to her and Sarah sat down and began to cry. Professor Schmidt said she noticed that Sarah's ability to read music and her obvious fine playing seemed to be at two different levels. Sarah then opened up about her years in special education and her difficulty with reading and writing. Professor Schmidt asked if she had registered with the student disability services office, and Sarah said no. Sarah didn't know about it, but she also wanted to shake off the special education label and do things like an adult without extra help.

Professor Schmidt asked how she was able to develop such wonderful technique and sound on the bassoon when reading music was so hard for her. Sarah explained that her private teacher during high school would play with her in lessons and would record all the exercises and pieces she was studying onto a recording that Sarah would practice with at home. Sarah explained, "I learned the music by listening to the recordings on my Smartphone. I don't really read the music: I sort of memorize everything before my lesson." Professor Schmidt was stunned and thought, "Why did Sarah's previous teacher let her get away without learning to read music? Was the previous teacher enabling her by recording everything for her?"

Professor Schmidt asked Sarah, "Did your last teacher not care if you learned to read music?" Sarah said, "Oh yes, we used to work really hard on improving my reading, but I think my mother talked to him and he changed his way of teaching after that and started making the recordings. I never asked my mother what happened. I was just glad not to have to go through the difficulty each week in my lesson. I wonder if my mother mentioned that I was in special education and had trouble reading?"

Professor Schmidt and Sarah continued to talk about her difficulty with reading music, and Sarah said she would call her mother to find out if she thought it was related to her trouble reading and writing. The next week Sarah came to her lesson with a copy of her last Individual Education Plan (IEP) from high school. Sarah said her mother helped her remember more details about why she had received special education services kindergarten through high school. Sarah has dyslexia, and her middle school special educator believed that her dyslexia impacted her ability to process written notation quickly as well. When Sarah began to take bassoon lessons in high school, Sarah's mother called the former special education teacher, Emily, to ask her for some strategies to help the bassoon teacher since he was frustrated and Sarah was ready to *quit music altogether. Emily advised that Sarah's strongest learning mode was aural learning paired with tactile strategies whenever she was struggling with reading. Emily suggested that the bassoon teacher model and record the lessons for Emily so that she had an aural example to pair with the written notation. She also said the teacher might make suggestions like directing Sarah to focus on how it feels to play a certain passage that is difficult, such as thinking about her fingerings and how the reed feels, to help Sarah with alternative strategies for learning music. It worked very well.*

What hasn't worked well is Sarah's transition to college. She was used to her mother and the special educators seeing to her needs when it came to her learning disability. Sarah never really learned how to be an advocate for herself. Her mother was quite upset to hear Sarah was failing music theory and struggling in her lessons. She asked Sarah why she didn't talk to the professors when she was having so much trouble? Sarah wanted to see if she could figure it out for herself, but obviously that wasn't working so well.

STUDENTS LIKE SARAH with specified learning disabilities—in this case, dyslexia—are just one group who struggle for various reasons in undergraduate school. Chapter 5, Specific Learning Disabilities, explains more about how to recognize and help students with learning disabilities. It is important to emphasize here that students like Sarah are at risk of dropping out of college because they are embarrassed or unable to ask for help. We can accommodate students with learning disabilities (and all other disabilities) by making adjustments in our course syllabi, by how we set up classes, and by adjusting our expectations, but we have to know that the student needs accommodations.

For centuries, education has been dominated by two narrow methods of instruction—lecture and written text. Although many students have been successful through these two dominant mediums of teaching, there are many who find one or both challenging.

In this chapter, you will be introduced to two approaches to teaching more inclusively; Universal Design for Learning, and Understanding by Design. Both are widely used in education and are very useful strategies for creating a more inclusive learning environment. For professors overwhelmed with how to adapt for their students with disabilities, this chapter provides tools to make sure your students are successful in your lessons, classes, and ensembles.

UNIVERSAL DESIGN FOR LEARNING OR INSTRUCTION

The term "universal design" (UD) originates from architect Ronald Mace, who began using the term for accessible buildings in the 1970s in response to the

Architectural Barriers Act of 1968 requiring that all "buildings designed, constructed, altered, or leased with federal funds meet minimum accessibility requirements to remove physical barriers to individuals with disabilities" (Burgstahler, 2008). Architects soon realized that it was much easier and in many ways less costly, to design buildings from the beginning that were accessible to all possible users. UD "features in a product or environment are integrated into the design so that they foster social integration and do not stand out" (Burgstahler, 2008). A good example is doors that open automatically when a person approaches a building. Many people with physical disabilities rely on automatic doors to easily access grocery stores, the post office, malls, and other public buildings. Many people without physical disabilities also prefer using automatic doors when they have their hands full of shopping bags or are pushing a baby stroller. Indeed, many musicians wish more concert halls had automatic doors when they are carrying or pulling large instruments!

Universal design is focused on the premise that most people will be able to access a building inside and out, including people with disabilities. UD also embraces the social construct of disability in that disability is not about the person's deficit but rather society's lack of attention to designing products and buildings that are accessible. UD is also meant to be proactive rather than reactive, which is a very important concept to remember in terms of classrooms, rehearsal space, or applied studio space.

Universal design and universal design for instruction (UDI) or learning are gaining notice as a tool for social justice and multicultural postsecondary education (Hackman & Rauscher, 2004; Higbee, 2008; Higbee & Barajas, 2007; Johnson, 2004; Johnson & Fox, 2003).

> It is imperative that educators implementing UDI consider a broad range and multiple intersections of students' diverse social identities rather than focusing on disability. It is this notion of inclusion for all that prompted the term *universal*. Within the context of UDI, *universal* refers not to "one size fits all"; rather, it prompts universal access to learning for all students, including students with disabilities. (Higbee, 2008)

PRINCIPLES OF UNIVERSAL DESIGN

The Center of Universal Design at North Carolina State University first described the seven principles of universal design to be used in the "design of products and environments for all people, to the greatest extent possible, without the need for adaptation or specialized design" (Center for Universal Design, 1997). They are listed below with guidelines. As you read the principles consider how you might apply them to your teaching spaces.

UNIVERSAL DESIGN

PRINCIPLE ONE: EQUITABLE USE

The design is useful and marketable to people with diverse abilities.

Guidelines:

   1a. Provide the same means of use for all users: identical whenever possible; equivalent when not.
   1b. Avoid segregating or stigmatizing any users.
   1c. Provisions for privacy, security, and safety should be equally available to all users.
   1d. Make the design appealing to all users.

PRINCIPAL TWO: FLEXIBILITY IN USE

The design accommodates a wide range of individual preferences and abilities.

Guidelines:

   2a. Provide choice in methods of use.
   2b. Accommodate right-or left-handed access and use.
   2c. Facilitate the user's accuracy and precision.
   2d. Provide adaptability to the user's pace.

PRINCIPLE THREE: SIMPLE AND INTUITIVE USE

Use of the design is easy to understand, regardless of the user's experience, knowledge, language skills, or current concentration level.

Guidelines:

   3a. Eliminate unnecessary complexity.
   3b. Be consistent with user expectations and intuition.
   3c. Accommodate a wide range of literacy and language skills.

3d. Arrange information consistent with its importance.

3e. Provide effective prompting and feedback during and after task completion.

PRINCIPLE FOUR: PERCEPTIBLE INFORMATION

The design communicates necessary information effectively to the user, regardless of ambient conditions or the user's sensory abilities.

Guidelines:

4a. Use different modes (pictorial, verbal, tactile) for redundant presentation of information.

4b. Provide adequate contrast between essential information and its surroundings.

4c. Maximize "legibility" of essential information.

4d. Differentiate elements in ways that can be described (i.e., make it easy to give instructions or directions).

4e. Provide compatibility with a variety of techniques or devices used by people with sensory limitations.

PRINCIPLE FIVE: TOLERANCE FOR ERROR

The design minimizes hazards and the adverse consequences of accidental or unintended actions.

Guidelines:

5a. Arrange elements to minimize hazards and errors: most used elements, most accessible; hazardous elements eliminated, isolated, or shielded.

5b. Provide warnings of hazards and errors.

5c. Provide fail safe features.

5d. Discourage unconscious action in tasks that require vigilance.

PRINCIPLE SIX: LOW PHYSICAL EFFORT

The design can be used efficiently and comfortably and with a minimum of fatigue.

Guidelines:

6a. Allow user to maintain a neutral body position.

6b. Use reasonable operating forces.

6c. Minimize repetitive actions.

6d. Minimize sustained physical effort.

PRINCIPLE SEVEN: SIZE AND SPACE FOR APPROACH AND USE

Appropriate size and space is provided for approach, reach, manipulation, and use regardless of user's size, posture, or mobility.

Guidelines:

7a. Provide a clear line of sight to important elements for any seated or standing user.

7b. Make reach to all components comfortable for any seated or standing user.

7c. Accommodate variations in hand and grip size.

7d. Provide adequate space for the use of assistive devices or personal assistance. (The Center for Universal Design, 1997).

Figures 4.1 and 4.2 illustrate the UD principles with examples that might occur in school of music facilities and classes.

Understandably, we are required to make the best use of the facility we are given; however, when possible, try to organize your teaching space by considering maximum inclusion for all likely users. Sometimes small changes can make a big difference for certain students. For example, students who are blind rely on their memory of your rehearsal room to find their way to their place. If a grand piano is used in your rehearsal, make sure it stays in the same place, or meet the student at the door to guide him or her around the piano. Imagine how embarrassing and frustrating it might be to a student trying to be independent to run into the piano.

UNIVERSAL DESIGN FOR INSTRUCTION

Rose and Meyer (2002) refer to multiple means of representation as one important strategy to make the curriculum accessible. This is the *what* of learning by prompting the design of multiple, flexible options for presentation of content (Glass, Meyer, & Rose, 2013). This involves the professor offering a variety of ways that the student can acquire information. Technology has given educators electronic means for presenting

Universal Design Principles Applied to Postsecondary Music

UD Principle	Postsecondary Music Example
1. *Equitable use.* The design is useful and marketable to people with diverse abilities.	*Accessible Concerts.* University concerts are accessible to audiences with a broad range of abilities, disabilities, ages, and racial/ethnic backgrounds.
2. *Flexibility in use.* The design accommodates a wide range of individual preferences and abilities.	*School of Music Website.* A design that allows a visitor to choose to read or listen to content on the website. The design is accessible is uncluttered and meets Web Accessibility Initiative (WAI) guidelines.
3. *Simple and intuitive.* Use of the design is easy to understand, regardless of the user's experience, knowledge, language skills, or current concentration level.	*Assessment.* Assessments, tests and evaluations are predictable and clear.
4. *Perceptible information.* The design communicates necessary information effectively to the user, regardless of ambient conditions or the user's sensory abilities.	*Building elevator.* Button text is displayed through visual, aural and tactile modes. Floor numbers are announced via recording and Braille appear next to numbers and words.
5. *Tolerance for error.* The design minimizes hazards and the adverse consequences of accidental or unintended actions.	*Concert hall backstage area, stage risers, entrances and stairs.* Backstage equipment is stored in the same places with a clear pathway between large objects. Choir risers and lofts are accessible.
6. *Low physical effort.* The design can be used efficiently, comfortably, and with a minimum of fatigue.	*Storage of university instruments.* Instruments are stored in accessible spaces and are able to be moved in and out of storage with a minimum of effort.
7. *Size and space for approach and use.* Appropriate size and space is provided for approach, reach, manipulation, and use, regardless of the user's body size, posture, or mobility. (The Center for Universal Design, 1997).	*Rehearsal spaces.* Set-up of rehearsal is the same and music stands, chairs, large instruments are placed in the same places unless the director makes changes with advance warning.[1]

[1]Chart is adapted from Burgstahler, S.E. & Cory, R.C. (2008). Universal design in higher education, from principles to practice. Cambridge, MA: Harvard Education Press.

FIGURE 4.1 Universal Design Principles Applied to School of Music Facilities

information in many different ways. Many professors rely on lectures as their main method of delivering instructional content. There is often the assumption that students will take notes and use the notes to study for written exams. Thinking of Sarah, she might take notes but she writes so slowly that she will likely not be able to take notes that are helpful for studying for tests. Often students with learning disabilities that impact writing are allowed to have a note-taker as an accommodation. Sarah could also bring her laptop and type. However, even with typing, some students cannot type and listen well at the same time. Another good option that benefits all students is for

Universal Design Principles Applied to Postsecondary Music Instruction

UD Principle	Postsecondary Music Instruction Example
1. *Equitable use.* The design is useful and marketable to people with diverse abilities.	A professor's Web site (Blackboard, Moodle, etc.) is designed so that it is accessible to everyone, including students who are blind and use text-to-speech software.
2. *Flexibility in use.* The design accommodates a wide range of individual preferences and abilities.	Textbooks and course materials are available in print, audio files and in braille to accommodate varied learning styles.
3. *Simple and intuitive.* Use of the design is easy to understand, regardless of the user's experience, knowledge, language skills, or current concentration level.	Controls in class piano classrooms are labeled with text and symbols that are simple and intuitive to understand.
4. *Perceptible information.* The design communicates necessary information effectively to the user, regardless of ambient conditions or the user's sensory abilities.	A video presentation includes captions.
5. *Tolerance for error.* The design minimizes hazards and the adverse consequences of accidental or unintended actions.	Software used for online assessments provides feedback when a student does not complete steps as outlined.
6. *Low physical effort.* The design can be used efficiently, comfortably, and with a minimum of fatigue.	Doors to rehearsal halls open automatically for people with a wide variety of physical characteristics.
7. *Size and space for approach and use.* Appropriate size and space is provided for approach, reach, manipulation, and use, regardless of the user's body size, posture, or mobility. (The Center for Universal Design, 1997).	Student desks in classrooms are available for left- and right-handed persons and for large people.[1]

[1]Chart is adapted from Burgstahler, S.E. & Cory, R.C. (2008). Universal design in higher education, from principles to practice. Cambridge, MA: Harvard Education Press.

FIGURE 4.2 UDL Principles Applied to Music Courses

the professor to upload PowerPoints and notes to Blackboard, Moodle, or whatever course organization software the university uses. Some professors turn their lectures into podcasts, which allow aural learners like Sarah to *listen* to the lecture again. The important point here is that the professor makes the essential content of the course available in different formats so students can access important course content in a way that works best for their own learning style.

A second strategy is multiple means of expression or flexibility in the ways students can demonstrate they understand. This is the "*how* of learning by prompting the design of multiple, flexible options for demonstrating understanding, knowledge, and skills" (Glass, Meyer, & Rose, 2013). What happens if a written exam is the preferred way to demonstrate understanding by only 20% of your students? Would it be possible to assess students in different ways? Take-home tests would allow students different ways to turn in their answers. Instead of trying to write an essay, Sarah could record an audio file and email it to the professor. It is likely that Sarah's speaking skills are better than her writing skills. Alternatively, she might use Dragon Dictation to speak an essay format exam into her computer and then edit it and print or email a copy to the professor. It is quite possible that Sarah might have another method that we might never think of that she has discovered after years of struggling with reading and writing. Flexibility is important to remember.

Multiple means of engagement are the ways you motivate and capture the attention of your students. For example, when I teach music education majors in my general music methods course about why pentatonic scales are so accessible to children, I show a three-minute video of Bobby McFerrin teaching the pentatonic scale to a room full of scientists at https://www.youtube.com/watch?v=ne6tB2KiZuk. McFerrin engages the scientists in singing with him in a very inventive way.

Students learn best when they are actively engaged in learning. You might include more small-group discussions, hands-on activities, or guest speakers, including speakers who talk to your class via Skype or another remote video process. UDI should avoid barriers to students with mobility, sensory, language, learning, or social challenges by offering multiple ways of representation, expression, and engagement.

Bowe (2000, pp. 5–6) developed a "Tip Sheet for Universally Designed Teaching":

1. Become aware of your culture's teachings and how those affect you as an educator.
2. Provide students with options for demonstrating knowledge and skills.
3. Offer instruction, and accept student work, at a distance.
4. Alert students to availability of digitized texts (e-books).
5. Offer students information in redundant media.
6. Provide support students need to improve accuracy and speed.
7. Translate important materials to other languages as needed by your students.
8. Choose physically accessible locations for your classes.

FAIR IS NOT ALWAYS EQUAL

Occasionally professors question all of this flexibility as "dumbing down the curriculum," not having high enough standards, or not expecting students with disabilities to live in the real world. What is fair or equitable is not always equal. To be successful teachers and learners, flexibility is essential.

START WITH YOUR SYLLABUS

A terrific website on Universal Course Design (UCD), located at http://universal-coursedesign.org/ucd-strategies, divides universal course design into four categories: Course Curriculum, Instruction, Assessment, and Environment. There are strategies for implementing UCD in courses with and without the required use of technology. The website has a large collection of examples that can be downloaded and used to help you plan your UCD. I start with my syllabus and look at all the things the students will be learning and doing in my course and think about the seven UD principles to see whether I have an accessible course for all the possible learners I might have in my class.

Sometimes even our syllabus is not fully accessible, and with a few adjustments, we can make it more so. For example, Sarah was hesitant to speak to her professors about her disability. Your syllabus can provide information about other options to meet with a student via Skype, through email, or as a virtual chat or discussion in your online course software. If your syllabus obviously welcomes students with disabilities and assures sensitivity and outreach, they will be more likely to speak to you early in the course. A student information sheet can be distributed on the first day with the question, "Is there anything that I should be aware of that might have an impact on your participation in this course (examples: a documented disability, absences for religious reasons, or ensemble tours, sports, or other school related travel, etc.)?" (Higbee, J. L., 2008). On the accompanying website are examples of syllabi for a music education methods course, a general education music course, and a voice studio.

Good UD syllabi include the following as a way to reduce the amount of text:

- photos
- maps
- tables of information
- web links to online sources for buying books
- section on how to receive peer tutoring and/or help from the professor
- important information appearing in both visual and text modes

Once you have completed your syllabus you can use the online validation tool at http://ucd.eeonline.org/validator/ to check that everything is readable by different assistive technologies that students might use. Only PowerPoint and Microsoft Word formats will work with this program. You can use this tool throughout the development of your class on your tests, rubrics, and handouts you give students.

To reduce student anxiety about failure:

- allow students to re-do assignments for a better grade.
- assessments should be varied to allow multiple means of expression.
- build many assessments into the course that are worth smaller chunks of points rather than one or two that are worth most of the grade.

UNDERSTANDING BY DESIGN

Continuing with the approach to design as a means toward inclusion, Understanding by Design (UbD) is an approach to curriculum developed by Grant Wiggins and Jay McTighe (2005). The authors addressed this question, "How do we make it more likely—by our design—that more students really understand what they are asked to learn?" Although it is difficult to summarize an approach to curriculum, instruction, and assessment, there are several basic principles to UbD.

Backward design is the first step: planning your course or curriculum from the exit goals and figuring out how to construct the course so all possible learners will be able to complete the goals or objectives for your course. For example, if one of the goals is that students will be able to analyze a Bach chorale, then you have to figure out how to teach your students the skills in a sequential way so they can do this.

SIX FACETS OF UNDERSTANDING

Wiggins and McTighe (2005, pp. 84–103) include another principle they call "The Six Facets of Understanding." The six facets, listed below, help us to recognize whether students truly understand what we have taugh:

Facet 1: Explanation. Students can explain—via generalizations or principles, providing justified and systematic accounts of phenomena, facts, and data; make insightful connections and provide illuminating examples or illustrations.

Facet 2: Interpretation. Students can interpret when they tell meaningful stories; offer apt translations; provide a revealing historical or personal dimension to ideas and events; make the object of understanding personal or accessible through images, anecdotes, analogies, and models.

Facet 3: Application. Students can apply when they effectively use and adapt what we know in diverse and real contexts—we can "do" the subject.

Facet 4: Perspective. Students demonstrate they have perspective when they can see and hear points of view through critical eyes and ears; they can see the big picture.

Facet 5: Empathy. Students find value in what others might find odd, alien, or implausible; perceive sensitively on the basis of prior direct experience.

Facet 6: Self-Knowledge. Students show metacognitive awareness; perceive the personal style, prejudices, projections, and habits of mind that shape and impede our own understanding; are aware of what we do not understand; reflect on the meaning of learning and experience.

As you develop your curriculum think about how you can integrate each of the six facets in your course, but more important, how will you know it if you see it?

We tend to develop our courses and use learning modes that are our own personally preferred ways of learning and teaching. Learning modes that are aural characterize people who prefer listening to others explain ideas, discuss thoughts with others, or read books and text. Visual learners gravitate toward images, charts, graphs, color, and video. Kinesthetic and tactile learners prefer hands-on activities, movement, and having actual objects they are studying on hand to interact with. For example, many instrumentalists who easily pick up and play new instruments are kinesthetic/tactile learners. Of course, no one uses only one learning style; but we do tend to be more comfortable thinking and teaching in one style.

To help you think about your students, ask them to fill out one of the many learning style surveys available online before class starts or early in the class schedule. I currently recommend this website's learning style inventory for college music majors: http://www.educationplanner.org/students/self-assessments/learning-styles.shtml.

Ways to engage students in participating in individually comfortable ways:

- Encourage students to turn in an index card with questions about a particular topic.
- Students who thrive on teaching or speaking on a topic of interest to them can be invited to make a presentation to the class
- Pecha Kucha presentations are a more visual way to present. Pecha Kucha is web-based tool where the student presents 20 images in 20 seconds (pechakucha.org).

Some students are better able to focus and organize their thinking if they are provided an agenda or, in the case of a rehearsal, a list of pieces that will be worked on during that day's rehearsal. For example, students on the autism spectrum tend to be very concrete and structured and are less likely to become frustrated if they know ahead of time what will be covered in class or rehearsal that day.

Music students are a blend of extroverts and introverts. Class discussions and small-group discussions can sometimes be challenging for introverts. I find that introverts respond much better in writing or in one-to-one talks with the professor. This is a difference that our culture does not always recognize or honor. Clearly, not all introverts have disabilities, but they will generally be more likely to listen than talk in large groups (Cain, 2013). Introverted professors might also struggle with leading discussions. If this describes you, prepare questions you might use before the class.

Be aware of speaking slowly and clearly. This is particularly true if you have any type of accent. Students with specified learning disabilities that impact their aural processing have great difficulty following lectures and discussions, especially when the pace is quick and the professor is from an area of the country or the world where language sounds a little different.

If you present text on slides, be sure to give students enough time to read it. This means giving more time than it takes for you to read the slide. Some students will read slower or need time to think about something you present in the slide. Slides should use graphics and primarily be visual. Text should be brief and only summarize points (Rose, Harbour, Johnston, Daley, & Abarbanell, 2008). If there is too much text to read, then the students with processing disabilities will have difficulty listening to the professor talk while reading text. Using images, charts, and limited text is keeping within UD principles.

At important points in the class stop and check for understanding. "Does that make sense?" "I know that concept can be confusing, would anyone like me to explain that again?" Sometimes I will say that and see nods from students and often another student will summarize what I say but in different words. It is particularly valuable when students compare the idea to something they might have learned in another class and explain it in relation to prior learning, which deepens understanding. Ending class a minute or two early on days when there might be confusion or when a test or assignment is approaching allows time for students to quickly ask you a question that they are reluctant to ask in front of their peers.

A great idea when presenting new information is shared in the UCD Strategies for Implementing UCD into Your Course website (http://universalcoursedesign. org/ucd-strategies). You can help to tap into the three different learning modes by using these cues while teaching: "say it–show it–do it." In a conducting class, you would first explain one way to conduct a cut-off, then model it, and of course then have the students try it. In this way, you have connected with all the learners in your class.

Of course when you "show it" you should get into the habit of describing what you are doing as you do it. "I am holding my fingers together then making a half circle." If you have a student with low vision, you can even model this a couple of times with one time encouraging the student to feel your fingers together and the movement your hand makes when you make a half circle. Students with hearing loss rely on speech reading, facial expressions, and gestures to understand what professors say. Get into the habit of speaking only when you face the class. The "say it" then will be accessible to those who speech-read.

Here are some additional instructional strategies:

- Use speech-to-text software (i.e., Dragon Dictation) that can be used to capture your lectures and change them into text.
- Post notes, slides, and any audio files on the course website.
- Create video podcasts of your lectures and post those on the course website.
- Provide links to podcasts from professors from other universities on the same topic, so students can hear content explained by someone other than you.
- Hyperlinking word and concepts can help students explore a topic in more depth.

When asking students to complete an assignment using technology,

- provide step-by-step instructions with screen shots or screen video recording as you model using the technology;
- consider making videos of important skills like making an oboe reed or directing choral warm-up exercises;
- use a gooseneck document camera hooked up to a Smartboard to demonstrate something hard to see;
- use smartboard software to capture additional notes you write on the board.

ASSESSMENT

Assessment is the process of gathering and discussing information from multiple and diverse sources in order to develop a deep understanding of what students know, understand, and can do with their knowledge as a result of their educational experiences; the process culminates when assessment results are used to improve subsequent learning (Huba & Freed, 2000). Of course, in the case of music, assessments can be extended to include conducting, singing, playing instruments, and performances that include compositions, improvisations, or arrangements.

Thompson, Johnstone, and Thurlow (2002) developed seven elements of universally designed assessments, listed here:

1. Inclusive assessment population (e.g., all populations who might take an assessment are considered during assessment development).
2. Precisely defined constructs (i.e., intended material or skills to be tested are transparent).
3. Accessible, nonbiased items (i.e., test items should not be biased against particular populations).
4. Amenability to accommodations (e.g., the test design should allow for the use of accommodations).
5. Simple, clear, and intuitive instructions.
6. Comprehensible language.
7. Maximum legibility (in both print and graphics).

It is important to be very clear about how students should submit assignments, when the assignment is due, and if you have an expectation for participation in class discussions. Rubrics should be created for all assessments of assignments, jury performances, teaching episodes, or presentations. It is helpful to provide examples from previous students that represent "A" work; these should be representative of multiple means of expression. Examples of rubrics that correspond to the syllabi are on the accompanying website for this book.

Provide descriptors of what "A" work looks like. Continue with B, C, and D work. An F is assuming the student did not do the work. Rubrics work best if they are developed in class with input from the students. It takes time but students consider it fairer and they also seem to do a better job in my experience. Display a rubric you used from a previous class and ask students if they agree with the method of assessment. If not, ask for suggestions for improvement. You can also suggest items to be assessed if you feel they are missing. Generally, the class will agree with your suggestions if they are tied to important enduring understandings in your syllabus.

Rubrics work best with a limited number of items, or else they become too cumbersome for everyone involved to use them effectively. I use between 4 and 10 items. Include use of technology options in the rubric; some students will do beautiful work in different types of software. Students who are good with website design might be encouraged to design a website that addresses a topic in class with links and visuals. Students should use a website accessibility checker to ensure that all users will be able to use the website. Use the Web Accessibility Initiative website to find checkers and guidelines for design (http://www.w3.org/WAI/eval/Overview.html).

Assign two or three students to take notes each class and upload their notes to the course software to be available to the other students. Other students can then focus on what is happening in class and retrieve the notes later. Having two or three versions of the notes allows for different ways individual students might understand the notes. Some students might draw flowcharts or notate musical ideas that can be easily captured by scanning the notes or taking a picture of the notes. Students with poor handwriting should take notes on a computer or tablet. All notes should be emailed to the professor to put on the course website. Students who record the class with audio or video recorders should share the files as well to be included in the course website.

Encourage and allow various types of items in assignments such as photographs, musical examples, diagrams, or color coding that help the student demonstrate understanding. Allow opportunities for students to select and adapt assignments according to their own personal interests. I had a wonderful music history professor in graduate school who believed each student should prepare and be responsible for teaching the class. She provided a list of topics that included everything from Woman Composers to Instrumental Styles. She was flexible enough to allow a student from Scotland to talk about Scottish composers, and he brought his bagpipes and talked about how one composer wrote for bagpipes and demonstrated on his! I still clearly remember this class that occurred 20 years ago and that experience became an unintended enduring understanding for me. I'll always remember how long it takes to produce that first pitch and how composers had to remember that when writing for bagpipes. I am also still impressed with the course and the professor's ability to support student interests but also to be flexible with their presentation styles.

If students are required to write a paper or complete a big project or assignment, consider allowing multiple opportunities for students to receive feedback before the final copy is due. Consider being flexible with due dates. I have learned that with my music education students, some are very overextended depending on the week and what is required in their lessons, ensembles, and recitals. If a student has his or her senior recital during the week a big project is due to me, there is no reason he or she could not turn that project in a week late. Students will do better work if they have a more flexible due date should they need it. However, there are some assignments that cannot be late. In music education, we must have acceptable lesson plans before we allow pre-service teachers to teach children. Even so, we can schedule the due date so students have a few days they can use to re-do the lesson plan or turn it in late if they have some sort of emergency. You need to decide which assignments you can be flexible with and which you cannot. For most of us, we are not usually able to grade big projects or papers all at once, so there is no harm if someone needs to turn in a paper a few days late when you are finishing up grading anyway.

Group evaluations are another excellent way to get feedback. This can be achieved in small groups or from the entire class. If all students are tackling the same problem, some might have important insights that can be helpful to their classmates.

Some professors use different types of graphic organizers to get regular feedback from the students. You might ask students to list the main points covered in class with an opportunity to ask you if there is any confusion. You can also use regular checks with your students to see how you are doing as a teacher. Sometimes you need strong nerves to read these because if they are anonymous, students might tell you things that can be embarrassing. Mostly, students will share constructive comments that either confirm your teaching is going well or ask you to slow down or give more time for assignments. Address these in class without asking who the author was and make an effort to improve where you can. We are all works in progress and can learn to be more effective instructors from literally anyone.

For professors who give tests, provide study tips and do not ask questions on material not covered. Even though it might be mentioned in the textbook, try to emphasize in class the all-important points that you would include on a test. Ask students for ideas on how best to assess skills or knowledge; they might have a better way than multiple-choice tests filled out on an electronically read form.

Consider giving online tests in the computer lab or making the test available online. This is especially valuable to students who might be distracted by sound from other rooms. This allows students who need extra time to have it and use resources they have available to them. Tests that evaluate students on short-term memorization of facts will likely not become enduring understandings; you might consider other methods of evaluation that either allow students to look up these facts or summarize what they understand based on your lectures, small-group discussions, and assignments.

Develop a glossary; students define terms discussed in class and post definitions online. Give credit for contributions and edit the final definition to make sure it is accurate.

Few universities provide training for faculty on development and evaluation of assessment tools. Other than music education faculty, school of music faculty are likely to have no training in assessment development. Faculty without experience in assessment development and evaluation are probably going to use assessment methods they experienced themselves as school of music students. The problem with relying on commonly used assessments is that faculty might be using tools that were never designed to be used with diverse student populations. Students like Sarah are unable to fit into rigid assessment structures that were designed for typical students.

Professors need to clearly define course outcomes or enduring understandings and the skills necessary to accomplish the outcomes. Consider as well skills needed by the student in order to access the intended construct. For example, Sarah needs to be able to process music notation through her visual mode. Speed and accuracy are going to impact Sarah's ability to visually understand music notation. The music theory professor is assuming she has those skills when in reality, Sarah is being assessed on a skill that is weak due to her learning disability. The professor does not offer her an alternative so Sarah is struggling to pass music theory. The assignments/assessments are not universally designed. All assignments/assessments in Sarah's music theory course are assessing students the same way and there is no variety. Not only will many students with similar learning disabilities have difficulty in music theory, but students with vision loss will also be unable to successfully complete written assignments/assessments.

It is probable that most music theory courses are taught this way because it is the way most of us experienced music theory ourselves in music school. Indeed, research in other academic areas in higher education affirms that professors who have never received training on varied methods of assessment and instructional approaches will continue to teach the way they were taught (Adams, 1992; Ambrose & Ambrose, 1995; Ehrmann, 1995; Felder, 1993). Conway and Hodgman (2009) encourage professors to consider innovative approaches to the preparation of musicians, and those without any training in teaching tend to use the "transmission model" of teaching. "A good instructor cannot simply transmit knowledge and expect students to learn it" (p. 3). One size definitely does not fit all and I am guessing that most schools of music notice that first- and second-year undergraduate students struggle the most with music theory. They fail the course and some are so hopeless about their ability to ever pass music theory that they end up dropping out of college or switching majors. Does this sound familiar?

The characteristics of universal design of assessment allow for students to use different learning modes (visual, aural, kinesthetic/tactile) for both input and output of information and can be achieved in all courses, ensembles, and lessons that are designed with flexibility (Dolan et al., 2005).

Using principles of understanding by design will help you determine whether your course and assessments are universally designed and if you have identified the enduring understandings that music students will need to know along with flexible methods to attain those understandings. As you use backward planning to develop your course curriculum, consider the skills students will need to be successful in your course and whether you are making false assumptions about the abilities of some music students.

ENVIRONMENT

Environment is sometimes the most difficult for us to control but there are some things we can attend to that might help students with disabilities in our classrooms. Our classrooms, rehearsal spaces, and studios should be comfortable for students, include accessible access and noise control, and allow for preferential seating. Comfort means more than room temperature; it also refers to the tone of the professor in regard to welcoming all types of students.

Welcoming everyone to your class helps to create an inclusive class climate. Avoid stereotyping students; for example, a professor often refers to African American students from low-income urban school districts as only prepared to sing Gospel music. This is obviously a stereotype that puts African Americans, who potentially want to audition for entrance into this professor's music school at a disadvantage. The professor is likely not to be open about the students' ability to sing other styles of vocal music.

Schools of music can be welcoming to students with disabilities and other marginalized groups by first looking at how their image is portrayed online. A full-service disability-friendly school, has an ADA map of the school of music with images of people with disabilities (Figure 4.3). The map should feature icons that show where automatic doors are located, accessible restrooms, and other features that students with disabilities appreciate.

Darrow (2016) discusses social interactions and acceptance of people with disabilities by persons without disabilities. Wright (1983) found that social interactions of people without disabilities included conversations that were terminated early, less smiling, and signs of restlessness or discomfort. In addition, people without disabilities often do not make eye contact and keep a greater physical distance from people with disabilities. Darrow cites more recent studies that show little progress has been made in improvement of social interactions (Michalko, 2002; Putnam, Greenen, Power, Saxton, Finney, & Dautel, 2003; Smart, 2009).

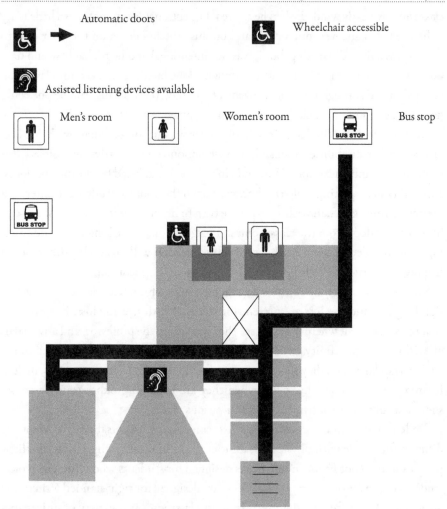

FIGURE 4.3 ADA School of Music Map

Try to make a point of making eye contact with students as they enter and smile or say hello to them by name, particularly to students with vision loss. Notice if a student with a mobility problem needs help or if access is blocked or difficult for him or her. I have noticed on my own campus that accessible entrances are sometimes at the opposite end of the building where I teach. Therefore a person who might already be moving slower than the typical student has farther to go to get inside the building and up the elevator to my classroom. It is essential for teachers to be flexible when students with disabilities are a little late. I once had a student with cerebral palsy who walked with crutches. It was important to him to walk and stay as physically mobile as he could even though a powered wheelchair would be faster. He was always 10 minutes late to class and was clearly winded when he arrived. His entrance was sometimes a little noisy as he tried to maneuver into a chair and put his crutches down on the floor next to him. It was a little distracting, but it was not intentional and he probably would have been on time had he not had to walk through a long building to reach my classroom. Others entered through the more convenient entrance, but with his crutches, he could not open the doors of the closer entrance unless someone was there to help.

Noise control is a challenge in schools of music, but for a student with ADHD or many other disabilities, focusing on instruction can be nearly impossible when someone is singing next door. We can help reduce sound bleed by closing our doors. I am guilty of forgetting to do this because I open the door for students to enter, and they enter through a hall with a 90-degree turn to my classroom. I cannot see or easily access the door from the classroom, so I forget. Consider asking for soundproofing to be installed in rooms with lots of sound bleed. It will make a big difference in helping some students to follow what is going on in the classroom.

Some students with disabilities do much better with preferential seating. When sign language interpreters are present for students with hearing loss, it is essential that the students sit where they can see the interpreter, the professor, and any visuals all within close proximity. Students who use wheelchairs are often relegated to the back of the classroom; they should have the freedom to sit at different places, including next to friends or other peers when they are in small groups. Your classroom should ideally allow for students to sit in various places.

Student desks can be problematic when considering universal design. Many are difficult for people with physical disabilities to get into easily. Big people and little people often do not fit in student desks designed for students who represent typical students of the 1960s and '70s. Most desks are designed for right-handed writers and are awkward for left-handed writers. In most classrooms in a variety of universities where I have taught there have only been right-handed desks. Tables are more accessible to students of different sizes, especially if the chairs are adjustable. Tables create other problems, however. They are hard to reposition and take up a lot of room. In active classes they will likely be problematic.

Furniture should be flexible enough that it can be moved around to accommodate different types of learning situations. If the chairs are fastened to the floor, then small-group work is difficult to achieve. Music education rooms should be equipped with technology and set up to resemble classrooms as they will appear in K–12 schools. Secondary ensemble courses should be in rooms where music can be played or sung. Elementary general music classes should be in rooms large enough to accommodate dancing, instruments, and areas where students can sit on the floor. All spaces should include technology, instruments, and furniture that would appear in typical classrooms that accommodate learners of all abilities.

Smartboards are great in all classrooms but essential in music education class-rooms. They provide a level of interactivity that is so important for diverse learners. Imagine a lesson on chords and a student being able to drag notes into a chord and tap the chord to hear it while others in the class watch. For some students with disabilities that impact brain processing, the opportunity to learn by manipulating music through touch provides a different way for brains to access and understand critical information. Sarah might actually keep up in music theory if she had that type of multi-sensory learning approach.

Smartboards and similar devices allow text and visuals that might be difficult to see in the textbook to be greatly enlarged. When you are discussing a visual, put the image on a slide that you can show in a much larger form than students can see in notes, textbooks, or even on their own computers. Sound, including your speech, should be audible by all learners. Some professors use a microphone, especially when there is competing sound around the classroom. Some students with hearing loss may bring assisted listening devices to help amplify the professor's voice directly into their hearing aids (this is further discussed in Chapter 10).

In classes lasting an hour or longer, provide breaks and changes in structure of the class. For example, you might divide the class into small groups, or have stu-dents play instruments, sing, stand, and conduct. How can you deliver instruc-tion that incorporates more of these types of active learning? If the class piano lab is available or could be made available for your theory or music history class, it would be appropriate to incorporate actual music making into your typical class sessions. Dalcroze realized this problem when he observed music theory stu-dents at the Geneva Conservatory studying theory without ever making a sound or connecting with the expressive qualities of music (Mead, 1994). Eurythmics, or expressive movement, emerged as a way to address a gap in musical under-standing. Everyone understands the importance of conductors being expressive through movement. Dalcroze applied eurythmics to theory and harmony, and it is used today in music education and conducting primarily. More enduring understandings might result in deep connections if they are presented through more multi-sensory learning modes.

If you teach in a large classroom, be sure you repeat students' questions so those in the back can hear. Student questions can often help clarify content in ways you would never dream.

Be sensitive to cultural, ethnic, religious, LGBT (lesbian, gay, bisexual, and trans-gender), and gender diversity. Thinking about a universal design classroom helps us to consider all the possible students who enter our classroom, including the groups named above. Of course, it is not unusual for a student with a disability to also be a member of a minority group along with being a terrific musician!

SUMMARY

Universal design is highly effective when used to make facilities and instruction accessible to all students. Beginning with a course syllabus, focus on creating materials and curriculum that include multiple methods of representation, expression, and engagement. Understanding by design is an approach to curriculum development that focuses on identifying course outcomes by identifying enduring understandings, concepts you hope students will remember ten years from now, and scaffolding a sequential curriculum to guide students in flexible ways to reach enduring understandings.

Universal design in postsecondary education can be implemented on many levels in postsecondary schools of music. Figures 4.1 and 4.2 offer guidelines for universal design in instruction, services, music, and information technology as well as physical spaces.

SPECIFIC LEARNING DISABILITIES

Greg has a beautiful tenor voice. He was a standout in high school choir and had a lead in the school musical for two years. He participated in the All-State Honor Choir for three years and received a scholarship to a prominent summer music camp. He never considered becoming anything but a performer. He was specifically passionate about being a Broadway singer. Living close to New York City, he frequently traveled to the city to see musicals and has had a few lessons with a prominent Broadway star.

Greg has chosen to audition for music schools with strong voice performance instructors and excellent musical theater degrees. His first-choice school held auditions last Saturday, and although he nailed the audition on his prepared piece, he struggled with the sight-reading. He also was told during the interview at the admissions office that his ACT math scores were too low for him to be accepted. He mentioned this to the professor he has been communicating with who has already offered him a full scholarship for next fall. She said not to worry about being rejected because the school for music can ask for an exception for talent. The professor and others listening to his audition were disappointed in his sight-reading. His difficulties clearly were not due to nerves. He just couldn't read music. Greg has a specific learning disability called dyscalculia.

SPECIFIC LEARNING DISABILITIES (LD) are currently the highest occurring disability in the United States. It is estimated that 2.4 million or 5% of students in public schools are diagnosed with specific learning disabilities. Forty-two percent of the country's 5.7 million school-age children receive special education services under the Individuals with Disabilities Education Act (IDEA). Two-thirds of those students are male, and Black and Hispanic students tend to be overrepresented in many states while white and Asian students tend to be underrepresented in many states in the specific learning disabilities category (Cortiella & Horowitz, 2014).

Sixty-seven percent of high school students with LD enroll in postsecondary education within eight years of graduating from high school. Most initially attended a two-year college at nearly double the rate of typical students from the general population. Students with LD will attend four-year college at half the rate of typical students from the general population. The college completion rate for these students is 41% compared to 52% of typical students. Cost is cited as the most common reason students do not finish college. This is primarily due to the amount of time it takes a student with a learning disability to complete college and the limits on financial aid. Most students cannot afford to pay for college on their own, and students with learning disabilities struggle to work while they attend college because of the time demands from classes. Some students with LDs that impact their ability to read might need three to five times as long to absorb something a typical student would read fluently.

Before the adoption of the ADA Amendments Act of 2008 (ADAAA), federal courts frequently reasoned that a student could not have a learning disability if he or she had a record of academic success (Grossman, 2014). Many universities require burdensome proof of disability that requires students to be retested. This is not only expensive but it also is not necessary since learning disabilities do not go away as the individual grows older. Once a person is properly diagnosed, there is no need to prove that the learning disability still exists (AHEAD, 2012).

Another possible reason for lack of success in finishing college is that only one in four, or 24%, of students who received special education support in high school consider themselves to have a disability. These students are resistant to disclosing their disability to student services staff and professors, so they are not receiving support in college.

Of those who do disclose their disability, many report difficulty in satisfying the documentation requirements needed to receive support and services at postsecondary schools. Therefore, only 17% of college students received accommodations and supports in postsecondary education for their disability, compared to 94% of the same students in high school (Cortiella & Horowitz, 2014). To take tests successfully, many students with learning disabilities need a quiet environment and no time limits, for example, but if they are not registered with disability services, they likely will not have that accommodation.

Returning to Greg's story, the statistics for secondary students with learning disabilities who receive average or above-average scores on math or reading assessments, compared with the typical population, is 12% to 26%. Students with learning disabilities in high school earn lower grades and experience higher rates of course failure in high school than typical students, and one-third are retained at least one year during their K–12 education. One of every two students with LD faced school disciplinary action such as suspension or expulsion in 2011, yet students with LD have the same aspirations and goals to attend college and have careers as typical students.

The good news is that in recent years, there have been major changes in K–12 special education that help to identify struggling students with learning disabilities through a system in place in most schools, Response to Intervention (RTI). Previously, teachers would identify students who were having difficulty and refer them for testing; after a year, there would be a meeting with a team of professionals to talk about what educational, emotional, and medical needs a student needs in order to be successful in school. Instead of waiting a year for assistance, students are now given support immediately. This timely intervention prevents children from falling behind their peers.

Most children with learning disabilities are delivered the same curriculum as their typical peers with support in the general classroom. This means that although the student's learning disability will never disappear, students will be coming to college with a better understanding of their learning disability even if they choose not to advocate for themselves. A very important skill that special educators instill in all students with disabilities is self-determination. When individuals understand their abilities and disabilities and what works best for them in learning, social, or many other contexts, they will be able to ask for what they need or simply provide what they need for themselves.

As of 2015, we see a mix of postsecondary students with self-determination skills. Sarah in Chapter 3 never learned to be an advocate for herself and was accustomed to her teachers and parents anticipating and meeting her needs. Greg disclosed his disability to the professor with whom he was communicating in the school of music in the hope that this professor could help to explain his difficulties and advocate for him on the university level. Once accepted into the school of music, he will then need to meet with staff at the disability services office with all of his most-recent documentation. This will enable him to get the accommodations that he needs.

In the future, schools of music can anticipate an increasing number of students with identified learning disabilities auditioning and attending postsecondary education. A study funded by the US Department of Education has followed students with disabilities aged 13 to 16 years of age beginning in 2000 and ending in 2009 when the same students were 21 to 25 years old. The National Longitudinal

Transition Study-2 (n.d.) was a replication of the NLTS begun in 1985 and completed in 1993. Both studies provide the following information:

- Describe the characteristics of secondary school youth in special education and their households.
- Describe the secondary school experiences of youth in special education, including their schools, school programs, related services, and extracurricular activities.
- Describe the experiences of youth once they leave secondary school, including adult programs and services, social activities, etc.
- Measure the secondary school and postschool outcomes of youth in the education, employment, social, and residential domains.
- Identify factors in youths' secondary school and postschool experiences that contribute to more positive outcomes (n.d.).

The two NLTS longitudinal transition studies show an 18% increase in students with disabilities enrolled in postsecondary education in 2005 compared to 1990. This study provided much information on changes in how students with disabilities are prepared for entering college and their success rates by disability once they enroll.

Keep in mind that most students with learning disabilities do not disclose their disability or ask for help once they reach college, yet results of another survey (Markow & Pieters, 2011) found that students with learning disabilities or attention deficit/hyperactivity disorders placed the same importance on a college education as other students; however, they had lower aspirations regarding their own future in higher education. The students reported having less confidence of achieving their goals for the future and were less likely to receive guidance from teachers and school counselors about how to prepare for college.

LEARNED HELPLESSNESS

Psychologist Martin Seligman (1975) first identified a behavior he later termed "learned helplessness" as a result of studying dogs being given electric shocks while unable to escape. The animals began to behave as if they were helpless to change the situation, similar to the way people with depression experience some situations. People with depression will easily give up, a behavior also observed in people with disabilities, especially people with learning disabilities. "Persistence is a byproduct of success, and if success is repeatedly out of reach of the student, he or she learns not to try" (p. 23). "Students exhibit *learned helplessness* when there is not a good match between learning objectives and student attributes; therefore, one single set of standardized objectives cannot be expected to meet the unique learning abilities of individual students in inclusive classrooms" (Stainback, Stainback, Stefanich, & Alper, 1996, p. 210).

Students at the postsecondary level will occasionally exhibit learned helplessness, particularly when they find themselves in a situation where they have previously experienced frustration and failure. Students with learning disabilities like Greg will become easily frustrated and give up when forced to read traditional music with the expectation that because of his considerable talent, he should be able to read fluently. The savvy professor will quickly recognize this and talk to Greg about a more efficient way for him to learn or adapt the notation in a way that is less overwhelming for him.

In summary, students with learning disabilities are enrolling in postsecondary education at record numbers. You should expect these students to be as talented and motivated to become fine musicians, teachers, and therapists as your students without disabilities. However, it will be critical for you to keep these cautions in mind:

- They are easily frustrated and will give up.
- If they feel as though there is no hope for passing a course or making successful progress toward a degree, they will often give up and drop out of school.
- Most students do not disclose their disability to disability services or to professors.
- Most students do not think they have a disability.
- Most students with LD do believe they will go to postsecondary schools and have good careers.

In some cases, the studio professor will be the first person the student with a learning disability encounters who may realize there is a problem. The professor who is supportive and accepting is likely to make it much easier for the student to be comfortable disclosing his or her disability. Once the student talks about the disability you can encourage him or her to register with disabled services. In the meantime, there are many strategies for studio professors, classroom professors, and ensemble directors to use that will be helpful for the student and reduce stress and feelings of helplessness.

WHAT IS A LEARNING DISABILITY?

Bateman (1965) was the first researcher to identify learning disabilities as related to an achievement-aptitude discrepancy. The US government sponsored two task forces to investigate learning disabilities during the late 1960s. One task force was composed of medical researchers and the other was a group of educators. The task forces could not agree on a single definition until 1968 when a new committee developed this definition adopted by the US Office of Education:

> Children with special (specific) LD exhibit a disorder in one or more of the basic psychological processes involved in understanding or in using spoken or written language. These may be manifested in disorders of listening, thinking, talking, reading, writing, spelling, or arithmetic. They include conditions which have been referred to as perceptual handicaps, brain injury, minimal brain dysfunction, dyslexia, developmental aphasia, etc. They do not include learning problems that are due primarily to visual, hearing or motor handicaps, to mental retardation, emotional disturbance, or to environmental disadvantage. (US Office of Education, 1968, p. 34)

Until recently, children with specific learning disabilities were identified through the use of a discrepancy formula based on results of educational tests compared to the child's IQ score. For example, if the child had an IQ of 130 (above-average) but in some math tests tested five grade levels below his or her current grade level, the discrepancy between the two indicated there was a learning disability. The child typically has average or above average intelligence but functions below his apparent intelligence level in one or more specific areas. The discrepancy is where the disability exists. Response to Intervention (RTI) is used in public schools to intervene quickly to help prevent delays in providing students with support for reading, writing, and math.

With 41% of all children receiving special education services for specific learning disabilities, this is the category with the highest incidence. Learning disabilities are also referred to as hidden or invisible disabilities. This is because LDs do not manifest themselves physically or through the senses; it is hard to tell that a person has a learning disability by just looking at him or her.

Trying to explain learning disabilities can be complicated but for music professors, it is important to understand that the brain processes information coming in (input), processes information going out (output), or makes sense of information once it is in the brain. Recently, there have been brain studies using fMRI (functional magnetic resonance imaging) machines to look at brain function when individuals do activities that impact their learning disability, like trying to remember a string of numbers. We are also beginning to understand that learning disabilities affect how a person understands music and sound, knowledge that was impossible to have before we could do very music-specific fMRI brain studies (McCord, 2015).

It is also not unusual for children to be identified "twice-exceptional," or having traits of a disability along with traits of giftedness. When this happens, it sometimes seems even more impossible to imagine that the student could have a disability. Greg is a student who would be "twice-exceptional."

Many times, students with learning disabilities are called lazy or unmotivated because they seem to not be applying themselves to the task at hand. For example, it is not unusual to see children in beginning instrumental music classes writing the names of the notes in their method books. Music educators are taught to quickly stop students from doing that and make them erase everything they have written because it is a "crutch." I believe music teachers should encourage and praise students who do this, no matter what age. This is a self-adaptation that enables the student with a cognitive processing disability to function well in band class.

DYSLEXIA

Dyslexia is often referred to as a specific reading disability (SRD) in children who are labeled early as poor readers.

> Dyslexia is a specific learning disability that is neurobiological in origin. It is characterized by difficulties with accurate and/or fluent word recognition and by poor spelling and decoding abilities. These difficulties typically result from a deficit in the phonological component of language that is often unexpected in relation to other cognitive abilities and the provision of effective classroom instruction. Secondary consequences may include problems in reading comprehension and reduced reading experience that can impede growth of vocabulary. (Lyon, Shaywitz, & Shaywitz, 2003)

In addition, nonlinguistic deficits such as difficulty with concentration, poor short-term memory, and challenges with organization may also be present (Helland & Asbjornsen, 2000; Reid & Green, 2007). Students with dyslexia tend to not learn well from written material and rely heavily on classroom discussions and visuals (Oslund, 2014). Dyslexia varies in different languages due to unique linguistic features and cognitive demands on the language (Besson, Schon, Moreno, Santos, & Magne, 2007; Chung, Ho, Chan, Tsang, & Lee, 2010; Lam, 2010). This is due to the differences in alphabetic and character-based languages.

Dyslexia and other learning disabilities do not disappear as the individual grows older, so there is a need for students to learn adaptive strategies and to receive support throughout their life span (Nalavany et al., 2011). Auditory processing disorder

> This is an example of text written in the DYSLEXIE font. It is more comfortable for students with dyslexia to read text written in DYSLEXIE, especially when printed on white paper with black text. Printing should be on matte paper or sometimes students prefer colored paper or reading with a screen overlay of colored plastic.

FIGURE 5.1 Example of Text Written in DYSLEXIE Font

is present in about half of individuals with dyslexia (King et al., 2003). This will mean that students take longer to process verbal information, they may have trouble retrieving words, or they may use an incorrect word that sounds similar to the one intended— for example, saying the word "saxophone" instead of "xylophone." Other common problems that occur in individuals with dyslexia are difficulties with fine motor coordination and gross motor coordination (Ramus, Pidgeon, & Frith, 2003). Students with dyslexia sometimes respond well to speech therapy to help with processing language.

Many students with learning disabilities, especially dyslexia, do poorly on standardized tests. Many universities have cut-off scores for tests like the GRE (Graduate Record Exam) without considering students with learning disabilities. In most schools of music, when faculty know a student has talent and want to accept the student despite the low test score, they will often request an allowance, particularly if the student discloses the disability.

A new font has been developed that makes reading much easier for individuals with dyslexia. The font, dyslexie, is designed for people with dyslexia to read with less effort. Each font character counteracts the symptoms of dyslexia that include changing, rotating, and flipping characters. A sample of dyslexie is shown in Figure 5.1. I now create any Powerpoint visuals with text using dyslexie. Information on purchasing the font can be found at www.dyslexiefont.nl.

MUSIC AND DYSLEXIA

Research on children with dyslexia and music began in 1985 with Atterbury, who discovered that children with dyslexia had difficulty identifying rhythmic patterns and trouble reading notation. Goswami (2011) found that when children have difficulty perceiving amplitude rise time this is probably an indication of a developmental learning difficulty. Rise time refers to the amount of time required for a pitch to reach maximum intensity. Different instruments respond faster or slower, and musicians learn how to compensate for rise time by adjusting speed of air, bow, pressure from a mallet, or other modifications. Children with dyslexia have significant difficulty in their ability to gauge rise time as compared with typical peers.

Other studies showed that children with dyslexia have a difficult time hearing strong and weak beats in music compared to their typical peers (Huss et al., 2011). Goswami found that both children and adults demonstrated difficulty with the ability to follow rhythmic patterns. "Children and adults with dyslexia were much more erratic than controls in tapping in time with a metronome at 2 Hz" (Goswami, 2012).

All of these documented difficulties are due to sluggish processing within the brain. There are no therapies, medication, or "growing out of it." Learning disabilities do not heal, but the musician can develop strategies for compensating for known problems. Universal design for instruction is immensely effective in including musicians with dyslexia. A multi-sensory approach to teaching students with specific learning disabilities has long been a top recommendation to music teachers (Atterbury, 1990; Hammel, 2013; Heikkila & Knight, 2012; McCord, 2004; Overy, 2003; Pratt, 2008; Register, Darrow, et al., 2007; Westcombe, 2002). For example, Heikkila and Knight (2012) encourage music teachers to assist students who have difficulty identifying high and low pitches to project notation on a screen and have students follow the pitch contour with their hand as they sing. Using a combination of aural, visual, and kinesthetic/tactile approaches to learning a musical concept supports learning. In the studio, professors may not have Smartboards for projection; however, it is easy to use the hand to follow the pitch contour. Also, consider incorporating movement to feel rhythm or other multi-sensory strategies.

Besson et al. (2007) found that children with dyslexia had difficulty discriminating strong pitch changes compared to typical children; this might indicate problems with tuning and balance when playing or singing with others. These authors also found that pitch processing in music and speech can be improved through music experiences and practice.

READING MUSIC

Postsecondary music students probably have some ability to read music or they would not have been accepted into music school. However, dyslexia now appears to impact music notation reading in varied ways according to the type and severity of the dyslexia. Professionals have developed alternative notation systems that simplify notation so the reader has less to process. The first to do this with documented success was Margaret Hubicki and her Colour-Staff System in the 1970s (2001). Using images or colors in place of black notational symbols provides memory supports and requires less processing. At the Resonaari School in Helsinki, a system developed for individuals with intellectual disabilities, FigureNotes, is being used with young typical children as a way to slowly introduce music notation. It appears to be an inclusive way to gradually introduce music notation to all children and is universal design for learning in that respect.

Musicians with slow processing in reading notation generally process music notation by looking for pitch contour, chunks of rhythm as "fast" or "slow," and then everything else (meter, key signature, clef, dynamics, and other expressive markings) in that order. Depending on the ability of the musician with dyslexia, errors will likely occur with rhythm since many musicians do not actually count rhythms but make something like an educated guess about them. If they hear the music first, musicians will be much more accurate; in fact, this is one of the preferred ways for musicians with learning disabilities to learn music. Seeing and hearing the notation at the same time greatly improves accuracy. Therefore, recording lessons and providing recordings or links to recordings with excellent models of a piece, exercise, or improvisation are the most helpful if they can be provided ahead of time.

Ensemble directors and studio teachers can create web pages with links or embed recordings of ensembles or individuals performing the piece being prepared. A free program called the *Amazing Slow-Downer* allows the student to import an MP4 file and see and hear it played at slower tempos without changing the pitch. This is an excellent way for students with learning disabilities to practice at slower, less frustrating tempos. College musicians with learning disabilities have probably developed incredible skills in learning by ear as one of their strongest self-accommodations. In many schools of music, this is not a skill that is typically celebrated by traditional professors and ensemble directors. I have often wondered whether many of the musicians in the early Count Basie bands had learning disabilities and never learned to read music. It is well documented that many of the great early arrangements were taught by ear. Maybe because these musicians were listening so closely to each other is why those bands are accepted as the most rhythmically swinging bands of all time.

You may not be interested in creating rhythmically swinging bands, but all ensembles care about intonation, balance, blend, and beautiful sound. These are all related to the development of sophisticated aural skills. They are also concepts in universal design, and developing multi-sensory approaches to working on these would be easy.

DYSCALCULIA

Dyscalculia, arithmetical learning disability, or specific mathematics disability, occurs in about 3% to 6% of the population to the degree that they are considered disabled. Many children with dyscalculia also have dyslexia. People with dyscalculia misuse signs, forget to carry, misplace digits, or approach problems from left to right (Shalev, 2004). Students with dyscalculia will often forget dots next to notes and read the value of the note as not dotted; forget key signatures, especially if they change within the piece; and sometimes struggle with reading left to right.

Some students with dyslexia and dyscalculia read slowly from left to right. They are slow to look ahead to the next word or in the case of music, the next measure or phrase. They end up being behind the ensemble. In special education, a strategy is to have an aid use a device called Reading Rulers or Reading Helpers that are made of cardboard with a little plastic window inserted into the middle. The aid guides the student to read ahead by moving the window on to the next word or sentence. This has been helpful for students who have difficulty with getting stuck on words as they read. It can be used similarly in music. A less intrusive way is to input music in electronic software and set the tempo and read the music at tempo as the file plays silently. For example, in a music notation software after hitting the play button, the music scrolls along in tempo. Much like the Reading Ruler, the musician is visually nudged forward in the music as the software displays. iPads are able to accommodate notation programs that are played back as the student reads the music. Some programs highlight each measure or show a cursor over each beat. The highlighting or blinking cursor ends up functioning like the special education aid that uses the little window device. In lessons, the window device is effective, but the student will need someone to do that when he or she practices or will need an electronic solution as mentioned above. This is an assistive technology solution and can be requested through the university's disability services. Depending on software used, the ideal would be a tablet mounted on a stand. The iPad solution is a more universal design because it is more seamless and allows musicians to read music from a music stand like others in the ensemble.

Other students experience music notes visually as jumping around on the page or disappearing altogether. A very common solution used in the special education classroom is a plastic colored overlay to reduce some of the bright contrast between the black notes and white paper. Looking at music can be quite fatiguing for many musicians with disabilities and the colored overlays reduce the fatigue. On the cover of this book is an example of the overlay being used in an oboe lesson to make reading music less fatiguing.

Poole (2001) recalls having common problems with reading music: "rather than try to memorize written notation, I try to remember visual patterns that my fingers can then play. My piano teacher would never accept that I needed time to think in silence about what I was about to play. If I played a wrong note, I needed to pause before attempting to correct it—I needed the time to work out where in fact my fingers ought to have gone" (p. 55).

DYSGRAPHIA

Dysgraphia, or specific writing disability, is seen in children with typical motor development but with handwriting problems. Handwriting for the individual with dysgraphia is an orthographic learning disability characterized by frequent spelling errors. Visual memory is required to spell accurately and children with dysgraphia experience difficulty in recalling spelling of words or trouble with finding written words to express ideas. In the most current special education literature, specific writing disability is now termed "dyslexia." There are no published studies on music and dysgraphia but these students likely would have difficulty writing music, particularly writing notes within a space or on a line.

DYSPRAXIA

Dyspraxia or developmental coordination disorder is often referred to as clumsy child syndrome. Children with dyspraxia have trouble planning and completing fine motor tasks that require single steps or multiple steps. Buttoning clothes and tying shoes involve performing multiple small steps and can be difficult for the child with dyspraxia. Imagine children with dyspraxia putting together a wind instrument; the process is likely to be highly frustrating for them. Others have trouble coordinating muscle movements involved in speech and some have problems estimating space, including difficulty moving objects from one place to another. Some children have trouble distinguishing left from right hand. There are no published studies of dyspraxia and music, although musicians with dyspraxia might possibly struggle with playing instruments that require muscle coordination and embouchure control. It is likely students with dyspraxia self-select out of playing some instruments because of their negative experiences struggling with learning to play an instrument.

Students with dyspraxia often respond best to physical or occupational therapy to help the brain create new neural pathways for processing motor-sensory stimuli. Writing down steps to remember when performing a multi-step physical task can be helpful to individuals with dyspraxia.

STRATEGIES FOR TEACHING MUSICIANS WITH LEARNING DISABILITIES

One of the primary features of a learning disability is slow cognitive processing when the individual is trying to access the area that the specific learning disability impacts. Because processing is slow it is important to give wait time for students to respond. Wait time needs to be silent. Resist the urge to give clues or talk as the student thinks; this only jumbles up the information in the students' mind and makes it hard for them to remember the question.

When the person with a learning disability experiences anxiety or stress it becomes more difficult to process efficiently. A common problem that occurs while processing is distractions: visual, aural, or even tactile. The student literally loses her place and has to start over. For example, the teacher asks, "What is the fingering for F sharp?" The student has to retrieve the fingering from memory, and she might first think about the familiar F natural fingering, but she knows she has to do something different to make it an F sharp. At this point, in her processing someone in the room drops a mouthpiece cap and it bangs on the floor. Her thinking process is interrupted, and she loses her place and has to work through the process again to come up with the answer. Occasionally these students become so lost in their thinking that they need to ask the teacher what the question was again.

Reading choral music is very overwhelming for students with many kinds of disabilities. Octavos contain too much information, and it is hard for the student to find and stay on his or her part. Add to that frustration the need to read notation (something almost impossible for many students with LDs) and words at the same time!

Allowing extra time is essential for the student with a learning disability. This can look different depending upon the music; for example, a student is learning the alto part of a choral piece in the university chorus. The director could provide a recording of only the alto part before the piece is introduced in the choir rehearsal. The student is then able to learn in her most comfortable learning style. She might elect to learn the alto part completely by ear and not use the music notation at all. She could also listen to the music and follow the words with her finger, eventually also making some connection to the music notation. She might look at an adapted score with all other parts left off except the alto part shown with colored highlights appearing in each space of the treble clef. Color overlays might be used or the music can be printed on colored paper or with enlarged notation or combinations of these. This is an accommodation with which disabled services can help. They provide note-takers for students who have difficulty listening and writing. This would be a similar need; the choral music needs to be adapted in the most appropriate way for the student, so she can participate without getting lost in the music. A choral student without the disability could sing the part and record it for the student who needs to learn aurally or adapt the written notation in a way that is helpful to the student who learns best in another way.

Music professors need to be aware of setting students up for success by allowing for adaptations such as the ones illustrated throughout this chapter. It is likely that typical students within the class or ensemble benefit from some of the same adaptations as well. All of this should be worked out with the student privately first. The student needs to decide for himself or herself if the adaptation works or if something else works better. The student also might decide that he or she would rather try to learn the same way the other students are learning, and the professor should then support the student in pursuing that avenue. *Self-determination* is an important skill that students with disabilities need to learn.

Individuals with learning disabilities do not like being confronted by the unknown; it is strategic to establish routines and develop trust as soon as possible to help them relax and do their best learning. Avoid asking students with learning disabilities to read or play by themselves in front of peers without asking them first. If professors want them to do this, it is best to let them know several days before so they have time to prepare.

Many people with learning disabilities talk about the amount of concentration and effort it takes to process difficult content. For some, it creates fatigue and can eventually make the task or activity something the student tries to avoid. This is quite prevalent among children with reading disabilities; they grow to dislike reading because it is so exhausting. Professors can help by recognizing when a student becomes frustrated or gives up easily; they can adapt by requiring fewer problems or tasks connected to an assignment or assessment than for typical students. Students with disabilities also respond well to a distraction-free place to work on assignments, and to taking tests that don't require completion within a certain time.

Use of repetition with added multi-sensory supports is immensely helpful and is often appreciated by typical students. Professors should sequence information and activities so students do not become overwhelmed by having to hold too much material in their memory. For example, when teaching a student to improvise over a specific chord structure using patterns or scales, the professor might introduce one chord at a time and review the pattern or scale that is associated with that chord rather than giving the student a page of music that includes chord symbols and patterns/scales notated with the chord. The student should apply the pattern or scale on his or her instrument for each chord one at a time and then add perhaps four chords and practice those, then maybe eight chords with time to practice and finally put the entire sixteen measures together. This helps to keep the student from becoming frustrated.

Many students with learning disabilities also struggle with short-term memory problems. It is difficult for them to hold material in short-term memory without losing it. Through many repetitions, a student can then transfer new material to long-term memory and remember content better.

Hammel (2013) advises teachers to consider using what she calls the "Big Four." The Big Four are used to assist students in reading music and include Color, Size, Modality, and Pacing. Color has been discussed and may include overlays, printing on colored paper, or highlighting music in color. Size can be used to make music larger and bolder, which is easier to read. Hammel gradually adds more information beginning with a blank score. Referring back to choral music, the teacher can sequence learning by beginning with only the notation of the alto part, perhaps even removing the time and key signatures, title, and other information. In the following week if the student is mastering the pitch, duration, and words, then those removed items can be added. Then add the slurs and possibly in the next lesson or rehearsal add the full score. The printed music can be supplemented with recordings that gradually add these items in as well. Modality has been discussed earlier in this chapter as multi-sensory learning. Hammel advocates teaching music in at least three ways using visual, aural, and kinesthetic learning modes. She records lessons or rehearsals and allows students to review the recordings at home. In addition, Hammel suggests that teachers allow students to respond in their strongest learning mode when being assessed—for example, students with writing difficulties can answer questions verbally.

Auditions create concerns for many students with learning disabilities. If processing music notation is identified as a difficulty, why do we continue to make students with disabilities sight-read in auditions? Auditions are stressful, and musicians with learning disabilities are already going to struggle in that sort of environment, but if music reading is difficult, they will likely not compare well with other musicians. Audition judges and teachers should ask themselves if sight-reading fluently is really a necessary skill for students to demonstrate. If it is, then recognize that students with learning disabilities will likely do poorly on an audition requiring sight-reading.

Finally, Hammel (2013) defines pacing as allowing for individual needs regarding a person's speed in learning new material. She provides a valuable list of steps that students with organizational challenges can use to learn a new piece. A checklist that helps organize their practice routines will help to ensure that the musician is provided guidance and support for learning music away from the teacher.

When you are thinking of strategies to help, look to the student as a resource; he has been making music for many years before he came to you and will likely have strategies that have gotten him through to music school. Ask him! Perhaps between the professor and student additional strategies can be developed that will work even better. Flexibility and a positive, supportive approach will help the student to trust you and will let the two of you work together.

- PATIENCE—processing time is slower and if you try to hurry the student it only creates anxiety and makes it harder for him or her to process.
- Use recordings to offer another mode of learning.
- Connect the kinesthetic/tactile sense as much as possible to learning. Encourage students to stand and move.
- Allow students to write in their music, even if it seems they are writing things like names of notes.
- Encourage students to use colored highlighters in their music if they lose their places.
- Use reading rulers and National Reading Styles Institute (NRSI)colored overlays for students with dyslexia.
- Enlarge music to increase size of notation.
- Eliminate or reduce high-stakes sight-reading.
- Give frequent breaks, especially if students develop headaches or begin to rub their eyes.
- Use checklists and visual supports, especially for new fingerings or techniques.
- Encourage the use of assistive technology
- Whenever possible use color, size, modality, and pacing to help provide adaptations that will help students with learning disabilities.
- Use less material but at the same difficulty level.

SUMMARY

Students with specific learning disabilities are not uncommon. Professors will likely have at least one student, and in large classes and ensembles, perhaps as many as a dozen. Each student has unique needs and capabilities. Adaptations that work for one student might not work at all for a different student, but many teaching strategies will help all students including those without any disabilities. Specific learning disabilities include dyslexia, dyscalculia, dysgraphia, dyspraxia and combinations of one or more. The student may be functioning well below your typical students in one or more academic areas. The primary challenges are listening, thinking, talking, reading, writing, spelling, or arithmetic (and I will add reading music notation). Students may also appear disorganized and use avoidant behaviors such as choosing to watch televison over reading assignments. Students with learning disabilities describe fatique associated with trying to focus on tasks that engage their learning disability.

Learning disabilities are a high-incidence disability, the most common disability in the general population. Learning disabilities are hidden, a person cannot see the disability when looking at the student. Learning disabilities do not disable the student from being musical, musicality may present differently than in typical students yet the student is still a competent musician.

6

SPEECH AND LANGUAGE DISORDERS

Jay is a music education major and trumpet performance double major. Jay is an honor student and president of the Phi Mu Alpha Sinfonia student chapter. Jay is taking his first music education methods course this semester and has confided to his trumpet professor that he is worried about teaching children for the first time. Jay has a stuttering disorder and he is concerned that it will cause the students to laugh.

Jay had a very difficult time getting through his lesson with first graders due to his stuttering. There were some giggles, and a few children echoed the way he spoke. Jay turned red but kept going and eventually during the part of a lesson where the children learned a new song, Jay modeled the song flawlessly.

Jay's stuttering impacts his speech but does not occur when he sings. As Jay's students learned the song and responded well to his singing, he began to relax and enjoy the children. Each time he taught he struggled with his stutter, but the children learned to be patient with him. He noticed that the more comfortable he became as a teacher, the easier it was for him to talk without stuttering.

As Jay's student teaching semester approached he worked with a speech therapist to see if he could smooth out his speech. Stuttering slows down the pace of his lesson, and children lose focus during the lesson when they have to wait for him to get his words out. Through very intensive work, Jay did become more confident and in control of his stuttering, and his teaching improved.

SPEECH AND/OR LANGUAGE disorders, the second highest occurring disability, creates problems with communication. They are invisible disorders because you can't see them by looking at the person. Delayed development of speech and language can range from little to no impact on daily living and socialization to the complete inability to produce speech and understand language (Gargiulo, 2012). Fortunately, most college students with speech and language disorders have received therapy over the years but some have a few lingering problems.

Students might come to college with delays in speech or language or both. Because speech/language disorders can profoundly impact development of reading and social skills, postsecondary students are likely to continue to show signs of delays.

Communication disorders can have a severe impact on children socially. Some communication disabilities are discovered when a child develops speech slower than is typical, while some are secondary to other disabilities, such as specified learning disabilities, autism-spectrum disorders, intellectual disabilities, and traumatic brain injury.

SPEECH DISORDERS

It is easy to take speech for granted, but if you think about it, speech is a very complex mode of expression. Speech requires the coordination of the neuromusculature of the breathing and voice-producing mechanisms, as well as integrity of the mouth or oral cavity (Gargiulo, 2012). For speech to occur, air is forced up from the lungs, into the trachea, and into the vocal tract. The main components of speech production are the lungs, the larynx, and the vocal tract with the nasal and oral cavities (Hurley, n.d.).

Speech impairment occurs when an individual's speech interferes with communication, attracts negative attention, and adversely affects listeners, the speaker, or both (Bernthal, Bankson, & Flipsen, 2009). Three types of impairments are identified as speech disorders: articulation disorders, fluency disorders, and voice disorders.

Articulation disorders occur most often and are errors in the production of speech sounds. They include omissions (*dum* for *drum*), substitutions (*wotary* for *rotary*), distortions (*wist* for *wrist*), and additions (*footspedal* for *footpedal*).

Fluency disorders are problems with rhythm and timing of speech (Gargiulo, 2012). Such a disorder is "an interruption in the flow of speaking characterized by atypical rate, rhythm, and repetitions in sounds, syllables, words, and phrases. This may be accompanied by excessive tension, struggle behavior, and secondary mannerisms" (American Speech-Language-Hearing Association, 1993, p. 40).

When most people think of speech impairments, stuttering frequently comes to mind. Stuttering is characterized by rapid-fire repetitions of consonant or vowel sounds, especially at the beginnings of words, prolongations, hesitations, interjections, and complete verbal blocks (Ramig & Shames, 2006). More than 3 million people in the United States have a stuttering disorder (NIH National Institute on Voice, Speech, and Language, 2010). Students who stutter in their speech are usually successful in singing fluently. These students can often work with a speech therapist who uses the student's fluent singing as a starting place for better production in speaking situations (E. Bernstorf, personal communication, December 18, 2014). This is likely what Jay's speech therapist did to help him improve his speech.

Stuttering can be situational and worsen under anxiety. Jay experienced more problems with his stuttering when he taught the first-grade children his first time, but stuttering can worsen when one speaks in front of a group or speaks to someone the student considers important. Stuttering is more common in males than females, and stuttering is also fairly common in twins (Ramig & Shames, 2006).

Speech therapists use a number of different approaches to treat stuttering including teaching the person to employ a singing voice for speaking and gradually regulate the singing to more speech-like communication. Another technique is having the person learn to elongate certain sounds or speak slower to get past blocks. Some children seem to outgrow the problem with no treatment at all (Owens et al., 2011; Ratner, 2009).

A sometimes-related disorder is cluttering, which is characterized by excessively fast and jerky speech. Cluttering is often disorganized speech planning, which results in talking too quickly or talking in spurts or simply being unsure of what you want to say (Gargiulo, 2012). People who stutter are usually aware of their speech. However, people who clutter are often not aware of their speech problem.

Other types of voice disorders may appear problematic in voice lessons. These problems occur in the way the person uses his or her voice, or they may be disorders of the larynx. The American Speech-Language-Hearing Association characterizes these problems by "the abnormal production and/or absences of vocal quality, pitch, loudness, resonance, and/or duration, which is inappropriate for an individual's age and/or sex" (1993, p. 40). This might include excessively hoarse voices or speech that lacks inflection.

Voice nodules can occur when the student is stressing the voice and is more common in adults than children. They are primarily a concern with singers; however, they can occur in wind instrument players. Singers who do not properly warm up their voices can gradually develop callus type growths on their vocal folds. Occasionally wind instrumentalists can develop vocal nodules by playing with poor posture or breath support. This can contribute to vocal stress, too (Benninger, 1994).

LANGUAGE DISORDERS

Between 6 and 8 million people in the United States have language disorders (NIH National Institute on Voice, Speech, and Language, 2010). Language disorders occur when there is a delay or complications with mastery in one or more areas of the five components of language: phonology, morphology, syntax, semantics, and pragmatics. The speech/language therapist generally resolves these by the time the student enters college. However, with the high numbers of veterans entering college, language disorders like aphasia as a result of brain damage are becoming a concern. Students with traumatic brain injuries will occasionally experience aphasia.

Aphasia is generally thought of as an elderly language disorder resulting from a stroke. Aphasia impacts communication as a result of damage to parts of the brain that control language. Aphasia may cause difficulties in speaking, listening, reading, and writing, but it does not affect intelligence. Individuals with aphasia may also have other problems, such as dysarthria, apraxia, or swallowing difficulty (American Speech-Language-Hearing Association, 1997).

A person with dysarthria may demonstrate the following speech characteristics:

- "Slurred," "choppy," or "mumbled" speech that may be difficult to understand.
- Slow rate of speech.
- Rapid rate of speech with a "mumbling" quality.
- Limited tongue, lip, and jaw movement.
- Abnormal pitch and rhythm when speaking.
- Changes in the voice quality, such as hoarse or breathy voice or speech that sounds "nasal" or "stuffy."

In addition to resulting from traumatic brain injury or stroke, dysarthria can also be a result of tumors, Huntington's disease, or multiple sclerosis. Professors who interact with the student who has dysarthria should use these strategies:

- Reduce distractions and background noise.
- Give your full attention to the speaker.
- Make eye contact with the person as he or she speaks or talks.

- Let the speaker know when you have difficulty understanding him or her.
- Repeat only the part of the message you misunderstood so that the speaker does not have to repeat the entire message.
- If you still don't understand what the person says, ask yes/no questions or have the speaker write down what he or she is trying to say (American Speech-Language-Hearing Association, 1997).

Apraxia of speech in adults is a motor speech disorder. The brain process involved with language becomes disrupted from the brain to the mouth. The person cannot move his or her lips or tongue in the right ways to make words. When apraxia of speech is severe, the person may use an assistive technology device for communication.

ANKYLOGLOSSIA OR TONGUE-TIE

A medical condition that impacts speech is ankyloglossia. The lingual frenulum is a small fold of tissue that secures the tongue to the bottom of the mouth. In some cases, the frenulum is attached to the tip of the tongue (tongue-tie) and especially when the frenulum is short, it prevents movement of the tip of the tongue and interferes with speech. Dovel (2010) identified similar problems with playing wind instruments in people with tongue-tie. "Clarinetists may be incapable of bringing the tip of the tongue to the tip of the reed, and trumpeters may be unable to bring the tongue to the intersection of the front teeth and the hard palate." In addition, some wind players lower the jaw to achieve low notes; tongue-tie prevents the student from lifting the tongue to the roof of the mouth when the lower jaw is dropped. Dovel further explains that dorsal tonguing may be an effective adaptation (2010). Students can have a minor procedure, frenuloplasty, to correct tongue-tie. Speech therapy will likely be needed after the procedure for the person to learn to speak with a tongue that now moves easier.

SUMMARY

Speech and language disorders are a high-incidence disability, and it is probable that professors may encounter students with a variety of speech and language problems during their careers. The good news is that most students with these disorders are able to function well as musicians. Singing develops vocal/verbal confidence, especially in students who stutter.

Tips for Teaching Students with SLD

- Use echoing exercises in the voice studio so the student can hear and imitate the professor through singing. This frequently transfers to speech.
- Use echoing to build confidence in the student to sing fluently and experience how to be vocally fluent.
- Singing and playing instruments help the student to focus on breathing and muscle control, often a goal in speech/language therapy.
- Patience. Resist the urge to finish sentences or to correct a student's speech.
- Although there are no known studies on speech difficulties transferring to playing wind instruments, it is possible that articulation problems on the instrument might be related to an existing speech disorder. Ask the student if it seems to be persistent, or if you notice it in his or her speech.
- If wind players seem to struggle with articulations, check for tongue-tie by asking if you can see under the tongue. In tongue-tied individuals, a thin piece of tissue is attached to the tip of the underside of the tongue.

Assistive Technology

Students with severe communication disorders may use low- or high-tech devices for communication. These devices are referred to as augmentative or alternative communication (AAC). Low-tech assistive technology (AT) might include communication boards that allow students to point to words or letters to spell out words or to point to simple words or phrases, such as "I do not understand" or "I emailed you my assignment." More sophisticated devices include electronic talkers like the Dynavox, a device that can speak a series of words or phrases when the student taps small pictures or uses eye gaze to access the speech function. Other devices allow the user to input questions or answers and then the talker speaks what the student typed.

7

PSYCHIATRIC DISORDERS

Kyle is enrolled in an undergraduate music performance degree program in a large university. He is in high demand as a trumpet player and is performing in four ensembles in addition to a full schedule of academic courses including studio lessons. During the second semester of his third year he began to experience auditory and visual hallucinations. Kyle has always kept to himself and although his peers respect him for his performance skills, they did not otherwise socialize with him. Kyle's trumpet teacher did begin to notice that occasionally when Kyle was talking during his trumpet lesson, he did not make sense. At times Kyle's behavior was a bit unsettling, but as long as he continued to be prepared for his weekly lesson, Kyle's professor pretended not to notice the strange mumblings.

With three weeks left in the semester Kyle barricaded himself in one of the dorm bathrooms and was heard yelling at someone. With no success, the campus police tried to persuade him to unlock the door. Finally, a locksmith came and opened the door. The police and other students were surprised to find Kyle walking in circles talking to someone who wasn't there.

Kyle was diagnosed with schizophrenia and placed on medication. He returned to school the following semester and completed his degree.

WHAT ARE PSYCHIATRIC DISORDERS?

College students with mental illness are among the fastest growing population of students on campus. Collins (2000) reports that 2.6% of college students identified as having one or more psychiatric disorders in 1978. By 1998, the percentage rose to 9%, and in 2004, estimates of students with psychiatric disorders were between 15% and to 20% (Rickerson, Souma, & Burgstahler, 2004). Kupferman (2014) states that the largest subgroup of students with disabilities is those with psychiatric disorders. In a recent survey by the American College Counseling Association (Gallagher, 2014), 26% of students presenting for psychiatric evaluation are on psychiatric medication. This is up from 20% in 2013, 17% in 2000, and 9% in 1994.

Sandy Colbs, director of the Student Counseling Center at Illinois State University, suggests four reasons for the increase in students with mental health challenges: (1) the stigma has been reduced against people managing a mental illness diagnosis, (2) students at Illinois State University are coming from more affluent families that can afford psychotherapy, (3) technology and social media use reduces the development of social skills and develops expectations of immediate contact and access to parents and friends, and (4) students seem to be less resilient than they were five to ten years ago. Colbs attributes this to a parenting style in which parents are increasingly more involved with their children and in control of their highly scheduled lives. "Students coming to college in 2015 have not learned emotional independence. They can't name what they feel" (S. Colbs, personal interview, June 10, 2015).

It is difficult to determine the exact numbers of students attending college with mental illness because many students never register with the disability services office. Students report that fear of disclosure is a common reason that many students who attend college resist registering with this office. A statistic that is even more troubling is that approximately 86% of students with psychiatric disorders withdraw from college before completing their degree (Kupferman, 2014).

People with psychiatric disorders experience a 90% rate of unemployment (Fleming & Fairweather, 2011; National Alliance on Mental Health, 2012; President's New Freedom Commission on Mental Health, 2003). Postsecondary education is a major factor in improving chances for employment; with that in mind, colleges and universities need to improve graduation rates of students with psychiatric disorders (Government Accountability Office, 2009; McEwan & Downie, 2013; National Alliance on Mental Illness, 2012). There are no statistics that track numbers of students with disorders in schools of music; it is not known if the rates of students with psychiatric disorders who are accepted and complete degrees in music are similar to statistics for the general university population. It can be assumed that music students with psychiatric disorders experience the same barriers that their non-music peers encounter. This chapter will explore some of these barriers and suggest solutions that may improve students' chances of completing a music degree and transitioning to employment.

DEFINITIONS

In the literature, the terms "mental illness," "mental impairment," and "psychiatric disorder" seem to be interchangeable. The Americans with Disabilities Act refers to mental illness as part of the broader ADA term "mental impairment" (Zuckerman, Debenham, & Moore, 1993). Mental impairment is not the same as mental illness. Mental impairment describes cognitive disabilities, traumatic brain injury, or specific learning disabilities. Psychiatric disorder is described as mental illness that significantly interferes with the performance of major life activities, such as learning, working, and communicating, among others (Zuckerman, Debenham, & Moore, 1993). Mental illness is a hidden disability; it is rarely apparent to others, but students with mental illness are at great risk for profound difficulty at some point in their college career.

The Americans with Disabilities Act Amendments Act (ADAAA) (2008) expanded the list of major life activities to include learning-related activities such as concentrating, reading, and thinking. Types of psychiatric disorders protected by ADAAA (2008) are depression, bipolar affective disorder, borderline personality disorder, schizophrenia, anxiety disorders, obsessive-compulsive disorder, and eating disorders. Substance abuse is a disorder that many students struggle with; however, it is not covered by ADAAA. Colbs (personal interview, June 10, 2015) explained that substance abuse is often a result of other ADAAA recognized disorders. It is not unusual for students to self-medicate using alcohol or drugs. For example, students with anxiety disorders will try to manage their anxiety by drinking to excess.

Mental illnesses can be managed or controlled through the use of medication and/or psychotherapy and can go into remission. Some people with mental illness will need no support or occasional support; however, people with psychiatric disorders will often need substantial and ongoing support.

There are four main categories of mental illness/psychiatric disorders: (a) schizophrenia and related disorders, (b) mood disorders, (c) anxiety disorders, and (d) personality disorders. According to the sixth annual report from the Center for Collegiate Mental Health, among the more than 100,000 college students who sought mental health treatment at 140 colleges and universities, the chief concern was anxiety. Previous surveys identified depression as the leading concern; in the recent survey, depression is now ranked as the second most common concern among students. The other eight concerns are, in descending order: (a) relationship problems, (b) stress, (c) academic performance, (d) family, (e) interpersonal functioning, (f) grief or loss, (g) mood instability, and (h) adjustment to new environment (Center for Collegiate Mental Health, 2015).

SCHIZOPHRENIA AND RELATED DISORDERS

The most severe disorder is schizophrenia. It affects individuals in different ways impacting their ability to think clearly, to sort out and interpret incoming sensations, and to act decisively. Individuals are defined by abnormalities in one or more of the following domains: delusions, hallucinations, disorganized thinking (speech), grossly disorganized or abnormal motor behavior (including catatonia), and negative symptoms (American Psychiatric Association, 2013). Individuals struggle with social functioning and display deficits in social skills (Flanagan, Zaretsky, & Moroz, 2010). Schizophrenia can vary in individuals, and symptoms can be constant or the individual may shift between episodes that are symptom-free and periods of severe impairment.

Other related disorders include schizophreniform disorder, which applies when two or more symptoms of schizophrenia are present, but the duration of the disability is less than six months, and schizoaffective disorder, in which symptoms of schizophrenia are accompanied by depression and/or mania (Flanagan et al., 2010; Gladding & Newsome, 2009).

MOOD DISORDERS

Mood disorders are classified under two categories: depressive disorders and bipolar disorders. Mood disorders are very common. Approximately 10% to 25% of women and 5% to 12% of men will experience a major depressive episode during their lifetime (Flanagan et al., 2010). Symptoms of depression include negative or pessimistic beliefs, distorted negative self-image, suicidal thoughts, and difficulty concentrating. Depression can also involve physical symptoms such as lethargy, insomnia or hypersomnia, loss of appetite or overeating, and lack of sexual interest (American Psychiatric Association, 2013). Depression varies widely in terms of severity and duration. Fisher (2004) reported that clinical depression most often appeared in adolescence, and mood disorders that emerge in college are likely to be life threatening.

Bipolar disorder can limit functionality more significantly than depression. Bipolar disorder differs from depression primarily by the added presence of mania or episodes of elevated or irritable mood (Gladding & Newsome, 2009). Manic episodes can last from days to months and in the most severe form, bipolar disorder involves frequent alternation between manic and depressive episodes. Bipolar disorder is classified by two types: bipolar I and bipolar II. Bipolar I represents the classic manic-depressive disorder first described in the 19th century. Bipolar II disorder requires a lifetime experience of at least one episode of major depression and at least one hypomanic episode. Bipolar II is no longer thought to be a "milder" condition than bipolar I disorder, largely because of the amount of time individuals with this condition spend in depression. The instability of mood experienced by individuals with bipolar II disorder is typically accompanied by serious impairment in work and social functioning (American Psychiatric Association, 2013).

ANXIETY DISORDERS

Anxiety disorders are the most common psychiatric disorder on college campuses (CCMH, 2015) and in the general population (Flanagan et al., 2010). Individuals with anxiety disorders can identify their anxiety and are in touch with reality (Gladding & Newsome, 2009). Anxiety disorders can occur with other psychiatric disorders and with other disabilities not considered psychiatric disorders. There are four types of anxiety disorders: (a) panic disorder, (b) post-traumatic stress disorder (PTSD), (c) phobic disorder, and (d) obsessive-compulsive disorder (American Psychiatric Association, 2013).

Perhaps the most severe of the four types of anxiety disorders are panic disorders. Panic disorders are characterized as sudden and unanticipated attacks that signal an imminent sense of doom. These attacks often occur with increased heart rate, difficulty breathing, dizziness, and a sense of terror (American Psychiatric Association, 2013).

PTSD is becoming more common on college campuses with the influx of veterans. Many veterans who experienced combat undergo an extreme emotional reaction to a life trauma. PTSD can also exist among persons who experienced rape, acts of violence, and accidents. The student with PTSD experiences flashbacks and nightmares that make it almost impossible to move on to life as it was before the traumatic event occurred.

Phobic disorders occur when a student experiences intense fear of an object, activity, or a situation that does not represent a real danger. A type of phobia is social anxiety disorder. Social anxiety disorder is familiar to those in the performing arts as stage fright. The *Diagnostic and Statistical Manual of Mental Disorders* (*DSM*-V) identifies a subgroup, social anxiety disorder-performance only, for people who experience anxiety primarily when speaking or performing in public (American Psychiatric Association, 2013). Stage fright is a fear of being embarrassed in public.

Obsessive-compulsive disorder (OCD) involves two behaviors, a recurring thought or impulse (obsession) and the ritualistic repetition of illogical behaviors known as compulsions. Related disorders include body dysmorphic disorder (perceived defects or flaws in physical appearance), hoarding disorder, trichotillomania (hair-pulling disorder), and excoriation (skin-picking) disorder (American Psychiatric Association, 2013).

PERSONALITY DISORDERS

Personality disorders are enduring patterns of inner experience and behavior that deviate markedly from the expectations of the individual's culture; these are pervasive and inflexible, have an onset in adolescence or early adulthood, are stable over time, and lead to distress or impairment (American Psychiatric Association, 2013). Personality disorders are grouped into three clusters. Cluster A includes paranoid, schizoid, and schizotypical personality disorders. Individuals with these disorders often appear odd or eccentric. Cluster B includes anti-social, borderline, histrionic, and narcissistic personality disorders. Individuals with these disorders frequently appear dramatic, emotional, or erratic. Cluster C includes avoidant, dependent, and obsessive-compulsive personality disorders. Individuals with these disorders often appear anxious or fearful (American Psychiatric Association, 2013).

Cluster A describes individuals with a pervasive mistrust of others. Students with disorders in Cluster B include anti-social personality disorder (characterized as violation of rights of others with no remorse), borderline personality disorder (characterized by impulsivity and instability of interpersonal relationships beginning in early adulthood), narcissistic personality disorder (characterized by exaggerated sense of self-importance), and histrionic personality disorder (characterized by excessive emotionality and attention seeking) (American Psychiatric Association, 2013). Cluster C disorders consist of avoidant disorder, a pervasive pattern of social inhibition, feelings of inadequacy, and hypersensitivity to negative evaluation, beginning in early adulthood and present in a variety of contexts. Dependent personality disorder is typified by a pervasive and excessive need to be taken care of that leads to submissive and clinging behavior and fears of separation, beginning by early adulthood and present in a variety of contexts. Students with obsessive-compulsive personality disorder demonstrate a pervasive pattern of preoccupation with orderliness, perfectionism, and mental and interpersonal control, at the expense of flexibility, openness, and efficiency, beginning by early adulthood and present in a variety of contexts (American Psychiatric Association, 2013). Notice the number of disorders that begin to appear in early adulthood.

FEEDING AND EATING DISORDERS

Students with feeding and eating disorders are characterized by a persistent disturbance of eating or eating-related behavior that results in the altered consumption or absorption of food. The disorder significantly impairs physical health or psychosocial functioning. These disorders include pica (eating nonnutritive substances for at least one month), rumination disorder (repeated regurgitation of food for at least one month), avoidant/restrictive food intake disorder (lack of interest in eating food, avoidance based on sensory characteristics of food; concern about aversive consequences of eating), anorexia nervosa (intense fear of gaining weight or becoming fat that may include a distorted view of body weight or shape), bulimia nervosa (recurrent episodes of binge eating followed by inappropriate compensatory behaviors to prevent weight gain such as self-induced vomiting, misuse of laxatives, diuretics, fasting, or excessive exercise), and binge-eating disorder (eating, in a discrete period of time an amount of food that is much larger than what most people would eat in a similar period of time under similar circumstances). Obesity is not included as a mental disorder in the *DSM*-V (American Psychiatric Association, 2013).

Kaye et al. (2004), in a study of people with eating disorders, found a high level of anxiety in this population. Most stated that they were diagnosed with an anxiety disorder before they developed an eating disorder.

SUBSTANCE USE DISORDERS

The *DSM*-V describes substance use disorder as a cluster of cognitive, behavioral, and physiological symptoms indicating that the individual continues using the substance despite significant substance-related problems (American Psychiatric Association, 2013). The lists of categories within substance-induced disorders include prescription and recreational drugs, alcohol, caffeine, cannabis, and tobacco use and withdrawal (American Psychiatric Association, 2013). Substance abuse is a major problem on many college campuses and is connected to other behaviors such as rape, vandalism, bullying, and violence. Substance abuse is more often thought to be the result of the aforementioned behaviors rather than a psychiatric disorder like schizophrenia.

FUNCTIONAL LIMITATIONS

Mancuso (1990) cautions that the following behaviors of some students with psychiatric disorders may impact academic performance:

- Difficulty with medical side effects: side effects of psychiatric medications that affect academic performance include drowsiness, fatigue, dry mouth and thirst, blurred vision, hand tremors, slowed response time, and difficulty initiating interpersonal contact.
- Screening out environmental stimuli: an inability to block out sounds, sights, or odors that interfere with focusing on tasks. Limited ability to tolerate noise and crowds.
- Sustaining concentration: restlessness, shortened attention span, distraction, and difficulty understanding or remembering verbal directions.
- Maintaining stamina: difficulty sustaining enough energy to spend a whole day on campus attending classes; combating drowsiness due to medications.
- Handling time pressures and multiple tasks: difficulty managing assignments, prioritizing tasks, and meeting deadlines. Inability to participate in multi-task work.
- Interacting with others: difficulty getting along, fitting in, contributing to group work, and reading social cues.
- Fear of authority figures: difficulty approaching instructors or teaching assistants.
- Responding to negative feedback: difficulty understanding and correctly interpreting criticism or poor grades. May not be able to separate person from task (personalization or defensiveness due to low self-esteem).
- Responding to change: difficulty coping with unexpected changes in coursework, such as changes in assignments, due dates, or instructors. Limited ability to tolerate interruptions.
- Severe test anxiety: the individual is rendered emotionally and physically unable to take the exam.

SUICIDE

The Center for Collegiate Mental Health (2015) conducted a study that included more than 100,000 students from 140 colleges and universities. In addition to an increase in numbers of students receiving mental health services, the report also saw rates of self-injury and suicidal thoughts to be on the rise. Nearly 1 out of 4 students have self-injured and 1 out of 3 have seriously considered suicide. Nearly 1 in 10 have attempted suicide.

USA TODAY analyzed 620 deaths of four-year college and university students from 2000 to 2005 based on published reports and public records (Davis & DeBarros, 2006). They found that more than one-third of undergraduate deaths were freshmen, with 40% due to suicide. Half of all deaths were due to falls from windows, balconies, and rooftops usually related to drug and alcohol abuse.

CAMPUS VIOLENCE

Recent violence on campuses, including Virginia Tech University and Northern Illinois University, have increased media attention about mental illness and propensity for violence. The US murder rate is much higher overall than on college campuses and no matter how careful universities might be in protecting the safety of people on campus, there is no clear method for identifying potentially dangerous students. In a study conducted by the Secret Service in 2002 that analyzed 37 school shootings between 1974 and 2000, the report concludes that "there is no accurate or useful profile of the school shooter." McClelland and Teplin (2001) stress that the greatest predictor of violent crime is not the presence of mental illness but of alcohol consumption.

Universities that use profiles of potential violent shooters risk over-identification or not identifying students who actually pose a risk. The ADA and additional laws, including the Family Educational Rights and Privacy Act and the Health Insurance Portability and Accountability Act (HIPAA) protect students with psychiatric disorders. Universities cannot share their educational and medical information without student consent.

ACADEMIC STRESS

Nearly all students experience stress during college but almost half of all college students have mental health concerns related to academic stress. Reducing mental health distress in college has direct implications for student academics (CCMH, 2015). Schools of music can support students by reducing stigma and encouraging students with signs of stress to feel safe about disclosing their worries and anxiety about academics and pressure on them as student performers. Faculty that discount stress by telling students to learn to relax or ignoring signs that students are not managing their academic lives are not acting in the best interests of their students. Changes in appearance, excessive absences, falling asleep in class, or other unusual behavior should be viewed as red flags worthy of attention and support.

DISCLOSURE

Students with documented mental disorders cannot be denied admission to higher education institutions unless reasonable accommodations are not available, or the student poses a threat to self or others (Leibert, 2003). Students must register at the disability services office in order to legally receive accommodations. It is estimated that most college students with diagnosed psychiatric disorders do not register at the disability services office because of the following reasons:

1. Fear or concern about the impact disclosure would have on how students, faculty, and staff perceive them, including within mental health degree programs.
2. There is no opportunity to disclose.
3. The diagnosis does not impact academic performance.
4. Students do not know that disclosing could help secure accommodations.
5. They do not trust that their medical information will remain confidential. (Gruttadaro & Crudo, 2012)

Mental illness had a dark past until changes in the law and culture began to chip away at long-held beliefs; people in the past with psychiatric disorders were institutionalized (often against their will) or the person was cared for at home. Children and adults with mental illness were not welcomed into traditional schools and universities, and a psychiatric diagnosis brought shame to family members. Stigma and stereotypes continue to be the largest barrier for resisting disclosure (Gruttadaro & Crudo, 2012). Stigma can be reduced by helping to make disclosure more comfortable for students with psychiatric disorders, including support programs that help to reduce the stigma on campus (Gruttadaro & Crudo, 2012).

Unger (1992) noted that the onset of major mental illness often occurs between ages 18 and 25, a period when many students are entering postsecondary education, preparing for future careers, and developing relationships. Students often experience their first crisis in college. Faculty and staff members who are open and non-judgmental can be immensely helpful to students experiencing psychiatric difficulties. Faculty and staff members who refuse to acknowledge student behavior as resulting from a real mental health condition will contribute to student embarrassment and shame.

Students have a right to privacy. It is not necessary for schools of music or professors to know a diagnosis; what is essential are compliance with the ADA and 504 laws that provide reasonable accommodation. However, students will often feel more comfortable disclosing a psychiatric disorder to certain professors with whom they have developed a trusting relationship. Often studio faculty will be faculty members whom students perceive as safe. If a student discloses a psychiatric disorder to a faculty member, the faculty member needs to honor the student's right to privacy but at the same time encourage the student to register at the disability services office. Usually, disclosure occurs when a student is in crisis. This is often too late for immediate help because the disability office needs time to review the case and develop accommodations. If the student registers with the disability office before there is a crisis, then a support system will be in place if the student should need it.

Disclosure is a personal decision. If the student ultimately decides not to disclose to the disability office, that is her or his choice. Once the student is 18, parents have no legal means to force their child to disclose. A professor cannot contact parents if there is a crisis as that violates student privacy. The professor should contact the student counseling center only if the student seems to be a danger to himself or herself or others.

HOW TO DEVELOP TRUST IN YOUR STUDENT WITH MENTAL ILLNESS

Often students listen and look for signs that a professor can be trusted and will be open-minded about psychiatric disorders. You can help by becoming aware of these behaviors that can be perceived as judgmental by a student with mental illness:

- Use of derogatory language like "crazy," "fruitcake," "space cadet," or other words that poke fun at people with mental illness
- Listen and try not to diagnose or push a student toward disclosure
- Mirror what you hear the student saying and ask if you are correctly understanding what they are trying to say
- Use affirming statements like "it sounds like you have had a week of high stress"

- Encourage the student to call the student counseling center for an appointment
- Be careful about assuming a therapist role; there are experts for this on campus.

MENTAL HEALTH AWARENESS

Most students are aware that they are in crisis when it happens, and some will have researched what supports are available to them on campus before they disclose to a faculty member. Gruttadaro and Crudo (2012) asked students in a nationwide survey how they became aware of mental health resources available to them on campus; 33% of the students identified their college website as the first place they looked for support. Next listed was the student health center (27%), then others, including local mental health providers and information shared during a campus tour (23%). Some respondents (22%) credited a faculty or staff member with identifying mental health resources available on campus, and 20% were helped by friends and peers. Faculty and staff can discuss mental health resources available when school of music meetings are held for all students. This is a great opportunity to model acceptance and support for all persons with disorders. Students who have family members with psychiatric disorders will appreciate your candor.

STUDENT DROPOUTS

Gruttadaro and Crudo (2012) found that the overwhelming majority of students who leave college (64%) before completing a degree do so because of a mental health reason. Among the survey respondents who left college, the primary diagnoses were depression, bipolar disorder, and post-traumatic stress disorder. Of the group that dropped out of college, 45% stopped attending because they needed accommodations, but they did not receive them; 50% of these students admitted that they were not receiving accommodations because they had not registered at the disability services office.

Another reason for dropping out among students with psychiatric disorders is the loss of financial aid and/or scholarships as a result of a low GPA or changing to a part-time status. Often students who experience a crisis without accommodations or supports will find themselves with compromised grades as a result of poor attendance during the crisis episode, uncompleted assignments or exams, and in the case of music students, inability to learn assigned pieces in their studio lessons. Students on scholarship risk losing their scholarship or being placed on probation.

With the loss of a scholarship, it might be impossible for students to complete their degree program.

Most financial aid requires students to finish college in four years and to attend school full-time. Many students with psychiatric disorders do best when they attend school part-time. By reducing their course load to lower than full-time status, students are likely to lose their financial aid, and this can also cause some students to leave college before completing a degree.

Although it is not always possible to recognize students with psychiatric disorders before their issues grow to result in a crisis, faculty can try to proactively reach out to struggling students. It is helpful to promote and publicize available accommodations, services, and supports to all students. Remember, many students will experience their first mental illness episode while in college. Professors can help by not penalizing students for mental health issues. Instead of failing a student who ended up in crisis at the end of a mostly good semester, allow the student to take an incomplete and turn in assignments late. This will save his or her GPA. Even if they eventually drop out of school, having a low GPA will prohibit many students from being accepted in the future when they want to return to school.

Imagine an otherwise good student having her first depressive episode in the third semester of music school. The student has no accommodations because she had never experienced severe depression and did not see a need for registering with the disability services office. Professors believe it is only fair to fail the student who disappeared for three weeks and did not communicate with the professor. The professor might not realize that during those three weeks, the student was unable to function. She may eventually go to see a therapist on campus and be put on anti-depressants. but by the time she improves enough to return to classes she is so far behind that she doesn't not know what to do and is afraid to explain to her professors that she spent most of the past three weeks in bed and unable to function. She does not feel comfortable disclosing to the professor, especially when the professor responds in an inflexible, demeaning way. "You need to buck up and take responsibility!" or "If I allow you to have extra time then I have to let everyone have extra time."

CRISIS

College is inherently a time of high stress for all students. In some cases, music students have more sources of stress than many other majors because of high demands on academic work and musical requirements. Few other majors, with the exception of theater and dance, require students to attend and prepare for long rehearsals or memorization of pieces.

Among Gruttadaro and Crudo's survey respondents, 73% reported having a mental health crisis while at college. Many students likely had their first crisis at college, often away from parents and other familiar support networks. When asked what triggered their crisis, surveyed students responded with the following:

- Extreme feelings of anxiety, panic, depression about school and life
- Difficulty adjusting to a new routine and environment
- Feelings of homesickness, loneliness, and isolation
- Stress or feeling overwhelmed about course load
- Post-traumatic stress disorder episode triggered by class content.
- Medications that stopped working (Gruttadaro & Crudo, 2012)

Of responding students, 35% indicated that their college did not know about their crisis. Students either did not pursue help or were unable to ask for help. A student in his or her first year on campus who has a crisis may struggle with what to do (Gruttadaro & Crudo, 2012). "For a student who needs predictability and routine for symptom management and is uncertain in new environments this is a considerable challenge and extends well beyond the typical development tasks of independence and autonomy" (Belch, 2011, p. 79). The remainder answered like this: 21% of students reported their college had a good response to their crisis, 17% indicated a fair response, 14% cited a poor response, and only 13% said their college reacted in a way they would consider excellent (Gruttadaro & Crudo, 2012). Students in crisis are already struggling with clear, rational thinking; it is essential to respond to students with empathy and in a non-judgmental and understanding way. Reaching out to a student at risk for crisis helps him or her to know that you care. Be sure to follow up with them.

Stigma is the most difficult barrier to overcome for students with psychiatric disorders. In addition, Sandy Colbs (personal interview, June 10, 2015), director of student counseling at Illinois State University, noted that students in crisis are more likely to use off-campus mental health services and resources when they have student health insurance that has good mental health coverage. Many students do not want their parents to know they are seeing a therapist or participating in group therapy. They are particularly anxious about their parents discovering they have been hospitalized or are receiving outpatient services.

Often students with psychiatric disorders are overwhelmed with inadequate insurance coverage, the cost of medications, and the cost of testing to confirm a diagnosis (Blacklock, Benson, & Johnson, 2003). Students in crisis who need documentation to be registered with disability services have difficulty finding the energy and resources to go through psychological testing and comleting the detailed paperwork required to be accepted as a documented student with a psychiatric disorder.

Students who are in crisis and need to be away from campus are a challenge for universities to help. The Americans with Disabilities Act (ADA) prohibits discrimination and protects a student's right to privacy so except through a judicial process the university cannot forcibly remove students who would be better if they were not at school. For example, a student who is at risk for a drug overdose might be safer if she was removed from school and hospitalized or at a minimum removed from a group of peers who also abuse drugs. The law protects students so well that the counseling or student health center cannot step in and remove a student. The university is often put in a difficult position of weighing student rights against the responsibility of protecting the lives of the rest of the student body. The university must be very cautious about recommending removal unless it can be proved that the student is a danger to himself or herself or others.

SOLUTIONS

Teaching and providing emotional and educational support for students with mental illness can be draining and sometimes scary for faculty and staff not prepared for these students. It is hard to know when it is appropriate to provide support and when to better direct the student to professionals. Faculty and staff need to know there is also a support network for them on campus and many in the network routinely provide training and consultation.

Faculty and Staff Training

Libert (2003) noted that stigma and faculty perceptions about mental illness "are seeded [more] in myth than in reality" (p. 10). Faculty and staff expressed concern that students with psychiatric disorders will be disruptive, violent, dangerous, or unable to meet academic standards (Gladding & Newsome, 2009; Unger, 2007). For faculty and staff to respond in positive and helpful ways for students, they need training. Faculty and staff may not be aware of warning signs, symptoms, and the frequency of mental health conditions in students. Providing general training will help this group to recognize students who are at risk for a crisis and to guide them to on-campus resources. Many faculty are not sure how to support students and are uncertain about the limitations and boundaries associated with privacy laws. Faculty and staff do not need to know a diagnosis to help. They do need to recognize that mental health issues are prevalent on every campus and students deserve mental health care just as they do physical health care.

Student Training

Colbs (personal interview, June 10, 2015) believes that incoming freshmen need some sort of training about resiliency but is not sure how that would look or how much time it would involve. At Illinois State University, residence assistants and other peer groups on campus receive training on how to recognize students in mental health crisis.

Two groups that are frequently present on campus as student organizations are the National Alliance on Mental Illness and Active Minds. Both groups are open to students with and without psychiatric disorders. Groups like these help to reduce stigma, advocate acceptance and inclusion on campus for all, and provide a safe social network for students who often feel marginalized on campus.

Supported Education

Collins and Mowbray (2005) defined supported education as a psychiatric rehabilitation intervention that provides assistance, preparation, and support to students with psychiatric disorders enrolling in and completing postsecondary education. Brown (2002) further noted that supported-education programs offered the following core services: career planning (providing instruction, support, counseling, and assistance with vocational self-assessment, career exploration, development of educational competencies, time and stress management, developing social supports, and tutoring and mentoring services), and outreach to resources and services (facilitating referrals to campus and relevant human service agencies). Unger (1990) identified the need for supported postsecondary education to assist people with mental illness to access and graduate from college. Supported education consists of counseling, learning-related skills, and accommodations (Mowbray et al., 2005). Supported education is based on the definition of supported employment in the Rehabilitation Act Amendments of 1986 (Sharpe et al., 2004). Unger (1998) identified three prototypes for delivery of supported education: (a) a self-contained setting that supports students in being reintegrated into the postsecondary setting; (b) on-site support, where ongoing support is provided by the university's disability services support staff or a mental health professional; and (c) mobile support, where support is largely provided off-campus by community mental health service providers.

Currently, most universities provide supported education with support staff at the disability services office. This can be challenging for disability services staff who do not feel properly trained to provide the type of support needed by students with psychiatric disorders. Many students with psychiatric disorders require large amounts of time and expertise. The most successful supported-education programs involve collaboration between on-campus and community resources (Whelley,

Hart, & Zafft, 2002). Blacklock, Benson and Johnson (2003) advocate four strategies to remove barriers that keep supported education from being effective: (a) implementing universal design strategies to improve the learning experiences for all students, (b) fostering social connections for students with psychiatric disorders, (c) improving communication and collaboration among key stakeholders on and off-campus, and (d) promoting access to resources for all key stakeholders through information sharing and training efforts.

One of the goals of supported education is to improve career employment opportunities. Very few adults with psychiatric disorders are fully employed. However, Unger, Pardee, and Shafer (2000) found that supported education improved the completion of course work (90%); 50% of students were employed in a job that fit their education level; and the number of students living independently increased. Students who were most successful were those who were enrolled part-time (9.7 credit hour semester load or less). Students on average completed a community college associate degree in 4.3 to 5.3 years. The type of diagnosis had no bearing on the student's ability to successfully finish school (Leff & McPartland, 1998; Unger et al., 2000). These results point to one of the most effective methods of ensuring successful completion of college and gainful employment after college.

Sandy Colbs explained that many schools had behavioral intervention teams that can be assembled as needed and function much like a supported-education program. Creating these teams is very time- and staff-intensive, so schools will not routinely do this unless it is clear that having an intervention team in place is in the best interest of both the student and the university.

Supported Education and the Music Student

How might supported education look in an undergraduate music degree program for a student who had a crisis, which resulted in a diagnosis of schizophrenia during the student's third year of music school? Returning to Kyle, he was able to integrate back into music school with supports. Kyle's support team consisted of his off-campus therapist, a psychiatrist, the student counseling center staff, the disability services specialist in psychiatric disorders, a peer trained in supporting students with severe psychiatric disorders, and Kyle's trumpet professor. The team monitored Kyle closely for signs of stress, including social withdrawal and indications that he had stopped taking his medication. Kyle lived with a peer who helped to monitor his daily functioning and made sure he took his medication. The peer also included Kyle in social activities and helped him to develop needed social skills.

Kyle's off-campus therapist and psychiatrist worked with his emotional needs and made sure his medication worked with a minimum of side effects. The student counseling center staff worked with Kyle's peer live-in aide and helped to provide training along with arranging respite for the aide. The disability services specialist coordinated Kyle's team and met with Kyle weekly to make sure he continued to do well. Kyle's trumpet teacher was his liaison to the school of music faculty and helped to see that he was not participating in too many ensembles; he also checked with other music professors on how Kyle was progressing in his courses. The trumpet professor was trained by the disability services specialist to recognize signs of stress in Kyle and to work with music faculty to reduce stigma and to provide feedback on how Kyle best learns based on experience.

When Kyle had his crisis, many of the school of music faculty expressed concern that he might become violent. Some requested that he be dismissed from the school of music; they felt he was too much of a risk. Others advocated for Kyle, noting that he was the best trumpet player in the school and that he was needed to maintain quality in the trumpet sections of at least two ensembles. Kyle's trumpet professor facilitated a discussion in the music faculty meeting that helped to dispel some of the fears his colleagues had about Kyle.

Kyle returned to school on a part-time basis and reduced his course load to one ensemble, two classes, and his trumpet lesson. He did have some bad days, usually due to stressful events in his life, but for the most part, he managed well and was grateful to continue in music and still hoped for a position in a symphony orchestra someday. He graduated in three additional years and won an audition in an orchestra in a small Midwestern city.

Through supported education, Kyle was able to finish his degree and find employment (part-time) in an orchestra. Kyle will always need a live-in aide, a therapist, and a psychiatrist, but he is mostly able to function well. Typically, in most universities, Kyle would have been withdrawn from school and probably would not have finished his degree. If he had not earned a performance degree, it would have been more difficult for him to find a symphony orchestra position. He would probably have become more isolated and would likely have followed the scenario of most people with schizophrenia—unemployment, periods of crisis due to being off medication, and a loss of the one thing that kept him connected to others, music.

Supported education often does not happen in higher education because it requires good collaboration of all members on the person's team. Universities may not have enough trained personnel to manage a student with a severe psychiatric disorder. Some students would prefer to drop out of college or they become resistant to treatment and medication. Kyle was motivated, and the stigma associated with schizophrenia was addressed by most of the adults who encountered him. Kyle's trumpet professor was liked and respected by his colleagues and students. He was trusted and could model a positive approach to supporting Kyle in music school.

Accommodations and Supports

Kupferman (2014) identified common accommodations for students with psychiatric disorders in a study that included feedback from 402 disability service professionals about accommodations that were successful at their universities:

- Reduced course load
- Extended time for taking exams
- Administration of exams in distraction-reduced environments
- Utilization of note-takers
- Rescheduling of exams
- Possible relaxation of attendance requirements due to the cyclical nature of psychiatric disorders or the side effects of medication

CREATIVITY AND AFFECTIVE DISORDERS

It is a very common misconception that people who are creative and especially people in the arts are prone to psychiatric disorders (Oslund, 2014; Santosa et al., 2006; Srivastava et al., 2010). There is no convincing evidence to support this stereotype, which only furthers the stigma that musicians are particularly susceptible to major psychiatric disorders. Schlesinger (2012) uncovers the history of this myth of the mad genius and helps to dispel the expectation that truly creative people must be manic, depressed, psychotic, or suicidal in order to produce great art. Faculty and advocates for students with psychiatric disorders can help to end this disabling stereotype by correcting anyone who puts forth an assumption that the student has mental illness because he or she is creative.

SUMMARY

Students with mental health challenges or psychiatric disorders are the fastest-growing group of students on the college campus who receive accommodations from the university disability services office. Most students will be diagnosed when they experience symptoms or a crisis while a college student. This is problematic because when this occurs, the student is likely not registered with the disabled services office unless he or she had another documented disability such as Tourette syndrome. When students are in crisis, it is difficult for them to find the energy and financial resources to be tested and provide documentation for disability services, and of course they are not provided accommodations until they are documented and accepted. Many students are already behind on assignments, course and degree requirements because of the difficulty to attend to these requirements during a time when they are experiencing very high levels of stress.

Sensitive faculty can help to bridge the gap by supporting students when appropriate until they stabilize and can to attend to completing the disability services requirements. Flexibility can make a huge difference to a young musician in the middle of what must be a terrifying and isolating experience. Reducing stigma and showing patience and acceptance help to support the student.

Once accommodations are in place the faculty member can participate in supported education if the student has benefited from a team to assist with management and guidance to help him or her stay in school and complete the music degree. Speaking openly to classes and groups of students about the need to set a tone for acceptance of diverse learning styles and needs is critical for the success of all members of the college community.

8

AUTISM SPECTRUM DISORDER

I first became aware of Jennifer when a colleague in the College of Education mentioned a music education student in her class who was rude and disruptive. Jennifer would challenge my colleague openly in front of other students and repeatedly ask questions that had already been answered or were covered in the syllabus. To make things worse, at the end of every class, Jennifer would demand at least ten minutes of her professor's time by asking the same questions or sometimes just talking about herself. Students in the class were complaining, and my colleague was becoming so irritated with Jennifer that she felt the school of music should take some sort of disciplinary action.

Jennifer took a music education class I taught the following semester and before the class I met with her to talk over the education course from the previous semester. She was totally perplexed that the professor spoke to me about her behavior. She thought the class had gone really well.

I explained that I only heard secondhand about the problem but thought it was good timing that she was registered for my class; it would allow me to give her feedback on whether I noticed the same behaviors my colleague had observed. We made a plan that I would walk over close to her and pull on my ear if I felt she was being inappropriate in my class. This would be my signal to wind up her question and reflect about what she said and why I might feel she was unprofessional.

Jennifer had Asperger syndrome; those with this syndrome are considered high functioning on the autism spectrum. She was not registered with our disability office and denied that she had any behavior problems. The interventions made it manageable to have her in class; she was able to monitor her outbursts and long-winded questions. She still wrote daily emails to me asking questions or just writing to tell me about something in her life. I found these emails to be mildly annoying and usually did not respond. She still waited to speak to me after every class, but I would make her wait while I answered any other students first.

THE CENTERS FOR Disease Control and Prevention (CDC) estimate that about 1 in 68 children is now identified with autism spectrum disorder (2015). Autism spectrum disorder (ASD) is a low-incidence disability despite the perception that it has become a high-incidence disability. It is true that ASD has seemed recently to be more prevalent, and a review of CDC statistics suggests that there does appear to be a significant increase in the numbers of children diagnosed with ASD. For example, in the year 2000, it was estimated that 1 in 150 was diagnosed with ASD and in 2004 the statistic had changed to 1 in 125, and by 2010 the number of children diagnosed with ASD had risen to 1 in 68 (2015).

Autism spectrum disorder is more common in boys (1 in 42) than girls (1 in 189) and ASD occurs in all racial, socioeconomic, and ethnic groups (CDC, 2015). ASD appears to have a genetic connection: with identical twins, when one child has ASD, there is a 36% to 95% chance that the other child will also be diagnosed with ASD. Parents who have one child with ASD have a 2% to 18% chance of having a second affected child (CDC, 2015).

The term "high functioning" is often used to describe individuals with autism who have average to above-average intelligence. These people have Asperger syndrome. The autism spectrum includes a range of individuals. Those with severe autism are unable to engage at all outside of their inner world; these individuals often have intellectual disabilities and communication disorders. At the opposite end of the spectrum are those who have the ability to communicate and also have average to high intelligence. Some individuals with autism have average to high intelligence but lack the ability to communicate verbally. They would be considered high functioning, but because they have a communication disorder, they do not have Asperger syndrome. The students who will audition and be accepted into music degree programs will be those who are high functioning. I use the term "autism spectrum disorder" or ASD to refer to both types of high-functioning students.

Students with ASD have always been present on college campuses, but only in recent years do we seem to have a label and a sensitivity for the loner student with the unkempt appearance who stunned students and faculty with an incredible ability to analyze music in music theory classes and tuned pianos on the side; now we know he may have been a person with ASD. Increasingly, students with odd behaviors, including those who are confrontational or disruptive in classes, are at risk for leaving college before finishing their degrees (Bedrossian & Pennamon, 2007). There are many successful examples of musicians who are high functioning on the autism spectrum, and children and adults with more severe ASD have been known to demonstrate exceptional interest and abilities in music. Also on the spectrum are an unusual group referred to as autistic savants. Occasionally we even hear about autistic musical savants like Derek Paravicini, an exceptionally talented musician with severe challenges (Ockelford, 2007).

Students in the high-functioning range of the autism spectrum are fully capable of completing music degrees; however, only recently have students in postsecondary education with ASD begun with the university's disability office and receiving accommodations. Accommodations are enabling many students to complete music degrees who might not have been successful in college even 10 years ago.

WHAT IS AUTISM SPECTRUM DISORDER?

The *DSM-V* identifies autism spectrum disorder with persistent impairment in reciprocal social communication and social interaction, and restricted, repetitive patterns of behavior, interests, or activities (2013). Deficits in any of the following three areas of social communication and social interaction across multiple contexts are common:

1. Deficits in social-emotional reciprocity, ranging, for example, from abnormal social approach and failure of normal back-and-forth conversation; to reduced sharing of interests, emotions, or affect; to failure to initiate or respond to social interactions.
2. Deficits in nonverbal communicative behaviors used for social interaction, ranging, for example, from poorly integrated verbal and nonverbal communication; to abnormalities in eye contact and body language or deficits in understanding and use of gestures; to a total lack of facial expressions and nonverbal communication.
3. Deficits in developing, maintaining, and understanding relationships, ranging, for example, from difficulties adjusting behavior to suit various social contexts; to difficulties in sharing imaginative play or in making friends; to absence of interest in peers. (American Psychiatric Association, 2013)

Persons with ASD have restricted and repetitive patterns of behavior, interests or activities. The *DSM-V* recommends that when diagnosing an individual with ASD, two of the following four should be currently present or there should be a history of such behavior:

1. Stereotyped or repetitive motor movements, use of objects, or speech (e.g., simple motor stereotypies, lining up or flipping objects, echolalia, idiosyncratic phrases).

2. Insistence on sameness, inflexible adherence to routines, or ritualized patterns of verbal or nonverbal behavior (e.g., extreme distress at small changes, difficulties with transitions, rigid thinking patterns, greeting rituals, need to take same route or eat the same food every day).

3. Highly restricted, fixated interests that are abnormal in intensity or focus (e.g., strong attachment to or preoccupation with unusual objects, excessively circumscribed or perseverative interests).

4. Hyper- or hyporeactivity to sensory input or unusual interest in sensory aspects of the environment (e.g., apparent indifference to pain/temperature, adverse response to specific sounds or textures, excessive smelling or touching of objects, visual fascination with lights or movement). (American Psychiatric Association, 2013)

These symptoms cause the person to have significant impairment in social, occupational, or other areas of current functioning. The symptoms cannot be explained by an intellectual or a developmental delay (APA, 2013). With the new edition of the *DSM*-V, Asperger syndrome is no longer listed as a separate category but is instead listed under autism spectrum disorder.

The statistics for employment for adults with ASD are typically low. Shattuck et al. (2012) reports that 25% to 50% of adults with ASD are employed with pay. Those who work are often employed below their level of education and, likely because of their social problems, many have difficulty finding stable employment. It is in the best interest of society that high-functioning people with autism attend postsecondary education and graduate into a meaningful and engaging career.

LEARNING CHARACTERISTICS OF STUDENTS WITH ASD

It is difficult to group students with disabilities, even with a specific disability such as Asperger syndrome, with a set of accommodations that will work for everyone. Neurotypical learners (a current favored descriptor of people without ASD) are equally diverse. In general, students on the spectrum might benefit from having professors who are aware of common learning characteristics that might represent students with ASD in their classroom. Freedman (2010) provides some guidance for college professors:

- Students with ASD tend to be visual learners who typically have some challenge with auditory processing. Because processing time can be slow, their response time can also be delayed. It is important to wait for these students to organize their thoughts before they are ready to answer a question.
- Students with ASD have communication challenges; professors need to remember that communication challenges can impact the students' ability to successfully request accommodations for their learning needs.
- Students with ASD can experience sensory overload. Sensory over-stimulation can negatively impact learning.
- Students with ASD struggle with organizational skills and the ability to manage time well. Often these students need assistance in successfully completing assignments.
- Students with ASD are prone to depression and/or anxiety. These mental health challenges, in addition to their ASD, can negatively impact academic success.
- Students with ASD may need assistance in developing skills of personal independence and social adaptation on campus. This includes friendships, romantic relationships, and relationships with faculty. Often the student is not successful in relationships and ends up not feeling accepted.
- Students with ASD can appear to be uninterested, rude, or self-absorbed and do not use social courtesies that are expected by neurotypicals. (Freedman, 2010)

Students with ASD might also have difficulty with fine motor control. Handwriting that is messy or illegible is often an example of difficulty with fine motor control. Students who write on computers can avoid creating problems for others in trying to decipher their handwriting.

Sensory Processing Disorder

Sensory processing disorder (SPD) is a frequently occurring problem in individuals with ASD. The severity can vary among individuals.

Frequent triggers for SPD:

- Fluorescent lights, a common fixture in classrooms around the world.
- Sensitivity to high pitches, certain timbres, and volume.
- Sensitivity to smell—people can be very distracted by the smell of a room, perfume, or possibly even valve oil.
- Sensitivity to textures in clothing, material used in furniture, or the feel of a wire string pressed by a finger.
- Difficulty in copying words or images from a board or from other media to paper.
- Clumsiness, or occasional difficulty with estimating distance.

The following adjustments are often effective:

- Wearing sunglasses in classrooms with fluorescent lighting can help people who are visually sensitive.
- Irlen lenses are colored lenses that are reported to improve the way the brain processes visual input (Irlen, 1998).
- If there is natural light, turn off fluorescent lights.
- Allow headphones in class if there is distracting sounds during exams.
- Students who become overstimulated may need to get up and stand or move.

BULLYING AND VICTIMIZATION

Students who have odd behaviors that might seem rude or anti-social are often targets for bullying and sometimes can be manipulated by others. Individuals with ASD tend to be very literal and honest. They assume that others are honest, too. For example, if students are working on a group project together and figure out that the student in their group with ASD can be convinced to do most of the work, it is easy for many students with ASD to be taken advantage of by peers. Another common problem with group work is that some students will not include the student with ASD. For example, students within the group might decide to meet at a time when the student with ASD cannot be there, or they might decide not to share contact information with the student with ASD. Professors need to be aware of the potential for these types of problems. Universal design promotes flexibility in assignments, so instead of a group project, a student may elect to work individually and have a shorter or less complicated assignment.

NAVIGATING THE SOCIAL WORLD

College is an exciting time for most students. It is an opportunity to be independent and have new experiences. The social life of the college student is a major part of attending college. Imagine the student with ASD who is not sure how to make friends. Is the person who shares your stand in orchestra your friend? Is a friend someone who likes the same composer that you do? These can all be confusing for the student with autism. Moore (2006) observed, "One disability specialist in Minnesota says interventions to provide social skills training at college is the least they can offer. We would provide an interpreter for a hard-of-hearing person. Why don't we provide an interpreter [of social situations] for somebody with Asperger's?" (p. 37). Students with ASD who have mentors, tutors, and sympathetic peers who can help them translate social cues are the lucky ones. However, many students with ASD find themselves challenged in social situations, in professional situations, and with professors. It is common for students with ASD to alienate others without ever knowing why.

EXECUTIVE FUNCTION

"Executive function" is an umbrella term that describes a set of cognitive abilities that govern behavior regulation and goal-orientated activities (Welsh & Pennington, 1988). Skills in executive functioning involve planning, organizing, synthesizing information, delaying, and initiating activity (Wolf, Thierfeld Brown, & Kukiela Bork, 2009).

Executive functioning can be very challenging for individuals with ASD as it requires

- cognitive flexibility
- inhibition of irrelevant responses
- behavioral adaptation to environment
- understanding codes of conduct
- using experience to understand rules
- identifying essential from nonessential information
- ability to retain a goal and the steps needed to accomplish it in one's mind (working memory) (Freedman, 2010, pp. 20–21)

Imagine an undergraduate student in a music history course with an assignment to choose a composer from either the Classical or Romantic era and to write a paper that explores that conductor's unique contribution to the music of their time. Many professors will write no more than that description in their syllabus. The professor assumes that the student knows how to write a paper that requires researching the composer in the library and identifying important contributions to music that the student discovers through research. Students with ASD might know that they need to go to the library and look up the composer and check out books that are relevant, but they might not understand what to do next.

Executive function skills that involve discriminating between information on the composer and relevant information that the assignment calls for are going to be challenging to the student. Perhaps the student is also fascinated with pianos and chooses a composer who composed for piano. For some students, it is easy to become narrowly focused on topics or objects that are particular passions. If the student is caught up with learning everything there is to know about pianos, he might find himself off on a tangent about the types of pianos being built in the specific decade and country during the composer's time. Soon the paper becomes centered on unusual pianos that are only remotely connected to the composer because a patron happened to play one of the instruments.

The music history professor who receives a paper that rambles on about unique pianos is left wondering why the student turned in a paper that had no connection with the assignment described in the course syllabus. A kind professor might tell the student to revise the paper, but many professors will simply assign a low grade for a paper that did not meet the requirements described in the syllabus. The student is puzzled because he or she loved the paper and cannot imagine why the professor doesn't, too!

This example is very typical of problems that occur everyday in a university course. Students with ASD need assignments broken down into steps with very clear instructions. An example of a paper written by a previous student in the same class who wrote a paper that included information about the unique contributions that the composer made to music is a helpful resource to make available to students. There will likely be typical students who appreciate not only having a good example of the paper to refer to but also might appreciate an example from a paper that earned a high grade. Many professors feel that students should be able to write a paper on a topic independently. They might see providing that much support as inappropriate for college students. It also might be difficult for a professor to understand how to explain an assignment in more detail. How much detail needs to be provided and how does one know if the student is able to independently write the paper?

Students who receive accommodations are usually provided a tutor who helps them organize a writing assignment and checks in with them as they begin writing to make sure they are on track. A tutor helping to monitor the development of the paper would likely notice that the student was writing about pianos rather than a composer. Here is an example of clear directions a tutor might offer for this assignment:

Composer Paper

1. Choose one composer from either the Classical or Romantic era.
2. Research the composer in the library and on the Internet looking for the most important contributions that the composer made to music. For example, Clara Schumann was probably the most prolific and best-known woman composer of the Romantic era. Include pieces she composed that have been recorded and pieces that were listed as composed by her husband Robert Schumann but are actually thought to have been composed by Clara.
3. Be sure to provide references that you used to support the information in your paper. Use the Chicago Style for your references. You can find examples of references written in Chicago Style in the example paper under the assignment in Blackboard.
4. Good papers are long enough to cover the important contributions but usually longer than 5 double-spaced pages and shorter than 15 pages.
5. The paper should be spell-checked and printed from your computer.
6. The paper is due no later than May 1.
7. Refer to the example paper by Judy Jones from last semester that is located in Blackboard under this assignment. You will see her paper is focused on unique contributions that Berlioz made to music of his time. The references are written in Chicago style, and her paper is 10 pages double-spaced in 12-point font.

Pragmatic Communication

The rules for using language within a social context, including body language, are a core challenge for students with ASD. Pragmatics affect both the input (comprehension) and output (production) of speech and language. Pragmatics include rules for conversation for interacting with others. Language processing tends to break down in unstructured social situations in individuals with ASD (Wolf, Thierfeld Brown, & Kukiela Bork, 2009). Often speech and language pathologists work with students to improve pragmatic communication; however, it is important for professors to recognize some of the skills that fall into the category of pragmatic communication:

- Knowing that you have to answer when a question is asked. This skill involves also knowing how to ask for clarification if you do not understand a question, are confused, or there is a communication breakdown.

- Being able to participate in a conversation by taking turns with the other speaker. This involves recognizing when the other speaker has finished talking and, if unsure, asking the speaker if he or she has finished. It also requires the individual to appreciate and understand the purpose of sharing information (related to joint attention).
- Noticing and responding appropriately to the nonverbal aspects of language.
- Knowing that you have to introduce a topic of conversation in order for the listener to understand fully what you will be talking about, and that you have to check for understanding throughout your conversations.
- Knowing which words or what sort of sentence type to use when initiating a conversation or responding to something someone has said.
- Knowing how to end a conversation appropriately.
- Knowing how to ask for clarification when you do not understand something.
- Knowing how to provide clarification so that the listener understands you: this includes being able to "read" the listener's facial expression to know if the listener is following you.
- Knowing the importance of staying on topic, and being able to do so.
- Maintaining appropriate eye contact (not too much staring, and not too much looking away) during a conversation.
- Being able to distinguish how to talk and behave toward different communication partners.

Inability to Read Nonverbal Skills

Related to pragmatic communication skills are nonverbal communication skills. Body language and facial expressions are essential ways that people communicate. Students with ASD have great difficulty with deciphering nonverbal communication. Students in performing ensembles led by a conductor must be able to read nonverbal communication from the conductor. If a student with ASD struggles with responding to a conductor, the disability office might be able to help to find a professional who can help the student in interpreting the conductor's body language. Students with ASD who are studying conducting may also have difficulty relaying nonverbal meaning through their conducting. If the student is at risk of a lowered grade and is receiving accommodations, it might be helpful to talk with the counselor working with the student to see if support might be provided in expressive nonverbal conducting skills.

Rigid Behaviors

Individuals with ASD can be very rigid about changes, and they can also experience difficulty transitioning to new activities. They thrive on sameness and a stable and predictable world. Unfortunately, life and certainly college is neither predictable nor the same. Even though professors might include a statement on their syllabus that affirms that changes might be made in the syllabus during the semester, as needed, students with autism will likely become frustrated and sometimes angry when changes occur. The student might also become irritated when someone sits at the classroom desk that the student with ASD perceives as his or her seat. Some students become so upset they have to leave the class if their chair is taken by someone else. Universal design recommends that professors be flexible in all aspects of teaching, but the student with autism does not always appreciate flexibility.

Another area that might upset the student with autism is changes in ensemble seating. Some ensembles require auditions each semester to accommodate shifts in ensemble membership when students leave for student teaching or other internships. A student with ASD whose seat moves will usually not like changing seats, even if the new seat is considered better. Prepare students for changes by mentioning that auditions are likely to impact many in the ensemble and explain why. It might seem obvious to expect students to understand this routine, but even so, many still become very upset by what they perceive as someone taking their assigned seat.

Having an agenda for class or rehearsal written on the board helps the student with autism to anticipate the routine for the class. As the instructor, if you feel comfortable estimating about how much time you plan to spend on each piece or activity, you could make a note of this. Students with ASD like to know what to expect and predictability helps them to be less anxious. If the student knows you plan to discuss a topic for 20 minutes, then put students into small discussion groups to answer questions for 15 minutes, it helps the student with autism feel secure. Occasionally students who begin to feel over-stimulated feel like they need to get up and move or even leave the classroom. They might be able to wait five minutes if they know a transition will be coming. This helps students learn to self-regulate their behavior and leads toward more independence and of course, fitting in better with others. It also helps students who become frustrated by activities or music they do not like to practice patience by knowing that soon the activity or piece will change. Conversely, if students like an activity or piece of music, it might be hard for them to change to another piece that they may not like. Planning for a transition helps them to manage their emotions. Of course, typical students appreciate knowing what is planned, too.

THREE UNIVERSITY MODELS FOR INCLUSION OF STUDENTS WITH ASD

It is likely that your university has one of three philosophies for including students who are on the autism spectrum. Generally four-year schools have more rigorous music programs and are the least flexible in accommodating students with complex disabilities. Community colleges are recognized as being more welcoming and more accustomed to students with ASD than four-year schools. Depending on the philosophy and resources of your school you will experience different levels of support.

1. Colleges that provide the basic level of support that is required by law fall into the first level of inclusion. These schools provide quiet places for taking tests, note-takers, and extra time allowed for tests. Students with ASD require intensive support that can be very time-consuming. Students with ASD would likely not be very successful at this type of school, which requires more independent students who are able to advocate well for themselves.

2. The second level provides more support including better coordination across the campus and additional levels of peer tutoring, hands-on assistance from the disability office on a regular basis, and referral to community services (student is charged a fee).

3. The third type of school is very comprehensive with all of the supports of level two plus specific supports in time management, organizational skills, social skills groups, mentoring and coaching (peer or professional), and ASD-specific counseling or psychotherapy. Usually additional fees are charged for these intensive services but students with ASD tend to be most successful in this level of university. (Freedman, 2010)

Assistive Technology

An exciting assistive technology device being developed in the United Kingdom is *Brain in Hand*. Brain in Hand is a Smartphone app that enables the user to use built-in coping strategies when the user is anxious or experiencing stress. If the coping system is not enough, then the user can push a red button and reach a person who can provide immediate advice and reassurance.

Similar to Brain in Hand are biometric wrist bands in development in the United States that measure the person's heart rate, sweating, temperature, and other stress responses in real time. This information is combined with a camera that identifies when the person is experiencing stressful events and sends a message to a center that is able to intervene. Both devices enable individuals with autism to move about their environment more independently.

Advising

School of music student advisors should be trained in communicating with students with ASD. It is important that student advisors be approachable and aware that students with ASD could be reluctant to make appointments with their advisor. The advisor needs to reach out to students who are at risk for falling through the cracks.

Students with ASD will likely avoid required classes they are not interested in and instead try to schedule only classes they like. Advisors need to patiently work with students who avoid taking some classes. It is difficult for students with disabilities to manage a heavy schedule. A course load that is too heavy is a major reason many students with disabilities drop out of school before graduation. Students with ASD should consider taking general education required courses during the summer at a local community college; then they can focus more on music courses during the rest of the year. They probably will like their music courses more and this way they will complete their least favorite requirements without having them compete against music classes. Students who love performing or other types of music coursework should be careful not to schedule too many performing ensembles. Typical students might be able to manage a heavier ensemble load but remember that the student with ASD is going to struggle with organizational and social skills every day and will need more support to manage a packed schedule.

Music Students with ASD and Social Isolation

Music student organizations and ensembles offer many opportunities for interaction in formal and informal social groups. Music fraternities, clubs, student-led ensembles, and the official music ensembles that are part of the curriculum are all places where groups of students gather. It is easy for students with autism to feel as though they do not fit in with some of the more social groups. It is important that any groups that are provided meeting space within the university be open and welcoming to students with disabilities. Leaders of these groups can help by reaching out to students who might feel marginalized and forgotten. Depression is a common secondary disorder for many students with autism due to feeling socially isolated. Student leaders can also benefit from training about ASD; it would likely help them to feel more comfortable with how to approach a peer who seems very aloof and anti-social.

Accommodations

Students with ASD can benefit from a broad range of accommodations:

- Assistance with time management, including prioritizing, and dealing with procrastination.
- Learning self-limiting skills for dealing with specific interests in computers, video games, or the Internet.
- Having course loads broken down into smaller, more manageable chunks.
- Using visual schedules and sequences for chunking, especially with long-term assignments.
- Using voice recognition software for dictation of papers.
- Receiving help with organizing class materials.
- Having visual and concrete supports for understanding instructions.
- Having someone check for understanding of instructions, and/or clarification of material, on a regular basis until it is clear that the student's understanding is adequate,
- Use of "priming" to prepare for the next class/lecture (e.g., providing the student with advance notice of what will be covered next; giving the student notes for the current or next class).
- Study skills training.
- Getting specific guidance for working in groups.
- Having someone intervene as needed to help the student develop appropriate classroom behavior and reduce inappropriate behavior (correcting professor, asking too many questions, thought broadcasting).
- Being allowed sensory breaks so that the student can leave the classroom for short periods of time, as needed, to deal with sensory issues.
- Having mitigation for the distraction caused by fluorescent lights and noisy corridors (e.g., wear sunglasses/tinted glasses; headphones for sound dampening, so long as student is still able to hear the lecture).
- Living in a single dorm room.
- Having fluorescent lighting in dorm room removed.
- Receiving social mentoring to help deal with bullying, social manipulation, dating issues, personal space, eye contact.

- Receiving guidance in managing roommate issues: neatness, overnight dates, drugs/alcohol, sharing responsibilities in the room.
- Receiving advocacy training: learning to communicate needs to professors; disclose disability to other students; deal with public safety.
- Get assistance in finding appropriate activities/clubs, support groups, or student organizations for students with disabilities.
- Having instruction in managing independent living skills (e.g., money management, hygiene, health and fitness).
- Receiving referrals available for professional "coaches."
- Receiving on-campus counseling, free or cost-based. (Freedman, 2010)

Sympathetic professors can be very important in assisting students with ASD:

- Offer an alternative to essay exams for students with ASD.
- Offer students the option to submit outlines instead of papers when writing is a problem.
- Consider alternative assignments to group projects.
- When students ask too many questions or monopolize discussions (thought broadcasting), inform the student he or she can speak only when called on twice during the class.
- Be available for 5 minutes after class and encourage students to write down comments or thoughts they have during class that they weren't able to share.
- If assignments or exams are handwritten, allow the student to use pencil and erasure of mistakes.
- If you suspect a student has ASD with serious behavior problems but you have not received a letter with accommodations listed from disability services, you should refer the student to disability services before starting any disciplinary action.
- Use principles of universal design to make teaching and the classroom environment accessible.
- Make a printout of grades, missed assignments, and assignments and exams yet to occur at mid-term unless there is an online version of this.
- Use an audio recording device.
- Use preferential seating.
- Give the student copies of class PowerPoint presentations.
- Give the student priority registration.
- Prepare behavioral contracts for guidance.
- Give the student permission to attend other sections of the same course.

SUMMARY

The autism spectrum includes a range of individuals who all struggle with communication, unusual behaviors that include repetitive movements, and challenges with social skills. High-functioning students with ASD are often very bright and will have no difficulty gaining entry into the school of music; however, they may have difficulty with successful completion of a degree and employment that represents their educational level. It is not uncommon for students with ASD to avoid registering with the disability services office, but they will have an increased chance for academic and social success if they do. Students with ASD can appear to be bored, challenging, rude, and hard to understand if the professor has not had personal experience or training in how to interact with individuals with autism in their class or ensemble. Patience is essential, and collaboration with the student and other professionals on campus will ensure that the student achieves a music degree and continues on to a rewarding career in music.

9

LOW VISION AND BLINDNESS

Carol auditioned on flute as a music education major. The flute professor waived the sight-reading requirement and instead asked Carol to prepare an additional piece. During the audition, the flute professor also asked Carol to echo her playing to determine how quickly she could pick up phrases by ear. Carol was able to instantly play any phrase the flute professor played. Carol has low vision and has perfect pitch.

Carol was particularly interested in playing jazz and could easily improvise in any jazz style. She also plays tenor saxophone. She passed the audition with no problems and was awarded a full scholarship. She was off to a great start and felt as though she had picked the right school; the professors seem very flexible and supportive, and she believed she would be able to fulfill her dream of being a music teacher at a state school for the blind.

A barrier that no one considered emerged in Carol's sophomore year. She was required to have four years of marching band as an instrumental music education major. Carol did not want to be in marching band because the disability office was unable to provide her an aide, but she also saw no reason for learning marching band because schools for blind do not have marching bands. Carol's advisor suggested substituting jazz band for marching band, but the band department refused; they did not want to set a precedent and felt strongly that all instrumental music education majors needed experience in marching band. Carol was very disappointed and after much soul searching, she decided to drop music education and to become a special educator instead.

ACCORDING TO RAUE and Lewis (2011), 3% of students registering with their university disability office identify as having low vision or blindness. Low vision/blindness is a low-incidence disability, but most schools of music should expect to see students with vision loss auditioning for admission at some point. Loss of vision does not impact the ability to learn and perform music; obviously, the only barriers will occur when the student is expected to read music quickly or engage in other activities that require vision. Carol felt that participating in marching band was not only unnecessary for her career goals but she also imagined being frustrated and embarrassed in front of large numbers of people who would see her fumbling with movement on the football field.

WHAT IS VISION LOSS?

Very few people with vision loss are totally blind. There is usually some residual vision that allows people to function somewhat in a sighted world. "Partial sight" or "partial blindness" are other terms often used to describe low vision; however, "low vision" is the correct term to use today. Low vision is caused by eye disease and involves visual acuity to be 20/70 or less in the better-seeing eye. It cannot be corrected or improved with regular eyeglasses.

Low vision is uncorrectable vision that interferes with daily activities. People with low vision experience many of the same challenges as people who are blind. Individuals with low vision may have trouble accessing and using adaptive technologies; getting around in unfamiliar settings; finding transportation; reading print; or participating in recreational or athletic activities. It is obvious that activities requiring movement will cause the individual to be unsure and at times awkward.

"Legal blindness" or "statutory blindness" is what the US government uses to determine eligibility for vocational training, rehabilitation, education, disability benefits, low vision devices, and tax exemption programs. Visual impairment describes a wide range of visual function, from low vision to total blindness. Additional factors influencing visual impairment include contrast sensitivity, light sensitivity, glare sensitivity, and light/dark adaptation (American Foundation for the Blind, 2015).

Functional limitation describes visual functioning and loss of ability to perform activities of daily living. Common daily activities affected by vision loss are reading, safe pedestrian travel, self-care, cooking, and recreational activities (American Foundation for the Blind, 2015).

TEACHING STUDENTS WITH VISION LOSS

Many students with low vision see best with proper lighting and visuals made with black print on a white background for the best contrast. Some individuals with vision loss have trouble reading websites with black print against a darker colored background—for example, red background with black print. Some students with vision loss can read large print for a sustained period of time without discomfort or difficulty while others might experience discomfort reading the same print for only a few moments (Schneider, 2001). Musicians may be able to read music in large print with good contrast, however, depending on the size of the music; it might need to be so large that it either does not fit on a traditional music stand or it requires frequent page turns.

The disability services office will prepare large-print materials; however, the office will probably need several weeks to produce music and at least six weeks to create a large-print textbook. As much as possible, course materials should be in Microsoft Word for easier transfer to Braille. PDF files have to be converted into Word and then Braille versions can be generated. Sometimes the conversion process is not accurate and requires a person to read and compare the Word version word-for-word with the PDF version. This is very time-consuming and expensive. Many universities cannot afford someone who does nothing but text-to-Braille conversion; however, it is the best way to be certain that students with low vision have all materials in a format they can access. The same problem exists for text-to-speech software. Always provide a Word version of all your course materials to those who use text-to-speech.

Note-taking in class can be accomplished in several ways; most common are student note-takers who then either turn the notes into audio files or have the notes transcribed into Braille. Software programs such as Duxbury Braille Translation enable note-takers to import a traditional Word document into Duxbury that is then printed in Braille. Other options include devices that students with vision loss use themselves that convert to Braille when printed. Some devices—in particular, the more affordable Perkins Brailler—can be very noisy and distracting to others in the class. Different software is used for music notation to Braille music notation. It will be difficult for the note-taker to put text and music together in their notes.

Students with vision loss are able to do research in the library. With the conversion of print to electronic formats, many books and articles are now available in Braille or can be accessed through text-to-speech software. Notated music will be a little more challenging. The National Library Service for the Blind and Physically Handicapped administered by the Library of Congress has extensive holdings of journals, magazines, books, music, and scores in Braille. Many books are now commercially available as audio books as well.

Those doing survey research that might include individuals with vision loss can have research instruments evaluated for validity and reliability by the American Printing House for the Blind (APH) Accessible Tests Department.

Graphics or images can sometimes be transferred to tactile print to help the student with vision loss understand a particular image. For example, in a music history course, there may be discussion comparing Renaissance era string instruments and modern string instruments. The professor may decide to show photographs of instruments to supplement the lecture. Piaf is a company that produces a tactile printer that can translate a flat image to one that can be raised so the person with vision loss can feel the contours of the two instruments. Most disability services offices do not own these printers but may be able to arrange to have a few images produced in advance of a lecture.

Individuals with vision loss depend on accessible websites to access course materials and to retrieve information. Many websites are not accessible to people who use text-to-speech translation software; using an APH template will help schools of music and professors in designing accessible websites. Any graphics on websites need descriptions for text-to-speech software. So if you have an image of Mozart on your web page you should have a caption that says, "This is an image of Mozart as a child" in order for persons with vision loss to be able to make sense of the image.

Online courses must be accessible to people who use text-to-speech readers. The National Federation for the Blind (NFB) reviews many online websites and online-based software for accessibility. Blackboard, a popular course organization tool and program for online courses, is certified by the NFB as being accessible.

A major barrier that can occur in rehearsal rooms are changes in the room setup. People with vision loss memorize the room and go to their seats based on the path they remember. If the rehearsal chairs are not set up the same or if the piano or other instruments are in the way, it can actually be dangerous to the student. First, permit the student to take time to complete a careful orientation to the room, allowing time for the student to feel the piano and get a sense of how large it is or learn that the best way to get to the French horn section on the stage is through a stage door toward the back of the orchestra that has a straight path to the French horn chairs. It is always important to consider the safety of the student. It is best to have someone in the ensemble wait at the door for the student with vision loss and guide them to his or her seat. When guiding people who are blind, offer your arm to them. They will hold your arm just above the elbow and follow slightly behind you. Walk at a normal pace and if needed let the person know of any upcoming obstructions by saying for example, "We are coming to a step" or "Here is a microphone cable on the floor; be sure not to trip."

When speaking to a person who is blind, look directly at him or her and talk in a normal voice (there is no reason to raise your voice). Always tell the person your name, and if you exit the room tell the person with vision loss you are leaving. I always say who I am when I say hello as the student enters my classroom: "Hi Autumn, it's Dr. McCord." When you leave the room tell the student you are going; otherwise they will not know.

As with any person who has a disability, always ask to clarify with the student if he or she has certain needs or abilities. "We do a lot of dancing in my class; would you like to join or are you more comfortable having us describe the dance?" If the student chooses to dance, then I would ask if he or she wants assistance and what specific kind of aid is most helpful.

If you are a professor who uses the board, be sure to turn around after writing and describe or read anything you wrote. If you use a PowerPoint presentation, this will need description, too.

Discuss alternate methods for taking tests with the student to see if he or she has a preference. Written tests will need to be in Braille and answers will need to be written by someone else. This type of test will need to be completed in another room. Exams can be read to the student and answers audio recorded.

ABSOLUTE PITCH AND VISION LOSS

There is interesting research suggesting that absolute pitch occurs more often in people who are blind than in sighted people (Gaab et al., 2006; Hamilton et al., 2004). You may recall in the scenario about Carol that she was able to accurately echo back phrases from her flute professor. Musicians who are blind are likely to prefer learning by ear than through Braille music.

BRAILLE MUSIC

Louis Braille, the blind inventor of the Braille system, was a musician who not only invented the code for reading words through a raised system of six bumps, but he also created a similar system for reading music. Braille notation is an important way for conductors and musicians who are blind to access scores and music. The problem with Braille music is that using it can be tedious and cumbersome for musicians. Imagine a pianist learning a new piece through Braille. First, the student feels the

Braille music for the right hand for maybe two measures and memorizes it by playing the two measures with the right hand as they continue to feel the Braille music with the left hand. Then the left hand part is added, and the process continues. It is slow and is not a very musical way to learn music. Most musicians with vision loss prefer to learn by ear. Since musicians with vision loss have very good pitch, including many with absolute pitch, it is a more fluent process for them to learn music by ear. Braille music is fine for conductors, although it can also be cumbersome, because the conductor is able to use only one hand for conducting. Braille scores work better for score study and conductors with vision loss will memorize the score. Figure 9.1 shows the basic notation for learning pitches, and durations of quarter, half, eighth, and sixteenth notes in Braille.

Braille Music Notation

Quarter notes from A to G look like this in Braille music notation. Dark dots are raised and felt by the musician.

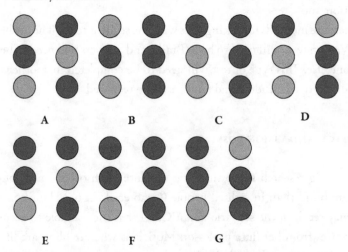

Durations are also represented in the same cell. For example, a half note C has dot 3 at the bottom.

Pitches with both 3 & 6 dots at the bottom are either a whole note or a sixteenth note. When there are no dots at 3 & 6, then the note is an eighth note.

FIGURE 9.1 Basic Notation for Pitch and Rhythm in Braille

There are collections of piano, vocal, choral, instrumental, and instructional method books available in Braille and many resources for learning to read Braille music. Taesch and McCann (2003) have written a free downloadable PDF for learning the basics of Braille music that is obtainable in a number of websites on the Internet. McCann, a musician who is blind, founded Dancing Dots, a company that primarily sells assistive technology and software for musicians with low vision and blindness allowing them to access music notation. The Lime Lighter is a device that magnifies music notation 1 to 10 times the original size. The color of the screen can be adapted to whatever is most comfortable for the musician. For example, instead of black notes on a white background, white notes on a black background might be preferred. A foot pedal is used to turn the pages of the music. Manhasset Stands makes a stand that adapts to hold the Lime Lighter video screen. The stand is about the size of the doublewide Manhasset conductor stand. The musician with low vision is able to read traditional music notation independently using a modified stand that fits in and is not noticeable to anyone in the audience.

Dancing Dots is the best source for musicians with low vision and blindness for low- and high-tech solutions for reading Braille music and text. It also works great for composing music using Braille software that works with common music software programs. The company sells Braille printers and scanners that can convert traditional music into Braille. For people who want to learn to read Braille music notation, Dancing Dots carries low-tech Braille music tiles. Note taking devices and other electronic equipment and resources are sold that help music students to be successful in a traditional music curriculum.

ACCOMMODATIONS

- Describe all visuals and read anything on PowerPoint slides or written on the board.
- Notify the disability services office at least six weeks in advance to prepare texts, music, and other materials in Braille.
- Ask the Disability services office to find Braille scores and parts or to lease the Lime Lighter so traditional music notation can be adapted and used.
- Accommodations for note takers should consider the preference of the student.
- Orient students to the classroom or rehearsal room and keep equipment, instruments, and furniture in the same place or make sure the student is safely guided.
- Meet the student at the classroom door and welcome him or her by saying your name.

- Provide preferential seating in the same place each session with room for a guide dog.
- Write music assignments in notation using assistive technology. Disability services will need to arrange for the devices and training.

SUMMARY

Students with low vision or blindness can be very capable music students. Their primary modes of learning are through hearing and touch. Musicians have excellent aural skills and many have absolute pitch. The most efficient and preferred way to learn music by students with vision loss is by ear. Braille music notation can be used to supplement learning and will be necessary for score study and completing music theory assignments.

There are many supports for music professors and students to ease translation of visual aspects of teaching and learning music. Students will often think of strategies or know of others they have used in the past; it is always important to ask them for ideas.

HARD-OF-HEARING, D/DEAF, AND DEAF

Sam is an undergraduate student with severe hearing loss. Sam wears hearing aids and is a percussionist. His hearing aids are barely noticeable but sometimes others notice him playing percussion in his bare feet and using American Sign Language (ASL) to communicate with others. He uses a sign language interpreter in his classes, but in lessons and rehearsals he relies on speech reading and gestures.

Sam began losing his hearing when he was eight years old after a series of ear infections. Sam's speech is good since he was already speaking when he began to lose his hearing. His audiogram shows that without his hearing aids, he would not hear speech or most of the instruments in the band. His hearing aid boosts the missing frequencies but is not able to restore the clarity experienced by people without hearing loss.

Sam plays drum set with a rock band and enjoys going to rock concerts. His audiologist recommended that he use custom earplugs without his hearing aids when he is in loud musical environments to save his residual hearing. He most enjoys playing music in rock bands without his hearing aids; that is when he feels like a "normal person."

THE NATIONAL INSTITUTE on Deafness and Other Communication Disorders (n.d.) estimates that 13% of people aged 12 or older have hearing loss in both ears, based on hearing examinations. Hearing loss is a low-incidence disability. However, music professors and music students are at high risk of developing noise-induced hearing loss themselves. Musicians are 3.6 times as likely as non-musicians to develop noise-induced hearing loss (Bond, 2014). Hearing loss is an occupational hazard for professors with regular exposure to large ensembles, particularly amplified music. Many musicians now use special earplugs designed for musicians that help protect hearing without loss of clarity of sound.

Blanchfield et al. (2001) estimated the percentage of people without hearing loss and those with loss in the labor force to be strikingly different. For the 18- to 44-year-old group, 82% of the US hearing population was in the labor force, and only 58% of the severely to profoundly deaf or hard-of-hearing population were employed. Deaf graduates will earn about 68% more during their adult lives than students who attend college but withdraw before completing a degree (Walter, Clarcq, & Thompson, 2001). Cheng and Zhang (2014) discovered that deaf or hard-of-hearing (DHH) students prefer degree programs in the arts because the arts tend to be more accepting of students who are different. Universities will continue to see an increase in enrollment of students who are DHH, particularly in the arts.

This chapter explores three issues: (1) students with hearing loss, (2) description of hearing loss, and (3) preparing your school of music for full inclusion of students with hearing loss and d/Deafness.

WHAT IS HEARING LOSS?

There are four types of hearing loss. They are conductive, sensorineural, mixed, and central losses. Schraer-Joiner (2014) defines conductive hearing loss as a type of loss that impacts the outer or middle ear and occurs when sound is not conducted efficiently through the outer ear canal to the eardrum and the ossicles (small bones) of the middle ear. Conductive loss results in a reduction of sound levels making it more difficult for the individual to hear soft sounds. Conductive hearing loss is the most common type of hearing loss and is often the result of ear infections, allergies, benign tumors, or impacted earwax. This is the type of hearing loss that Sam has as a result of frequent ear infections as a child (p. 10).

Sensorineural hearing loss is a result of damage to the inner ear, the pathways leading to the inner ear to the brain, or the central processing centers of the brain (Tye-Murray, 2004, p. 186). Sensorineural hearing loss is often irreversible and can range from mild to profound (Schraer-Joiner, 2014, p. 12).

Mixed hearing loss is a combination of both conductive and sensorineural hearing loss. A mixed hearing loss can include damage to the outer and middle ear in addition to the inner ear (Schraer-Joiner, 2014, p. 13).

Central hearing losses are unusual and occur as a result of damage to the central nervous system, the pathways leading to the brain, or damage to the brain (Baloh, 2009; Schaub, 2008). Schraer-Joiner (2014) describes individuals with central hearing losses as having inconsistent auditory behavior; people might respond to environmental sounds but not react to sudden loud sounds (p.13).

Understanding Hearing Loss

Hearing loss is often misunderstood because many have the image of older people turning up the television to hear well. Turning up the volume helps somewhat; however, hearing loss does not mean that all sound needs to be louder, just specific frequencies. Typically most hearing losses occur in the frequency range of speech. A typical audiogram represents decibels or intensity vertically and frequency or pitch horizontally. Figure 10.1 shows an audiogram with familiar sounds and speech represented in intensity and frequency. About two-thirds from the bottom

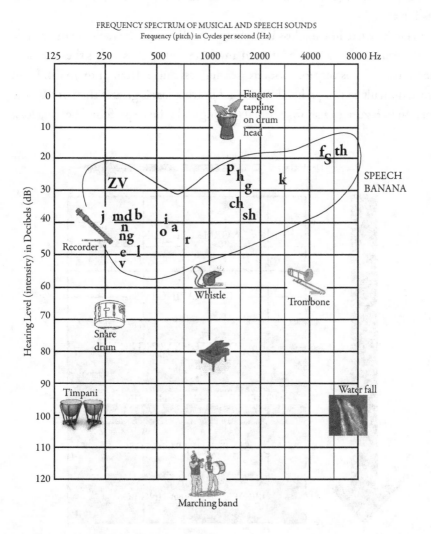

FIGURE 10.1 Audiogram of Familiar Sounds

of the audiogram is where most of the speech sounds occur. That area is referred to as the speech banana. If the speech sounds were circled the shape would look like a banana.

Hearing loss is categorized by degrees of hearing loss. Mild hearing losses are in the 25–40 dB range, in the speech banana. In very quiet settings, a person's function without hearing aids is fairly good, but in environments with competing sounds or several people talking at the same time, understanding will be more challenging for the individual with mild hearing loss, and he or she will miss up to 50% of class discussion (Schraer-Joiner, 2014, p. 15).

Moderate hearing loss occurs in the 41–55 dB range. A student with moderate hearing loss not using hearing aids will find it very difficult to function in the classroom. Schraer-Joiner (2014) estimates that this student will miss 50% to 75% of class discussions.

Moderately severe hearing loss is in the 56–70 dB range. It would be impossible for students in this range to understand anything said in class unless they are close to the source and it is very loud. Severe hearing loss ranges from 71 to 90 dB. Loud speech is difficult to comprehend. Profound hearing loss is greater than 91 dB. The audiogram in Figure 10.2 shows normal hearing and mild to profound hearing loss.

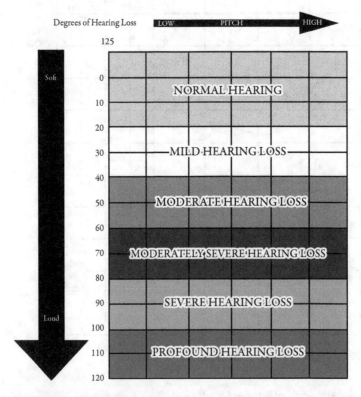

FIGURE 10.2 Degrees of Hearing Loss

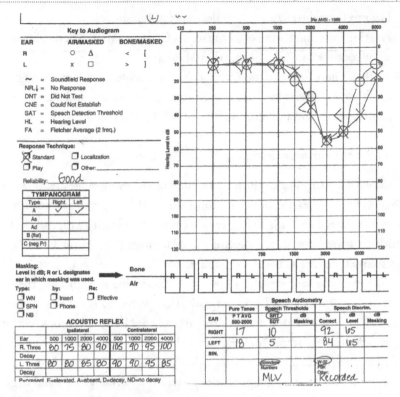

FIGURE 10.3 Audiogram Showing High Frequency Hearing Loss

Reading Audiograms

I recommend that music professors ask to see audiograms of their students with hearing loss. The audiogram will show hearing loss with and without hearing aids.

Figure 10.3 shows a typical audiogram of a person with high frequency hearing loss. The student will have difficulty hearing speech and may be more accurate in identifying instruments in the mid to low frequency range.

Reading the audiogram gives vocal and choral professors important information on the ability of students to sing with clear diction and balance and sing in tune in mixed voice ensembles. Students who use hearing aids will have audiograms that show hearing with amplification.

Hearing Loss Simulations

Perhaps the best way for musicians to understand hearing loss is by actually hearing music and speech simulations of various types of hearing loss. Many of these are available on the Internet; listed below are a few that include speech and music:

- Better Hearing Institute http://old.betterhearing.org/hearing_loss/ hearing_loss_simulator/index.cfm

- Hear to Learn http://www.hear2learn.org/CICSsim/
- Hearing Loss Simulation of a Flintstones Cartoon, Mild to Severe https://www.youtube.com/watch?v=ar1Dq-M20k4
- Cochlear implant simulation with 4 channel cochlear implants through 20 channel cochlear implants demonstrating both speech and music https://www.youtube.com/watch?v=SpKKYBkJ9Hw

Terms Used to Describe Individuals with Hearing Loss

Persons with hearing loss in the mild to moderately severe range are usually categorized as hard-of-hearing or HOH. Individuals with severe to profound hearing loss are considered deaf. Big D or Deaf are those who identify with the Deaf community via shared experiences, feelings, and language (ASL in the United States) (Christiansen & Leigh, 2002; Marschark, 2009). Prior to 1991, the term "hearing impaired" was used to refer to people with hearing loss. In 1991, the World Federation of the Deaf and other organizations voted to reject use of the term "impaired" to describe deafness (Marschark, 2009: NAD, n.d. People with hearing loss adopted the terms "d/Deaf" and "hard-of-hearing" (DHH) to describe individuals with hearing loss. Unlike other groups, the Deaf community prefers not to use person first language that is preferred by other groups and organizations. The Deaf community rejects person first language because it implies disability (Mackelprang, 2011, p. 441). They feel pride in their identity and do not adhere to the assumption that they have a communication problem because they have a language, American Sign Language, and therefore, are perfectly able to communicate.

Further, McIllroy and Storbeck (2011) define DeaF identity as the cultural space from which individuals with hearing loss transition within and between both the Deaf community and the hearing community thereby encompassing a fluid view of identity in that individuals can move from one identity type to another as they choose, depending on the roles, interactions, and contexts or settings in which the individual engages. The capital F indicates the fluid interactions.

D/DEAF AND HARD-OF-HEARING MUSIC STUDENTS

For completion of a four-year degree, the statistics for students with hearing loss are similarly dismal as for students with many other disabilities. Only 25% to 30% of the DHH students who enter college will complete a degree as compared to 50%

of peers without disabilities (Kuh et al., 2010; Newman et al., 2011). Most students leave during or after their first year (Boutin, 2008). Students who do persist often need five to six years to complete a baccalaureate degree (Hands and Voices, 2014). There are two reasons for poor graduation rates among DHH students. One has to do with academic readiness of DHH students, and the other is institutional readiness for DHH students.

Academic readiness among DHH students is related to significant delays in reading and comprehension. Hearing individuals generally have a single, auditory-based mode (listening and speaking) for both receptive and expressive language; DHH individuals may use varied language across different communication modalities (Boutin, 2008; Stinson, Scherer, & Walter, 1987). Students with DHH who use ASL rely solely on visual and manual communication. DHH students in the typical university must be able to manage well in an environment dominated by spoken language. In a recent study, Qi and Mitchell (2011) examined reading comprehension of DHH students on SAT test performance over five cohorts (1974, 1983, 1990, 1996, 2003) and found that the median performance never exceeded the fourth grade reading comprehension equivalent and mathematic problem solving never passed the equivalent of 6th grade.

American Sign Language Interpreters

It requires a very strong support system to see most music students with DHH through to graduation (Leppo, Cawthon, & Bond, 2013; Marschark et al., 2006). The most important accommodation for most students with DHH is access to high-quality sign language interpreters. For music students, interpreters must work with the student to develop signs to describe music terminology that might not have a sign in ASL. Highly qualified interpreters should be able to interpret music so the student with hearing loss is able to verbally describe live or recorded music.

For universities that are unable to meet the demands for highly qualified interpreters, Video Remote Interpreting (VRI) is an option. VRI is web-based and as long as the classroom has a high-speed Internet connection, VRI could be a solution, particularly if an interpreter can be regularly hired who is familiar with music and can also collaborate on signs with the music student (Simon, 2010).

Online instruction is a very accessible course delivery method for students with DHH. Instead of speech-heavy course delivery, online courses tend to be more text-heavy. Students can view materials at a pace that does not require a note-taker, and any online videos can be captioned prior to posting.

Students with hearing loss communicate in a variety of ways: speech, sign language, speech reading, writing, fingerspelling, or a combination of these. Body language and facial expressions help to relay the meaning of any verbal discussion.

Hearing Aids and Assistive Listening Devices

It is estimated that 30 million Americans have hearing loss but only 28.5% wear hearing aids (ENT & Allergy, 2011). Hearing aids can improve all levels of hearing loss. There are more than 1,000 different models of hearing aids in the United States, but all hearing aids are categorized in one of three different groups: ear-level aids, on-the-body aids, and bone conduction hearing aids (Northern & Downs, 2002, pp. 308–309).

Assisted listening devices help amplify the professor's voice, which is then transmitted directly into the student's hearing aids. The devices reduce background noise. Personal FM systems work similarly but use a microphone that can be clipped onto the professor's clothing. When using these assistive technology (AT) devices it is important to make sure the microphone or device is used not only for the professor but also for any students who speak or for other sound sources used (e.g., recordings, live music, Internet sites with sound). The professor should point the microphone or device toward the sound source while checking with the student that the AT device is not too close or too far away for optimal hearing. Be careful when holding a microphone too close to the speaker; the sound can be painfully loud to the person with hearing loss.

Cochlear Implants

Cochlear implants, a small biomedical electronic device that aids primarily in hearing speech, have been implanted worldwide in more than 300,000 people since 2012 (NIDCD, n.d.). A cochlear implant (CI) is a small, complex electronic device that helps to provide a sense of sound in individuals who are profoundly deaf or severely hard-of-hearing. One part of the implant is positioned behind the ear and another part is surgically implanted under the skin (National Institute on Deafness and Other Communication Disorders, (n.d.). Cochlear implants are somewhat controversial, particularly among adults, because the implant destroys any residual hearing. The quality of sound is improved with newer implants that have more channels than older models. If the cochlear implant simulations represent what people with these implants experience, then music is barely recognizable. CIs are primarily designed for speech, and compared with hearing abilities before the CI, speech is much improved.

If a student has a CI in your class or ensemble, it would be helpful if the professor to inquire about how many channels it has. The more channels the implant has, the more frequencies and intensities are available, and the more realistic music (with many frequencies) sounds. Children who receive CIs at a very young age seem to do better than children with severe and profound hearing loss using traditional aids. Professors will begin to see more students with CIs in the coming years as more children with CIs now reach college age.

Speech Reading

All people with hearing loss depend on speech reading, to some extent, to fully understand what another person is saying. It is essential to look directly at the person who is DHH when speaking so he or she can see your mouth and facial gestures. It is very hard to read speech; only 33% of English speech sounds are visible on the mouth (National Center on Deafness, 2009). Speech reading can be very tiring because the person with DHH has to focus intently to try to gain and decipher speech the best he or she can.

American Sign Language

ASL is a complete, complex language that uses signs made by moving the hands combined with facial expressions and postures of the body. It is the primary language of most North Americans with DHH who sign. There are signs for commonly occurring words, and letters that can be used to fingerspell. Fingerspelling is time-consuming but is used when there is no sign for the desired word. Many musical terms and musical instruments do not have a sign, so interpreters in a music class will need to know how to spell instruments, particularly words that do not sound the way they are spelled (e.g., djembe). If a lecture uses musical terms, it is helpful to the interpreter to have these words in advance. The interpreter will look for signs others have used or perhaps create a sign that will be used with the students.

Teaching with ASL Interpreters

Interpreters go through very rigorous training and testing. I teach at a university with a large deaf education program, and even deaf education professors are cautious about using ASL in any situation but casual discussion. If you have a student in your class who uses an interpreter and you do not know ASL, it will let the student

FIGURE 10.4 (a) Music/Song, (b) Hello/Hi

FIGURE 10.4 (c) Goodbye, (d) Play, (e) Listen

FIGURE 10.4 (f) Thank you, (g) Work, (h) Finished

know you care if you can learn a few basic signs. Figure 10.4a–h shows 10 words as signs in ASL; students will be very appreciative if you learn to use them.

I will sometimes refer to an app I have on my Smartphone called "Sign4Me." The app allows you to type in words or short phrases and then an animated person that you can look at from the front or the side translates the words into sign.

Most universities have an ASL interpreter they call for interpreting. Schools of music should provide interpreters for all major concerts. The Deaf community has very few accessible musical events, even in large cities. Even if only one or two people with hearing loss attend the concert, it still helps to send the message that the school of music is inclusive and welcoming of people with hearing loss.

Captionists

Captionists instantly transcribe the spoken word into English text using a stenotype machine, laptop computer, or real-time software (National Center on Deafness, 2009). The text is displayed on the student's computer or another device.

Accommodations

- Get the attention of the student with DHH before speaking.
- Speak slowly and clearly.
- Look directly at the person with DHH when speaking. If using an interpreter, avoid talking to the interpreter and instead face the person who is DHH.
- When speaking to a person with DHH, be careful not to talk with your hands in front of your face.
- Men should avoid mustaches that cover the lips.
- Avoid standing with light sources behind you.
- Use email or text messaging instead of phone calls.
- Collaborate with interpreters and the student to make sure music vocabulary is communicated well.
- Look for interpreters who are musicians.
- Use visual aids in addition to speech to offer more than one mode for understanding course content.
- Use note-takers.
- Assistive listening devices are helpful in classrooms, rehearsals, and for DHH audience members at concerts.
- Testing times should be extended to allow for slower reading comprehension.

SUMMARY

There are challenges for students with hearing loss in schools of music and university degree programs in general. It is well documented that DHH students are delayed in reading and math when compared to their hearing peers.

High-quality interpreters are difficult to locate in many areas of the country. A high-quality musically trained interpreter will be important for DHH music students. If the interpreter cannot adequately describe live or recorded music and be able to use music jargon, the college music student will struggle to succeed.

11

PHYSICAL DISABILITIES

Armando is voice performance major and is quadriplegic. He uses a powered wheelchair and attends one of the few universities with a highly competitive music performance program but also a school where he can receive the support he needs to live independently without his parents to take care of him. He chose this university because it offered physical care assistants (PCA), on-campus physical and occupational therapy, and transportation to classes, concerts, rehearsals, and dates with his girlfriend. Armando lives in a dorm designed for students with severe physical disabilities. He has a physical care assistant who happens to be a special education major and a music minor.

ACCORDING TO THE most recent US Census (2010), approximately 6% or 1.1 million of college undergraduate students have a physical disability. Although physical disabilities are a low-incidence disability, the numbers of students with these disabilities who are attending college are increasing as medical and technical advances make it possible for them to write papers, move independently, and of course create music from a seated position. Individuals with physical disabilities are living longer. For example, in 1987 individuals with a spinal cord injury at the age of 20 were expected to live to be 40 to 53 years of age. By 1995, the life span for this same cohort had increased to 55 to 65 years of age (Hedrick et al., 2006).

Students with severe physical disabilities have the most difficulty finding a university that can accommodate their complex needs. For those who are very intelligent or, as in Armando's case, highly gifted in music, there are few opportunities for pursuing music degrees in higher education. The cost of higher education for students with severe physical disabilities is considerably higher than for those with other disabilities because of the need for physical care assistants and sophisticated assistive technology. Most universities cannot afford the cost of modifying buildings and outdoor facilities to accommodate students with severe physical disabilities, including housing with the type of modifications needed for someone with ventilators, hospital beds, and special equipment to transfer a person to the toilet, shower, and other facilities for basic grooming and health needs. Very few universities can provide the level of support necessary for students with severe physical disabilities, which leaves students with the choice of staying at home and commuting to a local university, hiring a personal care assistant, or attending one of the few schools that provide full services, usually with a significant cost to the student. Students who hire their own PCAs will still require help with finding housing that can accommodate their physical and health needs. In most university cities, there are very few options for students who need to rent housing of this type.

In addition, the assistive technology (AT) needs for students with severe physical disabilities are considerable. Scherer and Glueckauf (2005) stressed that the ability to perform a variety of educational, recreational, or work-related activities, either aided by assistive technology or without, is important to a person's full participation in life. There have been remarkable advances in AT devices that substantially improve the lives of people with severe physical disabilities, and these improvements are having a significant impact on the ability of a person with severe disabilities to live more independently (Stumbo, Martin, & Hedrick, 2008). Even so, assistive technology can augment but not replace the need for human help for individuals with severe physical disabilities (Agree et al., 2005; Hoenig et al., 2003; Kaye et al., 2006; Kennedy, LaPlante, & Kaye, 1997; LaPlante et al., 2004).

WHAT ARE PHYSICAL DISABILITIES?

The Individuals with Disabilities Education Improvement Act (IDEIA) defines orthopedic or physical disability as "a severe orthopedic impairment that adversely affects a child's educational performance. The term includes impairments caused by congenital anomaly, impairments caused by disease (e.g., poliomyelitis, bone tuberculosis), and impairments from other causes (e.g., cerebral palsy, amputations, and fractures or burns that cause contractures" (20 U.S.C. 1401[3]); 1401[30]).

A severe disability as defined by Guralnik (2006) is one that causes an individual to require "help with three or more of the six [activities of daily living] (eating, dressing, bathing, transferring, using the toilet, and walking across a room) (p. 162). Orthopedic or physical disabilities can be further classified under three categories: neuromotor impairments, degenerative diseases, and musculoskeletal disorders (Gargiulo, 2012).

Neuromotor Impairments

A neuromotor impairment is an abnormality of, or damage to, the brain, spinal cord, or nerves that send impulses to the muscles throughout the body (Gargiulo, 2012). Complex motor problems are those that impact several body systems, causing problems such as these: incontinence, limited arm or leg movement, intellectual disabilities, seizures, or vision loss. The two most common neuromotor impairments are spina bifida and cerebral palsy.

Spina bifida usually occurs in the lower part of the spinal cord so the student will often have difficulty walking or will need to use a wheelchair. The student will need to catherize himself or herself to empty his or her bladder. Occasionally there are learning problems associated with spina bifida, including deficits in attention, memory, recall, motor reaction times, visual-perceptual skills, and organizational skills (Heller, 2009; Iddon et al., 2006).

Cerebral palsy (CP) refers to several nonprogressive disorders of voluntary movement or posture that are due to malfunction or damage in the brain (Beers et al., 2009; Miller, 2005). Cerebral palsy can be mild or severe. In milder forms, the only noticeable manifestation may be a person's somewhat uncoordinated movement. In more severe forms, the individual may be unable to chew food or speak. Tight muscles in one or more muscle groups characterize spastic CP. With athetoid CP, individuals have movements that are contorted, abnormal, and purposeless. Students with ataxic CP generally have poor balance and uncoordinated voluntary movements, and mixed CP is a combination of types. In addition, CP can impact one limb (momplegia), two limbs (paraplegia), one side of the body (hemiplegia), or all four limbs (quadriplegia) (Miller, 2005).

Degenerative Diseases

Degenerative diseases can affect motor movement. The student with certain degenerative diseases will need increasingly more complex adaptations and assistive technology to participate in academics and ensembles. Duchenne muscular dystrophy is the most common of degenerative diseases. Multiple sclerosis, another degenerative disease, is more common in women than men. It can be mild or severe, and often the person with multiple sclerosis experiences remission. Multiple sclerosis can impact muscle tone and strength and sometimes makes walking impossible.

Orthopedic and Musculoskeletal Disorders

Limb deficiency refers to a number of skeletal abnormalities in which an arm or leg is partially or totally missing. Most students with limb deficiencies wear a prosthetic device that allows for improved function.

Traumatic Brain Injury

Recently, there has been increased awareness of traumatic brain injuries (TBI) that may impact movement, learning, and mental health. Some of these are sports-related injuries, but most are war injuries, brought to the attention of universities as men and women with TBI return from military service and seek admission. TBI is classified as a physical disability if physical impairment is a result of the injury (Targett et al., 2013). TBI can require years of rehabilitation, and individuals may never recover totally from the injury. A TBI can have multiple symptoms and is often an invisible disability if there are not major physical disabilities. Common problems include poor attention, memory problems, decreased writing speed and accuracy, decreased stamina and endurance, and impulsive behavior (Gargiulo, 2012).

PHYSICAL DISABILITIES AND MUSIC

Music assistive technology (MAT) helps students with physical disabilities to better access the music curriculum. There are a variety of commercial products and instruments that would qualify as MAT.

One example of assistive technology that can be adapted for music ensembles is Bluetooth iPad page-turners. Several commercially available devices can control an iPad to change pages of a multipage music piece. The device can be configured to change with a tap of a foot, elbow, finger, chin, or just about any movement that the musician can make. The page-turners are a mid-tech device; most cost less than $150.

iPads and tablet computers offer solutions for many challenges that musicians with physical disabilities experience. The touch-sensitive screens offer tremendous accessibility for those with muscular dystrophy and low muscle control.

Electronic drum sets, individual electronic drums, and percussion pads are popular with mainstream drummers but are also very accessible to drummers with physical disabilities. Mesh drumheads on electronic drums can be adjusted for sensitivity. This is a very helpful feature in electronic instruments. Mesh drumheads can sense very weak touch and can also adjust for individuals who play very hard, such as individuals with somewhat uncontrolled movement. There are electronic keyboard percussion instruments made by Kat that are touch sensitive; these allow percussionists with low muscle control to play mallet instruments with a head stick, fingers, or traditional mallets.

A good instrument repairperson can adapt traditional acoustic instruments for musicians. Saxophone professor David Nabb had a stroke and lost the use of one hand. An instrument repairperson adapted his alto saxophone, so he could play it with one hand. Flute Lab in the Netherlands builds one-handed flutes, saxophones, and ergonomic flute head joints.

Occupational therapists are very good at building stands, supports, and other devices for people with physical disabilities to access their instruments. There are also online networks of people who will custom build stands and adaptive devices for people with physical disabilities. Adaptive Gear, Coalition for Disabled Musicians, Inc. is a website of ideas and success stories people have used to create access to musical instruments (http://www.disabled-musicians.org/adaptive-gear/).

The Association of Children's Prosthetic-Orthotic Clinics has an excellent website with specific strategies for adapting brass, woodwind, and other instruments for upper-limb amputees (http://www.acpoc.org/newsletters-and-journals/1974_10_009.asp). Clark and Chadwick (1980) have published images of dozens of adapted mallets, guitar strummers, and musical instrument stands, with directions for how to use them.

An excellent resource for occupational and physical therapists is *Guide to the Selection of Musical Instruments with Respect to Physical Ability and Disability* (Elliott et al., 1982). This book describes specific instruments and the amount of mobility needed in different body parts to play the instrument in the traditional method. For example, mobility without substitution or adaptation for playing the cello describes the amount of movement the following body parts need to play the cello: head, right and left shoulders, right and left elbows, right and left forearms, right and left wrists, right and left thumbs, right and left fingers and hips (p. 33). The therapist can consult with music professors or other music professionals in regard to whether the student has the necessary movement required to play the cello, or any of the other instruments listed in the guide. Occupational and physical therapists are very helpful for specific guidance on how to adapt instruments and in some cases, musical instruction to include students with physical disabilities.

Accommodations

There are certain strategies that will help to make classrooms, studios, and rehearsal rooms accessible to students with physical disabilities.

- Classrooms, studios, and rehearsal rooms should be accessible to students who use large motorized wheelchairs, walkers, crutches, and other orthopedic devices. Doors should be wide enough for the student to enter. Professors should have accessible offices or an alternative private meeting place that is accessible.
- Seating should be adaptive to accommodate large wheelchairs and desks should be easily adjustable. Figure 11.1 is a photo of classroom furniture in the school of music at Northwestern University. All furniture is on rollers to allow flexible classroom arrangements. Students in wheelchairs are not relegated to one place in the classroom but can sit anywhere.
- Students who need them should have note-takers or recording devices for taking notes.
- Instructors should provide notes or Powerpoint presentations, preferably prior to the class.

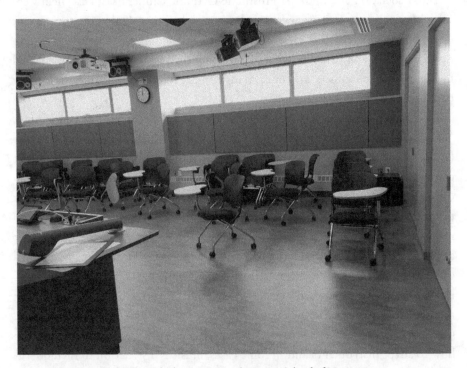

FIGURE 11.1 Universal Designed Classroom, Northwestern School of Music

- Assistive computer software and equipment, including speech-to-text software, word prediction, and keyboard or mouse modification are adaptations that should be considered.
- Give students with disabilities extended time for tests, a separate location, scribes, and access to adapted computers.
- Be flexible with assignment deadlines.
- Have adjustable tables to accommodate wheelchairs at different heights.
- Have an aide to set up computers, iPad page-turners, adapted instruments, etc.
- Plan activities that allow students to participate within their physical capabilities yet still meet course objectives.
- Provide audio versions of texts and audio recordings of music for lessons and rehearsals.

SUMMARY

Music students with physical disabilities may enter music school with a disability or disease. It can be life altering for a musician to suddenly find himself or herself unable to engage with music as before due to an accident. With so many available alternatives, including sophisticated and simple forms of assistive technology and music assistive technology, students may be able to finish their degree programs with the support of the school of music and consultants in occupational and physical therapy.

The cost to a university to educate a student with physical disabilities can be beyond reasonable accommodations because human and technology assistance is extremely expensive. If the student can live at home or has the means to manage these services, music degrees can be attainable.

12

CHRONIC ILLNESS

Tristan is a senior music education student who has Crohn's disease, a chronic inflammatory condition of the gastrointestinal tract. When Tristan was first diagnosed he was hospitalized for 11 days. He is managing his illness fairly well although he often has to travel for two hours to see his group of specialists for treatments. He frequently misses classes to see his doctors. He has a difficult time absorbing nutrients and tends to be very thin.

Tristan is a trumpet player and has high grades in his classes, lessons, and ensembles. He also works at a part-time job. Because he has been so successful in handling his medication and keeping his illness fairly well under control, he has not registered with the disability services office. He has not had any problems with his professors and generally does not disclose his illness unless it becomes a real issue. (T. Burgmann, personal correspondence on Crohn's disease by email, July 6, 2015).

THE CENTERS FOR Disease Control and Prevention (2009) estimate that 17.4% of women and 12.9% of men aged 18–29 have reported having at least one chronic illness. The three most common chronic illnesses for both women and men are asthma, arthritis, and hypertension. Other chronic illnesses include diabetes, cancer, and heart disease. Chronic illness is a low-incidence disability category.

Chronic illness, sometimes referred to as "other health impairment," is "a condition which: lasts for a considerable period of time or has a sequelae (a pathological condition resulting from a prior disease, injury, therapy, or trauma) which persists for a substantial period and/or persists for more than three months in a year or necessitates a period of continuous hospitalizations for more than a month" (Thompson & Gustafson, 1996, p. 4). The chronic illness can go into remission or it may cycle through periods of intensity and periods of relative calmness. Often the chronic illness is an invisible disability because the person may not appear to be sick.

CHALLENGES FOR STUDENTS WITH CHRONIC ILLNESS

A chronic illness can alter a student's life. In addition to missing school for treatments and medical appointments or because the student is not feeling well enough to go to school, the student may be responsible for managing special diets and medications and, in some cases, battling with insurance companies over payment for health care. The lives of most students with chronic illnesses are very different from those of their healthy peers. Students with chronic illness can be at risk of school failure and developing long-term mental health problems if their individual needs are not met by the university (Shiu, 2001). Students can also lose student loans or be required to begin repaying student loans if their enrollment drops to part-time status, yet many with chronic illness and other disabilities cannot manage a full-time schedule. Online courses help students with chronic illnesses to complete coursework from bed or hospital during acute episodes or recovery.

Students with chronic illnesses are attending college at higher numbers than in previous years due to better treatment options. More individuals are surviving serious illnesses that were once considered life threatening including leukemia, organ failure, and HIV (American Cancer Society, 2013; Bleyer, 2007). With improved devices, individuals can take care of many of their own complex health needs including catherization, tube feeding, respiratory treatments, and injections (Lehr, 1990).

The single most difficult issue for students attending college with a chronic illness is inflexible attendance policies. Maslow et al. (2012) found that significantly fewer young adults with childhood-onset chronic illness had graduated from college (20.7%) than their healthy peers (34.1%). Faculty are rightfully concerned with maintaining the integrity of the course while making accommodations for the disabled student's education. Edwards (2014) suggests working with students to "triage" deadlines and assignments so they can stay enrolled without putting their health in danger. The chronic illness is not a free pass for incomplete work; it is an extenuating circumstance that requires negotiation and mutual accountability.

Most four-year colleges and universities have an on-campus health care center, but one in six does not. Schools without health centers often do not provide 24/7 service, including emergency room-level care (Lemly et al., 2014).

Sometimes university staff are unaware of student needs; in a 2014 study of 153 college student health centers, 42% said their center had no system in place for identifying incoming students with chronic illnesses (Lemly et al., 2014). Universities should have a system for knowing all students on campus who have serious illnesses so they can be prepared in a crisis. For example, a student with diabetes who may come to the student health center after collapsing in class would receive essential treatment more quickly if the health center was aware of his or her diabetes.

Support for Students

A number of researchers have identified mentoring as the best way to ensure that students with chronic illnesses successfully complete their degrees (Houman & Stapley, 2013; Maslow et al., 2012; Royster & Marshall, 2008). One study found the college graduation rate for these students to be 13.5% higher among those with a mentor than those without (Maslow et al., 2012).

DePaul University in Chicago has established a comprehensive educational assistance program that focuses specifically on accommodations for students with chronic illness. The program, Chronic Illness Initiative (CII), was founded in 2003 as a research- and experience-based approach to serving chronically ill students on campus. One part of their very successful program is a special advisor advocate who coordinates questions and accommodations, acts as a liaison between faculty and students, and helps to minimize the complex administrative issues that can be overwhelming for a student with a chronic illness. The advisor also works closely with the financial aid office to help students navigate the confusing maze of financial aid options. In the first four years of their program, the enrollment of students with chronic illnesses increased from 50 to 200, and students enrolled in the CII program were more likely to maintain higher grade point averages, continue into their second year of college, and graduate (Royster & Marshall, 2008). The DePaul CII program also has support groups for their students with chronic illnesses.

CHRONIC ILLNESSES

There are many chronic illnesses that students manage while in college. The following are some of the more common illnesses that appear in young adults.

Asthma and Allergies

Asthma is a chronic lung disease that affects 18% of older adolescents (Akinbami et al., 2012). Asthma inflames and narrows the airways and causes recurring periods of wheezing, chest tightness, shortness of breath, and coughing. Asthma is among the most common chronic health conditions in college students. Although asthma is associated with substantial risk for disruption of school, work, and activities of daily life, symptoms can be managed with medication. However, the student needs to take an active role in order to keep asthma attacks under control. Students with their asthma under control can attend class and manage the disease without restrictions as long as they take their medication (National Heart, Lung, and Blood Institute, 2014).

Most colleges and universities offer a wide variety of foods, including vegan, low-calorie, gluten-free foods, lactose-free foods, and peanut-free kitchens for highly allergic students (Body and Mind, 2012).

Cancer

Cancers in young adults (ages 20 to 39) are usually different from cancers that strike children and older adults (American Cancer Society, 2014). Depending on the severity of the cancer and the type of treatment, the student may continue to attend classes while undergoing treatment or surgery. Studies document the incidence of neurocognitive deficits and depressed academic achievement associated with radiation and chemotherapy treatment in college-aged students (Brown & Madan-Swain, 1993; Findeison & Barber, 1997; Reeb & Regan, 1998); these are reflected in difficulties with attention, concentration, sequencing, memory, and visual-motor integration. Bleyer (2007) identified the most common cancers among 20–29-year-olds as lymphoma, melanoma, thyroid cancer, and testis cancer.

Crohn's Disease

Crohn's disease is a chronic inflammatory condition of the gastrointestinal tract. Men and women are equally affected, and it can occur at any age; however, it is more prevalent among adolescents and young adults between the ages of 15 and 35 (Crohn's and Colitis Foundation of America, 2015).

For students with Crohn's disease, the symptoms will likely impact their education and performance as a musician. They often need to use the bathroom urgently, and they frequently experience pain in the gastrointestinal tract. Other common symptoms are a loss of appetite, weight loss, fatigue, and fever.

Cystic Fibrosis

Cystic fibrosis (CF) is a chronic, life-threatening disease. It is a genetic disease that causes a thick buildup of mucus in the lungs; this mucus then traps bacteria that cause lung infections. The child/young adult with CF develops difficulty breathing along with trouble clearing mucus from the lungs. The person with CF coughs to clear the lungs and the CF cough sounds terrible, but is important to keep the lungs as clear as possible. Students will sometimes miss school because of hospitalizations. Videoconferencing software enables students to attend class and not fall too far behind.

Diabetes

Students living with type I diabetes are usually able to manage their disease with support from a good campus health center. Type I or juvenile diabetes is most often diagnosed in children and young adults. Regulation of insulin and secondary symptoms requires good health care that is available either in the student health center or in the local community. First-year college students with type I diabetes have been shown to experience difficulties managing their diabetes because of problems in finding appropriate health care and dealing with changes in insurance providers and routines (Balfe, 2009; Mellinger, 2003; Wilson, 2010). Lemly et al. (2014) reported that of 153 US college student health centers, most expressed confidence in caring for students with asthma or depression, but only half thought they were prepared to manage diabetes.

Epilepsy and Seizure Disorders

Epilepsy includes a spectrum of brain disorders ranging from severe, life-threatening, and disabling to benign or mild seizure disorders. Epilepsy cannot be cured but it can be managed with medication, diet, devices, and occasionally surgery (National Institute of Neurological Disorders and Stroke, 2015).

Students who have seizures may experience embarrassment and find that their independence is restricted; they may not be able to drive a car or engage in certain recreational activities, and they may be uncomfortable in social settings. Many students state that the effects of epilepsy and the medication to control it impact their alertness, information processing, attention and memory, and distractibility (Charlton, 1997).

Professors, friends, and advisors should know about the student's seizure disorder and what to do should a seizure occur. Students with epilepsy may experience difficulty with memory. Due dates and other critical dates should be recorded in a date book to help students remember upcoming concerts, assignments, and other important dates (DegreeJungle, 2013).

Fibromyalgia

Fibromyalgia is a disorder characterized by widespread musculoskeletal pain and is frequently accompanied by difficulty sleeping, fatigue, memory, and mood problems (Mayo Foundation for Medical Education and Research, 2015). The disorder occurs more often in women than men, and many people with fibromyalgia report tension headaches, temporomandibular joint (TMJ) disorders, irritable bowel syndrome, anxiety, and depression.

Current research suggests that fibromyalgia is a neurological condition that impacts the way the body processes pain (National Institute of Arthritis and Musculoskeletal and Skin Diseases, 2014). There is no cure for fibromyalgia, but medication can help to control pain and improve sleep.

Music students with fibromyalgia will struggle with fatigue, cognitive and memory problems at times. Students do best when they do not schedule too many courses or activities and try to take courses at their most productive time of the day, usually in the late morning and afternoon (Stewart, 2011).

Human Immunodeficiency Virus

Human immunodeficiency virus (HIV) can lead to acquired immunodeficiency syndrome or AIDS. Once it is infected, the human body cannot get rid of HIV, unlike other viruses. New HIV infections are most common in teenagers and young adults, ages 13–24 (Centers for Disease Control and Prevention. (2015). Many college students are a generation removed from the HIV/AIDS pandemic; consequently, they are less aware than that cohort of the dangers of contracting HIV and are at most risk for infection (Way, 2014).

Hypertension

High blood pressure in college-aged students primarily occurs in students who are overweight, African American, drinkers, or smokers, and those with certain chronic illnesses that increase blood pressure such as kidney disease, diabetes, and sleep apnea (Mayo Clinic Staff, 2015). Often individuals with hypertension are not aware of their condition. Medication and lifestyle changes are the most effective way to treat hypertension. Hypertension is a growing chronic illness among college students, particularly male students (Centers for Disease Control, 2009).

Lupus

Lupus is an autoimmune disease that most often strikes young adult females. Infections, toxins, and environmental factors trigger acute lupus. Sunlight seems to bring on painful episodes in 70% of people living with lupus (Benlysta, n.d.).

Migraine Headaches

Migraine headaches can be a disabling chronic medical condition for many students. Women are three times more likely to have migraine headaches than men and they are frequently diagnosed during puberty and early adulthood (O'Brien et al. 1994; Mayo Clinic Staff, 2013). Female students, in particular, may experience migraine headaches for the first time in college and they may have difficulty in finding a doctor who can help with medication and with identifing triggers for the headaches. During this time, the student will not be identified with the disability services office and of course will have no accommodations. There must be a diagnosis before accommodations and supports can be arranged.

Triggers for migraine headaches are varied and affect some individuals but not others. Professors should be especially aware of sensory stimuli that can bring on attacks in some students. Bright lights are migraine triggers in many people. What comes to mind first are stage lights, and many students report that projectors used for displaying presentations can initiate migraine headaches. Loud sounds sometimes create headaches, certainly a problem for students participating in some ensembles. Unusual smells such as fragrances, paint thinner, and secondhand smoke can also trigger migraines.

Multiple Sclerosis

Multiple sclerosis (MS) is an immune-mediated process in which an abnormal response to the body's immune system is directed against the central nervous system. Most people with this disease are diagnosed between the ages of 20 to 50 (National Multiple Sclerosis Society, n.d.). Multiple sclerosis is difficult to diagnose and symptoms may be misunderstood before there is a final diagnosis. Students will experience numbness in their feet and struggle with exhaustion. Before the diagnosis is made a music student may notice the first signs appearing with fumbles while practicing their instrument. The body does not respond the way the brain expects and at first the student may discount the symptoms. During the long process of diagnosis, it may be puzzling to studio professors and their student as to why the student suddenly seems to be struggling so much with certain fine motor control movements. The disease progresses at varied rates in different people, but students may find that they need to use crutches or a wheelchair for mobility.

Rheumatoid Arthritis

Rheumatoid arthritis (RA) is an autoimmune disease with symptoms caused in part by inflammation (Rheumatoid Arthritis, 2014). RA symptoms can include joint pain, swelling, stiffness, fatigue, and muscle pain. It is more common in women and is often diagnosed in young adults. In severe RA, people develop damage to their joints and in some individuals, joint replacement is necessary to maintain function. Medication and rest help to manage pain and damage to joints.

Music students with RA may need additional time to travel to classes, write, type, or complete any activity that involves physical strength or movement. Some students may use wheelchairs and need access to classrooms, studios, and buildings for their wheelchair. Most students with RA will have difficulty managing stairs and carrying heavy objects. Assistive devices that support instruments help the student with RA to manage holding and playing instruments. Fine motor control in the hands and fingers will be difficult during inflammatory episodes. Students may miss class during a painful inflammatory crisis, but with careful medical management from the students' rheumatologist, most students will be successful in completing their music degrees.

Sickle Cell Disease

Sickle cell disease (SCD) is a genetic, chronic disease with no cure and very serious side effects. Pain can be extreme when the person is in crisis. Although often thought of as a disease that only strikes African Americans, it can be present in persons with African ancestors and persons from Middle Eastern countries.

Students with SCD are frequently hospitalized for infections and blood transfusions. Common illnesses like the flu can quickly develop into life-threatening problems because of the inability of the blood to carry oxygen and nutrients throughout the body. Avoiding infections is critical, and using campus bathrooms, gyms, and even school-owned instruments that are played by others can easily infect a student with SCD.

Common Accommodations for Students with Chronic Illness

Accommodations (adapted from Chronic Action, 2013) will vary for individual students according to their specific illness and whether they are experiencing an acute phase of the illness.

- Extra time on tests.
- Stop-the-clock testing. If the student is not feeling well during the test, he or she can complete the test at a later time.

- Reduced course load and extra time granted to complete a degree program.
- Extra time to turn in assignments when ill.
- Ability to record classes.
- Permission to leave and rejoin the class to take care of medical needs.
- Permission to carry and take medications, water, or snacks as needed.
- Request to attend class via videoconferencing.
- Request to leave some lights on when overhead projectors are in use to reduce bright lights.

SUMMARY

The numbers of college students with chronic illness are increasing as better medical treatment makes it possible for them to function in a university environment. Students with chronic illness usually are not easily identified unless you know there is an underlying illness. It is easy to question whether a student is actually sick when he or she appears healthy. Many students with chronic illness experience cycles of acute health crisis and relative stability with their symptoms. Some chronic illnesses first appear in individuals when they are young adults. When this happens to a college student, he or she may have the first acute crisis of the illness on campus, away from family and other support systems. Such a student would not be registered with the disability services office. This creates difficulty for students who must to attend to their health needs without official support from the university.

13

ATTENTION DEFICIT/HYPERACTIVITY DISORDER

Jose is in your music history class. You notice that he seems very restless; he constantly bounces his legs and shifts around in his chair. He often sits in the back corner of the class, and although you have a policy of no cell phones in class, he brings his laptop and you wonder if he is actually taking notes; he smiles at the screen and types during times that recordings are being played in class.

On the mid-term exam, he was unable to finish the exam and failed the test. You ask him to meet with you and question him about the test. He says he couldn't focus on the test because he kept hearing the woodwind quintet down the hall rehearsing during the test. You ask him more questions trying to understand if he is paying attention in class. Eventually he explains that he has a difficult time siting and listening for very long, and it helps him to play games on his computer just to get through the class. Further discussion reveals he has ADHD and was taking prescription medication, but he has been going without it because he doesn't like the way it makes him feel. He says he is not registered at the disability services office; he doesn't like the disability classification. He said in his high school that students with disabilities were students with intellectual disabilities, and he never liked that classification for himself.

You explain that he could be getting accommodations for taking a test in a quiet place if he registered with the disability services office. He nods and seems uncomfortable, and you aren't sure whether he will follow through. You tell him that unless he registers you have to assume he can manage without accommodations. He nods his head again.

Jose begins missing class, fails the final exam, and has many unfinished assignments. He ultimately fails the class. You find out he has poor grades in most of his classes except his ensembles and studio lessons. At the end of the semester, he is put on probation by the school of music and will likely lose his music scholarship.

ATTENTION DEFICIT/HYPERACTIVITY DISORDER (ADHD) is a high-incidence disability. ADHD is characterized by developmentally inappropriate levels of inattention and distractibility and/or hyperactivity and impulsivity that cause problems in the ability to function at home, at school, and in social situations (Glanzman & Sell, 2013).

Individuals with ADHD are usually classified in one of three groups that apply to types of inattention: predominantly inattentive, predominantly hyperactive and impulsive, or combined inattentive/hyperactive (Turnbull et al., 2010). According to Wilens (2004), 50% of children retain their ADD symptoms into adulthood.

ADHD is considered a disorder rather than a disability. A disorder disrupts the daily functioning of an individual, interfering with a person's ability to carry out simple and more challenging tasks (Oslund, 2014). Disorders can improve and occasionally be overcome. In the case of ADHD, with medication and sometimes other therapies, the person may be without signs of inattention, hyperactivity, or impulsivity.

ADHD is prevalent in all cultures and occurs in about 2.5% of adults (American Psychiatric Association, 2013). Reports indicate an increase in college students with ADHD in recent years (Gaddy, 2008; Quinn, Ratey, & Maitland, 2000; Wedlake, 2002). Harbour (2004) conducted a national survey and found that students with ADHD are the second largest group of postsecondary students registered and served by university disability services offices. Students with learning disabilities are the greatest group. However, many students with learning disabilities also have ADHD. Wolf (2001) estimated that 25% of college students receive disability services for ADHD; 30% of high-school students with ADHD enroll in two-year college programs, and 6% attend four-year institutions (Wagner et al., 2005). Adults with ADHD obtained less formal education and/or had lower grades in high school than their typical peers (Barkley et al., 2002; Mannuzza et al., 1993). Of concern are the low numbers of actual graduates; only 28% of students with ADHD, about half the number that enter college, actually complete their degrees (Barkley, 2014; Faraone, Beiderman, & Lehman, 1993; Gaub & Carlson, 1997; Gregg, 2009).

POSTSECONDARY STUDENTS AND ADHD

University students with ADHD are at higher risk for difficulty with academics and underachievement than their typical peers (Heilingenstein et al., 1999). The challenge with college students with ADHD is that so many stop taking medication. Once they are away from their parents and high school special educators who make sure the child takes medication on time each day, many decide they want to be in control of their own lives. Oslund (2014) describes this common trend in college students:

> What people who do not take medication for an invisible disability do not realize is that those who are invisibly disabled have internalized the social myth that they look so much like others that they should be capable of acting like others, including functioning without daily medication. In effect, my "real" self is the one who *doesn't* take medicine because that is the way all the "normal people" get through life—without medication that impacts their reaction to their environment. (p. 61)

Comorbid disorders are common in those with ADHD. Kadesjo and Gillberg (2001) found that 87% of individuals in their study had at least one comorbid disorder, and 67% were living with two disorders. The most common academic disorder was in reading and writing (40%); 47% experienced developmental coordination disorder. In addition, 14% were diagnosed with autism spectrum disorder (Kadesjo & Gillberg, 2001). Autism and ADHD are frequently found together (Oslund, 2014). As many as 60% of children diagnosed during elementary school also present with oppositional defiant disorder (Oslund, 2014). Oppositional defiant disorder is a recurrent pattern of developmentally inappropriate levels of negativistic, defiant, disobedient, and hostile behavior toward authority figures (Hamilton & Armando, 2008). Biederman (2005) found a 55% rate of comorbidity in adults with ADHD and anxiety disorders. Learning disabilities and mood disorders are also common in adults with ADHD. Adults with ADHD, especially males, have a 35% addiction rate to alcohol and drugs (Biederman, 2005).

Addiction frequently occurs during the college years, particularly among students who choose to stop taking their medication and turn to alcohol and drugs to self-medicate. When students with ADHD try to function without medication, they often experience an increase in anxiety and impulsivity; by using alcohol and some types of drugs, they are able to deaden these feelings. It is also more socially acceptable in college to use alcohol and drugs.

Professors may notice students with ADHD often lose or forget daily items like keys, phones, or even music and instruments. A recent graduate of mine was unable to take her ADHD medication because it triggered migraine headaches. She was constantly forgetting her oboe, purse, and other items, and her roommate learned to check with her before she left for school to make sure she had everything she needed during the day. She was fortunate to have someone who could help her compensate for her inattention challenges.

It is not unusual for students with ADHD to run across professors and others who, when hearing that the student has ADHD, tells the student that they do not believe ADHD is a real disorder. Faculty can be unwilling to accept alternative assignments from students or provide special assistance to students with disabilities (Vance & Weyandt, 2008). In one study, faculty members younger than 40 years old were less tolerant and would not consider common accommodations for students with invisible disabilities, including ADHD and learning disabilities (Buchanan, St. Charles, Rigler, & Hart, 2010).

True ADHD is a real disorder; individuals with ADHD show diminished symptoms when taking medication. Those without ADHD are no different when taking medication. For example, a student with anxiety disorder may display restlessness and difficulty focusing, but if the student does not have ADHD, ADHD medication will not reduce the symptoms of anxiety. ADHD is classified as a neurophysical disorder with a strong genetic basis (Voeller, 2004).

Common forms of medication are stimulants, which actually have a calming effect on individuals with ADHD. Medication has been shown to improve students' quality of note-taking; scores on quizzes, tests, and worksheets; the amount of written-language output; and homework completion (Evans et al., 2001; Loe & Feldman, 2007). Stimulants, however, are not associated with normalization of skills in the domain of learning and applying knowledge (Rapport et al., 1994). Stimulant medication also does not appear to improve reading abilities (Forness et al., 1991; Forness et al, 1992).

A common problem among college students with ADHD is that typical peers without ADHD will ask to take the ADHD person's medicine believing it will help them to stay awake all night to study and help them to remember material before an important test. Upadhyaya et al. (2005) found that 29% of students treated with stimulants for ADHD gave or sold their medication to peers. The more responsible students with ADHD will not let other students know they take medication in order to keep enough of their medication for their own needs. However, because many with ADHD want to be liked by their peers, they will give their medicine to others.

Abuse of ADHD medication is common in college. Some students will go off their medication and actually sell it to other students as a way to make money. What they often do not realize is that selling any prescription drugs is illegal. Students can be arrested and charged with drug trafficking and end up with a criminal record. Selling medication without thinking of the long-term consequences of being arrested is an example of impulsivity. If the student were taking his or her medication, he or she probably would not be so impulsive, but because he or she stopped the medication in order to sell it and make money, he or she ends up behaving more impulsively.

SUPPORTING THE POSTSECONDARY MUSIC STUDENT WITH ADHD

Typical challenges for the college student with ADHD include these:

- Difficulty in attending to more than one issue at a time (Reaser et al., 2007).
- Struggling with courses that impact cognitive processes such as music theory and/or history that include detailed-oriented work, reading, and comprehension of readings.
- Having a preference for easy work.
- Not being able to get enjoyment from learning.
- Difficulty in persisting under pressure.
- Learning to rely on internal rather than external standards to judge their performance (Wallace, Winsler, & NeSmith, 1999).
- Having positive rather than negative attitudes
- Controlling internal restlessness (Tominey, 1996; Weyandt et al., 2003).
- Difficulty in selecting main ideas on tests and test strategies (Reaser et al., 2007).
- Lacking organizational skills.
- Forgetting to bring necessary items to classes and rehearsals.
- Sometimes submitting assignments in the wrong format.
- Having messy or illegible handwriting.

ACCOMMODATIONS

Studio professors can help by doing the following:

- Prepare outlines for lessons to keep students motivated and on track.
- Use templates for assignments required in a particular format.
- Make tasks salient, novel, or interesting (Carlson et al. [2002] found that students showed improved behavior or musical performance when this was done).

- Allow students to redo assignments that can be resubmitted for a higher grade.
- Post materials on a course web page, Blackboard, or similar course tool a day in advance of the class to help students with learning differences to inform the professor of their needs (Connor, 2012).
- Remember that students with ADHD are prone to confrontational and aggressive behavior under stressful situations (Weyandt & DePaul, 2008).
- Create more frequent low-stakes assessments rather than two or three that determine a course grade.
- Consider giving the class a break to stand up and stretch if you notice students fidgeting or having trouble focusing in class after a long period.

COACHING

Many students with ADHD benefit from ADHD coaching, a method of supporting students through focusing on their strengths and unique learning styles based in positive psychology (Costello & Stone, 2012; Gable & Haidt, 2005). ADHD coaches emphasize supporting students to develop their own systems and strategies in order to effectively engage in their academic programs and maximize academic performance (Parker & Boutelle, 2009). Coaches view students as creative and resourceful while helping them learn to take action and achieve the goals that are most important to them (Whitworth et al., 2007). Coaching is based on the premise that students are most challenged by their lack of skills in self-regulation and time management necessary to engage in and complete the study process (Swartz, Prevatt, & Proctor, 2005). In addition, coaching is designed to enhance students' self-concept, abilities, and personal interactions (Griffiths & Campbell, 2009). When used according to professional standards, whether life coaching, executive skills coaching, or academic skills coaching, this type of assistance serves as an example of how college support services staff, advisors, and sensitive professors can apply the tenets of positive psychology (Costello & Stone, 2012).

Rather than using a prescriptive framework, which is more common in therapeutic counseling, the executive function coach guides the student's thinking through asking about the student's preferences, beliefs, and ideas for solutions to particular challenges. Executive functions are defined as cognitive skills such as working memory, verbal learning, complex problem solving, sustained attention, and response inhibition needed to engage in self-regulated behavior (Katz, 1998). The coaching model is effective in supporting self-determination skills and produces long-lasting results for students (Costello & Stone, 2012). In a study by Parker and Boutelle

(2009) of 241 students enrolled in regular coaching sessions, ADHD students commented on their ability to eventually self-coach, which decreased their anxiety, allowed them to more effectively problem-solve for themselves and, in time, to activate a positive feedback loop. Effective interventions include strategies for better concentration, time management, and test strategies that include keeping a weekly planner, entering all reminders, planning and writing down all daily and weekly study goals, sitting in the front of the classroom, utilizing note-taking as a way to increase concentration, and developing specific strategies for essay versus multiple-choice tests (Reaser et al., 2007). Interventions should aid students with ADHD by helping them to internalize their motivation for academic and musical behaviors. This works best by first establishing their external goals and beginning with tasks that are their least favorite. A student might plan to practice a least favorite piece for choir for 15 minutes and then allow himself or herself to play a video game for a half hour (with an alarm at the end of the half hour).

Then students move to more intermediate goals. For example, "If I learn this difficult concerto I can audition for the concerto competition." Students then transition to internal motivations: "I will choose to write my jazz history paper on the group, The Bad Plus, because the group is my favorite." Having a choice when completing a difficult task helps students with ADHD to internalize motivation for doing something they dislike and to reduce procrastination.

ONLINE COURSES

Parker and Banerjee (2007) discovered that students with ADHD have difficulty with online courses. Some types of technology, software, and apps can provide support systems for students who need reminders, writing tools, and electronic locators for lost phones, tablets, or laptops. However, online courses present an opportunity for distraction that can interfere with learning.

SUMMARY

Students with ADHD are second only to students with specified learning disabilities as representing the most frequently occurring disability on campus. They often stop taking their medication for a variety of reasons, do not disclose their disability to disability services or professors, and end up with academic and social problems. They are at high risk for dropping out of school before completion of their degree. Three predominating behaviors mark students with true ADHD—inattentiveness, hyperactivity, and impulsivity.

14

TOURETTE SYNDROME, WILLIAMS SYNDROME,
AND OTHER SYNDROMES

Sam is a jazz piano performance major. He has Tourette syndrome and has constant physical tics and occasional verbal tics. They increase when he is asked to speak in class or sometimes when he is in social situations. On particularly bad days, he is exhausted by afternoon and has difficulty concentrating.

A secondary diagnosis associated with his Tourette syndrome is obsessive-compulsive disorder (OCD). For Sam, OCD permeates his life and makes it difficult to leave his dorm room because he worries that he forgot to lock the door. He also frets about germs and struggles with sharing pianos with other people. He has to sanitize the piano keys on any piano he plays and can be easily distracted by discoloration or marks on the piano keys.

When Sam plays the piano, there is a noticeable change in him. He relaxes and the tics disappear, and he smiles and moves with the music in obvious pleasure. Playing the piano is the only time during his day when he is free from Tourette syndrome. Some call it "being in the zone" or "lost in music," but Sam describes it as "opening the door of his jail cell." He is free.

WHAT ARE SYNDROMES?

A syndrome is a group of symptoms that occur together and characterize a particular disorder. Syndromes may have a genetic basis, can be environmental, or may be a combination of both (Simpson, 2013). There are more than 100 syndromes documented (Simpson, 2013); many impact intellectual ability or overall health, and some even seem to boost musicality in an individual. Like other disorders and disabilities, syndromes can have a range of severity and affect people differently.

Tourette Syndrome

Tourette syndrome (TS) is a neurological disorder that may originate in a specific gene, although studies have yet to be conclusive (State, 2011). TS symptoms include chronic vocal or motor tics. Obsessive-compulsive disorder (OCD) and attention deficit/hyperactivity disorder (ADHD) are often secondary features in individuals with Tourette. Males seem to be affected more frequently than females. Treatment is most successful through medication and habit reversal therapy (Robertson, 2015; Simpson, 2013).

Individuals with TS, OCD, and ADHD are at risk for poorer quality of life (Eddy et al., 2011; Storch et al., 2007). Studies show that young people with tics are rated less favorably and are less socially acceptable than those without tics. Students with ADHD and/or OCD are rated low on social acceptability scales by their typical peers (Bawden et al., 1998; Boudjouk et al., 2000; Friedrich, Morgan, & Devine, 1996; Stokes et al., 1991). Social acceptability increases when individuals are able to explain their symptoms to their typical peers (Nussey, Pistrang, & Murphy, 2014).

Tourette and Music

Musicians with Tourette experience relief from tics when they are involved in a musical activity, specifically playing a musical instrument or listening to music (Lees et al., 1984; Roessner, Banascheswki, & Rothenberger, 2004; Robertson & Cavanna, 2008; Sacks, 1995, 1998, 2006, 2007). Other activities that contribute to decreased tics include relaxation (Berardelli et.al, 2003; Eapen et al., 2004; Lees et al., 1984; Robertson et al., 2002), distraction (Berardelli et.al, 2003), habitual or automatic actions (O'Connor, Gareau, & Blowers, 1994), and attention and concentration (Berardelli et al., 2003; Caurin et al., 2014; Lees et al., 1984; Robertson et al., 2002).

In two studies by Bodeck, Lappe, and Evers (2015), musicians with TS were observed for decreased tics during performance and musical listening. Both activities demonstrated a decreasing effect on tics according to the musician's feedback. The researchers found significant tic-reducing effects related to musical, personal, and environmental factors.

Williams Syndrome

Williams syndrome (WS) is a developmental disorder that most often impacts intellectual disabilities. IQs are typically in the mild to moderate range for most people diagnosed with WS (Howlin, Davies, & Udwin, 1998; Udwin, Yule, & Martin, 1987). Individuals with WS are also described as having abnormal sensitivity to loud sounds, aversion to innocuous sounds, and attraction to other sounds (Klein et al., 1990; Levitan et al., 2005; Nigam & Samuel, 1994). Sensitivity and attraction to sound are related to a fascinating interest in music and strong musicality among those with WS.

Other Syndromes

Turner syndrome occurs in females only and identifying features are short stature, frequent hearing loss due to small ear canals, and sometimes vision loss. Intelligence is not affected and in one recent study, women with Turner syndrome achieved education and employment levels higher than the typical female population in the United States (Gould et al., 2013). Women with Turner syndrome should have no particular problems with participation in music degree programs other than physical challenges due to their height and possible hearing loss.

Fetal alcohol syndrome (FAS) is a neurological disorder that includes mild to severe disturbances of physical, behavioral, emotional, and/or social functioning (Streissguth & O'Malley, 2000). In addition, individuals have diminished pain and temperature sensation, occasional swallowing disorder, and decreased reflexes (Simpson, 2013). Some individuals will have below average IQs due to permanent brain damage that may impact cognitive abilities (Steinhausen, Willms, & Spohr, 1993). Many people with FAS have difficulty adapting to change, and problems with distractibility, memory, and executive function (Kerns, Don, Mateer, & Streissguth, 1997). Some individuals with FAS do not receive a diagnosis until they become adults (Chudley, Kilgour, Cranston, & Edwards, 2007).

Students with FAS are capable of becoming excellent musicians. A major challenge for them is completion of the degree because of their deficits in attention, memory, verbal learning, and executive function (Kerns, Don, Mateer, & Streissguth, 1997). Many students with FAS gravitate toward substance abuse, have mental health problems, and are at risk for dropping out of school. Sensitive professors will recognize these challenges and help to support the student toward developing skills in self-determination and self-advocacy. The temptation to express their frustration in negative ways will always be an area of difficulty for students with FAS; success in music can help to alleviate these challenges. Duquette and Orders (2013) caution that without dedicated support from a caregiver who lives with the student and solid academic and social integration support, most students will probably not complete their degree programs.

SUMMARY

There are more than 100 identified syndromes, and most are related to a genetic deficit. Because the cause of most identified syndromes is genetic, there is no cure; however, in some types of syndromes, medication can alleviate the symptoms, including secondary symptoms that often occur in particular syndromes. Students with Tourette and Williams syndrome can be highly musical and have improvement in their symptoms when they are engaged in music.

15

INTELLECTUAL DISABILITY

Anna is a young musician with Down syndrome. She would like to become a pre-school music teacher and is attending her local community college. She works part-time at the on-campus day care center and accompanies herself on ukulele when she teaches the children songs.

As long as her parents can remember, Anna has been passionate about music and dance. Anna takes piano and dance lessons. She does read music notation at a very basic level but excels more at learning by ear and through watching her piano teacher.

STUDENTS LIKE ANNA would never have been considered for college before the reauthorization of the 2008 Higher Education Opportunity Act (HEOA). The law includes a number of new provisions that increase opportunities for students with intellectual disabilities (ID) to attend postsecondary education (Grigal & Hart, 2010). Before 2008, students with ID were not eligible for financial aid because most did not receive high school diplomas, pass General Educational Development equivalency tests, or pass "ability to benefit" tests (Lee, 2009). HEOA allows students with ID to be eligible for Pell Grants, Supplemental Educational Opportunity Grants, and Federal Work-Study Programs (Grigal & Hart, 2010; Martinez & Queener, 2010).

Previously, the major barrier for most students with ID in regard to acceptance in college programs was the lack of a high school diploma, yet, today students with ID are attending college and some are completing a certificate or degree (Grigal & Hart, 2010). Often universities are concerned about the cost involved with providing accommodations for students with disabilities. Students with ID require very few accommodations and the cost to the university is negligible. The most common accommodation for students with ID is personal assistants or education coaches. The costs of assistants and coaches are usually not the responsibility of the university. (Grigal & Hart, 2010)

A college education is an important factor for increased employability and future earnings, greater job satisfaction, and healthier lifestyles (Baum, Ma, & Payea, 2010; Carnevale & Derochers, 2003; Marcotte et al., 2005). Education and employment for persons with ID are typically the lowest among all categories of people with disabilities (Newman et al., 2011). Postsecondary education greatly improves the opportunities for individuals with disabilities to find secure employment and become financially independent (Flannery et al., 2008; Grigal, Hart, & Migliore, 2011). It is difficult to estimate the numbers of community colleges and four-year universities with programs for ID students; however, Think College (2016) identified 242 schools that were offering opportunities for students with ID to attend college.

WHAT ARE INTELLECTUAL DISABILITIES?

Intellectual disability means significantly sub-average general intellectual functioning, existing concurrently with deficits in adaptive behavior and manifested during the developmental period, that adversely affects a child's educational performance (Council for Exceptional Children, 2015). Intellectual disabilities are generally classified by levels according to measured intelligence.

"Intellectual disability" is generally preferred over the term "mental retardation," because the latter in many cultures is a derogatory term. In many federal documents the word continues to be used; however, most educators prefer to use intellectual disability.

This chapter describes successful college programs and how these models can be adapted in schools of music and community college music departments. In addition, thriving music programs that exist in colleges, universities, and communities will be described as a model for building music offerings even if your school is not among the initial Transition and Postsecondary Programs for Students with Intellectual Disabilities (TPSID) grant institutions.

CATEGORIES OF MODEL FRAMEWORKS

Grigal and Hart (2010) identified three broad designs for service delivery to students with intellectual disabilities: the mixed/hybrid model, the substantially separate model, and the inclusive individual support model.

MIXED/HYBRID MODEL

In the mixed/hybrid model, students with ID participate in academic classes (audit, credit, or no credit) and social activities with their peers without disabilities. Support for students with ID may range from one-on-one support within typical college courses to special courses designed for students with ID to prepare them for life skills needed to participate socially and professionally in life as an adult. In some schools, employment internships (sometimes including paid internships) are incorporated as a way to provide customized job experience based on the students' personal career goals. In Anna's case, a mixed/hybrid college experience to reach her goal of teaching music in a pre-school might include music courses in elementary general music, class piano, music appreciation, and music technology. In addition to her music courses, Anna might also take a child growth and development course, early-childhood education courses, and dance and drama education. By working as an intern at the campus daycare center with guidance from university or daycare professionals she is provided on-the-job training that helps her apply what she learns in her courses. Further examples of mixed/hybrid models with greater detail including descriptions of activities students experience, funding structures, and other aspects of the model can be found in Grigal and Hart (2010), Casale-Giannola and Wilson Kamens (2006), Grigal, Dwyre, and Davis (2006), Grigal, Neubert, and Moon (2001), Hall, Kleinert, and Kearns (2000), and Hamill (2003).

SUBSTANTIALLY SEPARATE MODEL

As the title implies, students participating in the substantially separate model attend segregated classes with other students with disabilities and do not traditionally attend typical college classes. In some cases, the classes may already be in the curriculum as continuing education courses offered to the general community but with sections created for students with disabilities. Other classes might be specifically created for students with disabilities. Some community organizations that cater to local individuals with disabilities may collaborate with higher education institutions to offer courses in available classrooms at the college or university.

One particularly successful version of the substantially separate model is housed at George Washington University and consists of a four-year degree program created for students with disabilities that is taught by graduate special education students (Martinez & Queener, 2010). The George Washington University program is a vision-ary model that offers customized courses based on courses already offered to typical students with built-in supports. It also provides a unique opportunity for special edu-cation graduate students to teach and learn to adapt for adult students with disabili-ties. The benefits to special educators interacting with ID students is that it helps them understand how to better prepare ID high school students for transition to college.

Anna may not benefit as well in this model because it is unlikely that special education students would be prepared to teach music education courses; however, graduate music education students could certainly co-teach with special education students and offer an excellent experience for students such as Anna.

INCLUSIVE INDIVIDUAL SUPPORT MODEL

The inclusive individual support model focuses on providing students with indi-vidualized services such as educational coaching, tutoring, technology, and other natural supports in order to facilitate access and participation in college courses, certificate programs, and/or degree programs (Grigal & Hart, 2010). This model is based on individual career goals of the student, and those goals influence the types of courses and supports that the student requires to be successful. Students in the inclusive individual support model participate in all courses and social activities just like typical students. Although this type of model is ideal in many ways, it is also hard to administer due to the student's schedule and freedom to participate in any course or social event. Finding one-on-one supports that are available and flexible according to the student's needs and interests presents a challenge. The individual supports are determined by analysis of student interests, needs, and career goals. Educators, adult service personnel, and education/transition coaches are typically some of the professionals involved in delivery of the model (Hart, Zafft, & Zimbrich, 2001; Rammler & Wood, 1999).

Anna might have a family member who would be able to attend school with her and could serve as the education coach for Anna as needed. If Anna chose to attend a school in another location within or outside her state, her parents might investigate hiring either local students to attend classes and events with her, or adult service professionals who would meet her needs. The university would likely not be able to pay for these services, although there are some programs such as REACH—Realizing Educational and Career Hopes program at the University of Iowa—that specialize in college education (a two-year certificate of completion) for students with ID or autism. The University of Iowa model emphasizes four areas: (1) Inclusive Student Life, (2) Person-Centered Planning and Academic Enrichment, (3) Career Development and Inclusive Internships, and (4) Post-Program Support (Hendrickson et al., 2013). Anna would certainly be able to meet her career goal in the REACH program.

DUAL ENROLLMENT

Initially developed for high-achieving high school students, dual enrollment programs enable high school students to begin working on their college degrees while they are still in high school. Typically high school students travel to a local university to take one or two courses during each week. With online coursework now offered by many universities, students can also achieve dual enrollment without leaving their high school campus. In some cases dual enrollment is increasingly available to high school students with ID who have IEP goals for a college education. Many ID students are enrolled in high school through age 21 while completing their high school education and transition services (Hart et al., 2005).

The benefits of dual enrollment for students with ID include the ability to participate in age-appropriate transition-related activities such as these:

- Academic courses.
- Job shadowing.
- Internships.
- Learning self-determination skills.
- Learning how to use public transportation.
- Experiencing competitive employment.
- Engaging in social activities or events that occur on the college campus
- Other skills needed for adult living (Grigal & Hart, 2010).

There are numerous benefits of dual enrollment programs on college campuses for all students including students with ID:

- Enrich the course opportunities for districts struggling to fund programs.
- Advance course rigor of the high school curriculum.

- Help low-achieving students obtain academic standards.
- Increase students' aspirations.
- Acclimate the student to college life.
- Incorporate grades earned through dual enrollment as part of the students' permanent high school and college transcripts (Karp et al., 2007).

Here are some specific benefits to students with ID whose dual enrollment programs are connected to research-based transition programs:

- Students learn skills needed as an adult.
- Skills are tried out in the environments where they will be used.
- Students without disabilities provide an opportunity for natural supports and same-age peer role models.
- School districts meet the requirements of IDEA 2004 by educating students in the least restrictive environment.
- Students with ID have the same choices as their siblings and peers (Grigal & Hart, 2010).

Colleges and universities can prepare for inclusion of ID students by the following:

- Maintain high expectations for the future of the student with ID.
- Inform and instruct staff, professors, and other employees about universal design methods of instruction and access.
- Assure the campus grounds, technological resources, classrooms, and curriculum comply with the Americans with Disabilities Act.
- Investigate options for alternative or nontraditional methods of admissions (e.g., open admissions) and course load.
- Consider collaboration with researchers involved in investigations in postsecondary education for students with ID and consider applying for privately and/or publicly funded research and demonstration projects.
- Ensure that faculty and staff are aware of resources already embedded on campus through the disability support services offices.
- Seek to engage peers without disabilities to serve not only as class coaches, mentors, or supporters but also as friends (e.g., service clubs, students in professional preservice programs).
- Consider collaboration with public schools and/or support agencies as a means of service to the community, especially as a way to alleviate issues of limited space options on campus.

- Incorporate students with ID in work-study programs or other paid work experiences (Martinez & Queener, 2010).

SUMMARY

Students with intellectual disabilities are often the last group universities expect to show up in classes and ensembles, yet many postsecondary institutions are now launching programs for these students. It is important that the university maintain rigor but at the same time find opportunities for students to learn and make music alongside their typical peers.

16

TWICE-EXCEPTIONAL STUDENTS

April has a full scholarship as a trombone performance major. Her music school feels very fortunate that she decided to choose them knowing that she auditioned at 12 different schools and most also offered her a full scholarship. She is participates in several ensembles and is also in the honors program. Her schedule is very full, but her studio professor believes she is managing very well.

At the end of her first semester, she receives several D's in general education courses. It turns out these courses emphasize writing skills, and April has great difficulty writing. She was afraid to ask for help because she didn't want to alert anyone in the school of music about her long existing problems with writing. In high school, her mother helped her with every writing assignment, and that enabled her to pass courses with writing requirements. April's mother lives 460 miles away now and there is no one to help April. She was hoping by now she could manage on her own, but it is clear that her writing difficulties are not improving. Because of her GPA, she is put on probation and is at risk of losing her scholarship.

WHAT IS TWICE EXCEPTIONAL?

Twice exceptional, often referred to as 2e, is fairly common in all ages of music students. To be 2e means to have characteristics of a disability along with characteristics of giftedness. According to Abramo (2015), 2e students have asynchronous traits, meaning that the 2e individual has advanced abilities in some areas and delays in others. Many music students come to music school with exceptional talent, but they may also have ADHD, specific learning disabilities, autism, or mental illness. Learning disabilities are the most common disability associated in twice-exceptional people (Assouline, Foley Nicpon, Whiteman, 2010; Baum, 1984; Baum & Owen, 1988; Brody & Mills, 1997; Neihart, 2008; Nielsen, 2002).

The following characteristics are collected from experts who have observed, taught, and researched 2e students. These characteristics are especially true for students with learning disabilities (Higgins, Baldwin, & Pereles, 2000; Weinfeld, Barnes-Robinson, Jeweler, & Shevitz, 2006):

- Struggle with basic skills due to cognitive processing difficulties; need to learn compensatory strategies in order to master skills.
- Show high verbal abilities but extreme difficulty in written language; may use language in inappropriate ways and at inappropriate times.
- Experience reading problems due to cognitive processing deficits.
- Demonstrate strong observation skills but have difficulty with memory skills.
- Excel in solving "real-world" problems; have outstanding critical thinking and decision-making skills; often independently develop compensatory skills.
- Show attention deficit problems but may concentrate for long periods in areas of interest.
- Have strong questioning attitudes; may appear disrespectful when questioning information, facts, etc. presented by the teacher.
- Display unusual imagination; frequently generate original and at times "bizarre" ideas; extremely divergent in thought; may appear to daydream when generating ideas.
- Require frequent professor support and feedback in deficit areas: highly independent in other areas; can appear stubborn and inflexible.
- Are sensitive regarding disability area(s); highly critical of self and others including professors; can express concern about the feelings of others even while engaging in anti-social behavior.
- May not be accepted by other students and may feel isolated. May be perceived as loners since they do not fit the typical model for a student who is either gifted or learning disabled; sometimes have difficulty being accepted by peers due to poor social skills.

- Exhibit leadership ability; alternatively, the disability may interfere with the student's ability to exercise leadership skills.
- Show a wide range of interests but may be thwarted in pursuing them due to processing or learning problems.
- Have very focused interests—for example, a passion about certain topics to the exclusion of others.

Twice-exceptional students are often good problem solvers who can produce creative solutions and make connections between concepts that seem unrelated. These students have a deep interest in and commitment to projects and ideas that are meaningful for them (Abramo, 2015).

Students who are gifted and have learning disabilities show superior intellectual ability despite exhibiting a significant discrepancy in their level of performance in an academic area such as reading, mathematics, spelling, and written expression. Their academic achievement is below what is expected based on their general intellectual ability (McCoach et al., 2001). Al-Hroub (2014) found that students who are gifted/learning disabled will learn much better through visual learning modes than auditory learning modes.

Twice-exceptionality for giftedness and ADHD is common (Cramond, 1995; Reis & McCoach, 2002; Webb & Latimer, 1993). Students with ADHD/giftedness are frequently misdiagnosed (Chae, Ji-Hye, & Kyung-Sun, 2003; Harnett, Nelson, & Rinn, 2004; Reis & McCoach, 2002). Hyperactivity or ADHD can manifest with giftedness by demonstrated high but focused energy levels, which are direct and intense in the gifted child (Foley Nicpon et al., 2011).

Twice-exceptionality occurs with autism spectrum disorder, especially among higher functioning individuals (Klin, Volkmar, & Sparrow, 2000). Gifted students have similar characteristics as those with autism, including intense focus on certain subjects, uncooperative behavior, and difficulty making friends (Cash, 1999; Gallagher & Gallagher, 2002).

THE 2E MUSIC STUDENT

It is likely that many 2e music students will manage to go through music school without others noticing that they have a disability that impacts them outside of music. Many are so highly gifted that we tend to ignore their challenges because we are so impressed with their talent. This must be a tremendous relief to someone who struggled through K–12 education to finally be immersed most of the day in the area in which he or she excels.

Abramo (2015) recommends preceding lecture or extensive teacher talk with an active experience. When listening to a recording in music history, encourage all students to follow the melodic contour with their hand, draw a chart that shows transitions between sections, or better yet, get students up and moving to the music. Mixed meters are better understood through movement than hearing someone talk about them.

Campanelli and Ericson (2007) advise that twice-exceptional students are motivated by higher-level thinking rather than a grade. Motivation will increase if a professor does the following:

- Engages students in abstract thinking and problem solving.
- Pre-assess skills and knowledge in order to compact the curriculum, thereby eliminating unnecessary work, or repeating skills and knowledge that have already been mastered.
- Integrate creative thinking and problem solving.
- Use compacting or summarizing content to buy time for independent work.

SUMMARY

Twice-exceptionality is probably more common among music students than students in many other academic areas on campus because we tend to work with students who come to us with exceptional talent or interest in performing or scholarly study of music. It is the students who are identified as gifted in music or talented in music that frequently choose to pursue music as a career. However, these same students may also have a disorder or disability. Students with specific learning disabilities are the most frequent 2e students followed by those with ADHD and autism.

17

ASSISTIVE TECHNOLOGY AND MUSIC ASSISTIVE

TECHNOLOGY TO SUPPORT STUDENTS WITH DISABILITIES

Adam has a communication disability caused by autism. His IQ is above average and he is a talented pianist. His audition for music school was outstanding until the question and answer interview. The committee was surprised when Adam opened a communication device to type answers to their questions. His answers were straightforward and short.

One professor was very uncomfortable with accepting Adam based on his almost blunt communications; he was unsure whether Adam could successfully complete a college degree. Another professor reminded the others that in the performance audition, students should be judged by their musical abilities only and this young man certainly could play the piano. Another asked, "What about accompanying other students or choirs? Will he be able to collaborate with others? Will some students prefer not to work with him because of the awkward way he communicates?"

IN 1988, "ASSISTIVE technology device" was first defined in the Technology-Related Assistance for Individuals with Disabilities Act (P.L. 100-407), also known as the "Tech Act," and this definition was later used in the 1990 reauthorization of the Individuals with Disabilities Education Act. Assistive technology as defined in the Tech Act and subsequent laws refers to "any item, piece of equipment, or product system, whether acquired commercially off-the-shelf, modified, or customized, that is used to increase, maintain or improve the functional capabilities of individuals with disabilities" (US Congress, 1988). Bryant and Bryant (2012) explain further that "this definition is sufficiently broad to include just about any item or system, from electronic wheelchairs for people with mobility impairments to remedial reading programs for children with dyslexia." They also point out that there are three components of the definition of an AT device: *"What* it is, *how* it's made, and its *use"* (pp. 3–4).

What refers to the device or equipment itself. Adam used a Dynavox communication device that enables students with communication disabilities to use a computerized system to speak. The device is programmed to emulate speech based on words or pictures represented on the device. The user can tap or use eye gaze to activate the machine to talk "Is the book in the library?" This is an expensive high-tech device that the student usually owns and is not something a university provides. Assisted listening devices are often owned by the university and loaned out to students with hearing loss who are in large classes or ensembles. In noisy environments, students might benefit from having the professor wear a device that amplifies and transmits the professor's voice directly into students' hearing aids. Imagine a student in a large general-education class or even a music major singing in a large choir seated in the back of the chorus. Both devices enable people to participate more fully in life.

How refers to whether a device has been purchased to function a certain way or if it needs additional modifications to be used. For example, a French horn player who lost her left arm in an accident was no longer able to operate the valves of the horn with her left hand. Her horn was adapted by a good instrument repairperson to be played by the right hand. The musician would further need to have a special prosthesis made for the hand that goes inside the bell. The material for the prosthesis would need to be close to the weight and density of a human hand in order not to impact tone quality and pitch. The prosthesis could include a hook to easily manipulate mutes as well.

Use refers to how the person makes use of the device. For example, electronic drum controllers are made for those who want sampled and electronic sounds that are played by percussionists. Some drum controllers have rubber pads that are very sensitive to touch. A percussionist diagnosed with amyotrophic lateral sclerosis, known as Lou Gehrig's disease, may be able to continue playing percussion even as the disease advances and impacts his ability to hold or lift drumsticks and other hand-held instruments. By tapping sensitive rubber pads on the music assistive technology device, he can continue to play.

Assistive technology naturally brings to mind computers and electronic devices. Computers and electronics have contributed to improved access to music making and to the quality of life for countless individuals with disabilities. In general, digital learning tools would most likely qualify as assistive technology for students with disabilities (Edyburn, 2013). However, there is one exception. "Assistive technology" does not include "a medical device that is surgically implanted, or the replacement of such device" (IDEA 2004, Sec. 1401(1)(B).

LOW-, MID-, AND HIGH-TECH ASSISTIVE TECHNOLOGY DEVICES

Assistive technology can be low-, mid-, or high-tech. Even though some of the most exciting AT tends to be high-tech, we should not forget that there are many low-tech ways to achieve access for a person with a disability. A woman with very small hands has silicone risers on her saxophone that help to make her palm keys easier to access while reducing fatigue in her hands. The same musician uses a baritone saxophone support stand to more comfortably play a large and heavy instrument. Both low-tech devices are commercially available.

Mid-level AT has emerged primarily with the popularity of tablet computers and sophisticated applications (apps). The drummer with ALS can download any number of apps on his iPad that work similarly to touch-sensitive drum controllers. The sheer number of apps for music are impossible to even count because every day new ones are offered.

High-tech devices often have a steep learning curve in addition to their cost. I worked with a teenager who was on a ventilator and in a wheelchair with no movement except in her right eyebrow. Because of her low mobility and inability to communicate, she was more of an observer than a participant in life. An electronic musical instrument, the SoundBeam, changed her life in ways no one could have anticipated. The SoundBeam emits an ultrasonic beam from a sensor that translates movement into MIDI sounds (and now sampled sound). An occupational therapist and I focused the beam on this student's eyebrow and she could play three different pitches the first day. After two years of weekly therapy using the SoundBeam, this young student was eventually able to play a one-octave chromatic scale with her eyebrow. Because she was motivated and worked so hard to make music, she developed excellent control over her eyebrow muscles, which led to her being able to type on a computer using her eyebrow movement. This was the first time she had been able to communicate after 17 years of silence. That is not the end of the story; using the new version of the SoundBeam, her mother's voice was sampled. Her mother is a Gospel singer, and now the daughter sings with her mother's voice using her eyebrow.

The results are amazing, but the student and her occupational therapist had to work with the SoundBeam for several years to learn to use the device in a way that met their goals. Many high-tech devices require a specialist or someone with extensive training to use the device the way it was intended. Nonetheless, features of simplicity or complexity should be evaluated periodically when considering a device: does it match the students' anticipated needs, activity requirements, and task demands? Does it present barriers? (Bryant & Bryant, 2003; King-Sears & Evmenova, 2007; Scherer & Craddock, 2002; Zabala & Bowser2005).

Beyond the evaluation, special education law allows for a host of other services, including these:

- Purchasing, leasing, or otherwise providing for the acquisition of assistive technology devices.
- Selecting, designing, fitting, customizing, adapting, applying, maintaining, repairing, or replacing assistive technology devices.
- Coordinating and using other therapies, interventions, or services with assistive technology devices, such as those associated with existing education and rehabilitation plans and programs.
- Training or technical assistance for a child, or where appropriate the family of the child.
- Training or technical assistance for professionals (including individuals providing education and rehabilitation services), employers, or other individuals providing services to, employing, or otherwise substantially involved in the major life functions of a child. (IDEIA Sec 602 (1)(A))

College students who were evaluated in public school and had an active Individual Education Program while in high school continue to receive IEP supports until they turn 21. Under 504 of the Rehabilitation Act of 1973, students continue to receive training and support for the use of assistive technology in college. Public institutions must give "primary consideration" to the requests of persons with disabilities unless they can demonstrate another equally effective means of access (Simon, 2011). Both the Americans with Disabilities Act and Section 504 do not use the term "assistive technology"; instead they use "auxiliary aids and services for effective communication" and "modification to policies, practices, and procedures."

Disability Rights California published an online chapter that explains the rights of students with disabilities to assistive technology in postsecondary institutions:

Effective communication means that colleges must communicate with applicants and students who have disabilities as effectively as they communicate with others. 28 C.F.R. § 35.160. To do so, and to give you equal opportunity to participate in their programs, colleges must furnish auxiliary aids and services. 28 C.F.R. § 35.160(b)(1).

Auxiliary aids and services cover a wide range of services and devices. They can include these:

- Recorded texts
- Note-takers
- Interpreters
- Video displays
- Television enlargers
- Electronic readers
- Braille printers, or typewriters
- Closed caption decoders
- Open and closed captions
- Voice synthesizers
- Computer keyboards with large buttons
- Reaching devices for library use
- Assistive listening devices or systems

A university does not have to provide assistive technology if it fundamentally alters the nature of the program or creates an undue financial or administrative burden. This law is open to broad interpretation, which probably explains why it is challenged so often. Consider the phrase "fundamentally alter the nature of the program." Does it fundamentally alter the nature of a choir that performs standing up to include a person who is seated in a wheelchair? If the college decides there is an undue burden, an alternate aid must be suggested in order for the individual to participate in music or receive services from the student disability office. Under ADA, only the head of the public university may decide an action that would result in a fundamental alteration or undue burden.

The student cannot be charged a fee to use assistive technology provided by the university. Students, however, cannot expect universities to purchase personal devices such as wheelchairs, durable medical equipment, or prosthetic devices. Students should make a request in advance of when the device and training are needed to ensure optimum readiness when school begins. Colleges will likely require documentation of the disability and the need for the device or devices.

SUMMARY

Assistive technology devices or programs help an individual to access the curriculum. The devices can be low, mid or high-tech and can be custom designed or commercially purchased. Training for both the student and any faculty or staff who work with the student and the device is also provided under federal law. Devices are loaned to students if they do not have their own and the disability services office decides that the student needs the device to function in the academic setting.

If the device fundamentally alters the curriculum or is an undue burden on the university, the university does not have to provide the device. The burden is on the university to prove that the student can manage without the device.

References

CHAPTER 1

Berklee College of Music. (2015). *Disability services for students*. Retrieved from https://www.berklee.edu/counseling-and-advising-center/disability-services-students on October 27, 2015.

Flowers, C., Bray, M., & Algozzine, R. F. (2001). Content accessibility of community college web sites. *Community College Journal of Research & Practice, 25*(7), 475–485.

Gruttadaro, D., & Crudo, D. (2012). *College students speak: A survey report on mental health*. Fairfax, VA: National Alliance on Mental Illness.

Haller, B. A. (2006). Promoting disability-friendly campuses to prospective students: An analysis of university recruitment materials. *Disability Studies Quarterly, 26*(2), 1–19.

Kennedy, M. (2000). Gaining access. *American School & University, 73*(4), 14–19.

Mulvey, B. (2015). *Essentials for success: Opportunities for academic success with individualized and small group support*. Retrieved from https://www.berklee.edu/sites/default/files/pdf/pdf/counseling/PM-111.pdf on October 27, 2015.

Nelson, J. R., Dodd, J. M., & Smith, D. J. (1990). Faculty willingness to accommodate students with learning disabilities: A comparison among academic divisions. *Journal of Learning Disabilities, 23*(3), 185–189.

Stodden, R. A. & Roberts, K.D. (2008). Transition legislation and policy: Past and present. In F. Rusch (Ed.), *Beyond high school: Preparing adolescents for tomorrow's challenges* (2nd ed., pp. 24-53). Upper Saddle River, NJ: Pearson.

Stodden, R. A., Whelley, T., Chang, C., & Harding, T. (2001). Current status of educational support provision to students with disabilities in postsecondary education. *Journal of Vocational Rehabilitation, 16*, 189–198.

Thomas, S.B. (2000). College student and disability law. *Journal of Special Education, 33*:4, pp. 248–58.

US Census. (2012). *Nearly 1 in 5 people have a disability in the U.S., census bureau reports.* Retrieved from https://www.census.gov/newsroom/releases/archives/miscellaneous/cb12-134.html on October 27, 2015.

Wilson, K., Getze, E., & Brown, T. (2000). Enhancing the post-secondary campus climate for students with disabilities. *Journal of Vocational Rehabilitation, 14*(1), 37–50.

CHAPTER 2

Adamek, M., & Darrow, A. A. (2012). Music participation as a means to facilitate self-determination and transition to community life for students with disabilities. In *The intersection of arts education and special education: Exemplary programs and approaches.* Washington, DC: VSA/The Kennedy Center for the Performing Arts. Retrieved from https://www.kennedy-center.org/education/vsa/resources/Finalprofessionialpapersbook2013.pdf on October 31, 2015.

Ashmore, J. (2010). Transitioning from high school to college—Students with disabilities. *Disability Blog, September.* Retrieved from https://usodep.blogs.govdelivery.com/?s=Jean+Ashmore on October 31, 2015.

Burgstahler, S. (2007). DO-IT: Helping students with disabilities transition to college and careers. *National Center on Secondary Education and Transition.* Retrieved from DO-IT: Helping students with disabilities transition to college and c . . . on October 31, 2015.

Carter, E. W., Boehm, T. L., Biggs, E. E., Annandale, N. H., Taylor, C. E., Loock, A. K., & Liu, R. Y. (2015). Known for my strengths: Positive traits of transition-age youth with intellectual disability and/or autism. *Research and Practice for Persons with Severe Disabilities, 40*(2), 101–119.

Diament, M. (2015). Post-secondary programs see signs of success. *Disability Scoop.* Retrieved from http://www.disabilityscoop.com/2015/09/21/post-secondary-signs-success/20810/ on October 31, 2015.

Durlak, C. M., Rose, E., & Bursuck, W. D. (1994). Preparing high school students with learning disabilities for the transition to postsecondary education: Teaching the skills of self-determination. *Journal of Learning Disabilities, 27*(1), 51–9.

Dykens, E. (2006). Toward a positive psychology of mental retardation. *American Journal of Orthopsychiatry, 76*, 185–93.

Erickson, W., Lee, C., & van Schrader, S. (2014). 2013 disability status report: United States. *Cornell university employment and disability institute (EDI).* Ithaca, NY: Cornell University.

Gargiulo, R. M. (2012). *Special education in contemporary society: An introduction to exceptionality* (4th ed.). Los Angeles: Sage.

George Mason University. (2015). *The Mason LIFE Program.* Fairfax, VA: George Mason University.

Gomez, C. (2015). 5-day program helps students with disabilities transition to college more smoothly. *Disability Compliance for Higher Education.* Retrieved from http://www.disabilitycomplianceforhighereducation.com/m-article-detail/5-day-program-helps-students-with-disabilities-transition-to-college-more-smoothly.aspx on October 31, 2015.

Grigal, M., & Hart, D. (2010). *Think College!* Baltimore: Brookes Publishing.

Grigal, M., Neubert, D., & Moon, M. (2001). Public school programs for students with significant disabilities in postsecondary settings. *Education and Training in Mental Retardation and Developmental Disabilities, 36*, 244–254.

Hall, M., Kleinert, H. L., & Kearns, J. F. (2000). Going to college! Postsecondary programs for students with moderate and severe disabilities. *Teaching Exceptional Children, 32*, 58–65.

Harris, L. & Associates. (2004). *National Organization on Disabilities/Harris Survey of American with Disabilities.* New York: Author.

Hart, D., Zimbrich, K., & Ghiloni, C. (2001). Interagency partnerships and funding: Individual supports for youth with significant disabilities as they move into postsecondary education and employment options. *Journal of Vocational Rehabilitation, 16*, 145–154.

Hart, D., Zimbrich, K., & Parker, D. R. (2005). Dual enrollment as a postsecondary option for students with intellectual disabilities. In E. E. Getzel & P. Wehman (Eds.), *Going to college* (pp. 253–267). Baltimore: Brookes.

Holt, J., Chambless, C., & Hammond, M. (2006). Employment personal assistance services (EPAS). *Journal of Vocational Rehabilitation, 24*(3), 165–175.

Jellison, J. (1999). Life beyond the jingle stick: Real music in a real world. *Update—Applications of Research in Music Education, 17*(2), 13–19.

Kruse, D., Schur, L., and Ali, M. (2010). Disability and occupational projections. *Monthly Labor Review, 133*(10), U.S. Bureau of Labor Statistics, 31–78. Retrieved from http://www.bls.gov/opub/mlr/2010/10/mlr201010.pdf on October 31, 2015.

Landmark College. (2015). Transition to college program for recent high school graduates. Retrieved from http://www.landmark.edu/academics/summer-and-january-programs/transitions on October 31, 2015.

Miller, K. (2015). Academy for adult learning. Temple University Institute on Disabilities, the College of Education. Retrieved from http://disabilities.temple.edu/programs/inclusive/aal.shtml on October 31, 2015.

Moon, M. S., Grigal, M., & Neubert, D. (2001). High school and beyond: Students with significant disabilities complete high school through alternative programs in postsecondary settings. *Exceptional Parent, 31*(7), 52–57.

Mulvey, B. (2015). *Essentials for success: Opportunities for academic success with individualized and small group support.* Retrieved from https://www.berklee.edu/sites/default/files/pdf/pdf/counseling/PM-111.pdf on October 27, 2015.

Neubert, D. A., Moon, M. S., & Grigal, M. (2002). Post-secondary education and transition services for students ages 18–21 with significant disabilities. *Focus on Exceptional Children, 34*, 1–11.

Rogan, P., & Rinne, S. (2011). National call for organizational change from sheltered to integrated employment. *Intellectual and Developmental Disabilities, 49*(4), 248–260.

Rogan, P., Updike, J., Chesterfield, G., & Savage, S. (2014). The SITE program at IUPUI: A postsecondary program for individuals with intellectual disabilities. *Journal of Vocational Rehabilitation, 40*, 109–116.

Shogren, K. A., Wehmeyer, M. L., Buchanan, C. L., & Lopez, S. J. (2006). The application of positive psychology and self-determination to research in intellectual disability: A content analysis of 30 years of literature. *Research and Practice for Persons with Severe Disabilities, 31,* 338–345.

Smith, L. E., Barker, E. T., Seltzer, M. M., Abbeduto, L., & Greenberg, J. S. (2012). Behavioral phenotype of fragile X syndrome in adolescence and adulthood. *American Journal on Intellectual and Developmental Disabilities, 117*(1), 1–17.

Sparks, S. D. (2015). For students with disabilities, transition from high school requires self-advocacy. *Education Week, 34*(33), 8.

Stetser, M. C., & Stillwell, R. (2014). Public high school four-year on-time graduation rates and even dropout rates: School years 2010–11 and 2011–12: First look. *National Center for Education Statistics.* US Department of Education. Retrieved from http://nces.ed.gov/pubs2014/2014391.pdf on October 31, 2015.

Stodden, R., & Whelley, T. (2004). Postsecondary education and persons with intellectual disabilities: An introduction. *Education and Training in Developmental Disabilities, 39*(1), 6–15.

Targett, P., Wehman, P., West, M., Dillard, C., & Cifu, G. (2013). Promoting transition to adulthood for youth with physical disabilities and health impairments. *Journal of Vocational Rehabilitation, 39,* 229–239.

Trainor, A. A., Morningstar, M., Murray, A., and Kim, H. (2013). Social capital during postsecondary transition for young adults with high incidence disabilities. *Prevention Researcher, 20*(2), 7–10.

Turnbull, H., Turnbull, P., Wehmeyer, M., & Park, J. (2003). A quality of life framework for special education outcomes. *Remedial and Special Education, 24,* 67–74.

Turner, E. (2007). Personal assistance services. *PAS Facts, 1.* Virginia Commonwealth University. Retrieved from http://www.worksupport.com/documents/pasfactsvol1.pdf on October 31, 2015.

University of Missouri St. Louis. (2015). UMSL SUCCEED. Retrieved from http://www.umsl.edu/~pcs/succeed on October 31, 2015.

US Census Bureau. (2014). United States Department of Labor (2015). Youth employment rate. *Office of Disability Employment Policy.* Retrieved from http://www.dol.gov/odep/categories/youth/youthemployment.htm on October 31, 2015.

Virginia Commonwealth University. (2015). ACE IT in college. Richmond, VA. Retrieved from http://www.aceitincollege.org on October 31, 2015.

VonSchrader, S., and Lee, C. G. (2015). *Disability statistics from the Current Population Survey (CPS).* Ithaca, NY: Cornell University Employment and Disability Institute (EDI). Retrieved from https://www.disabilitystatistics.org/reports/cps.cfm?statistic=poverty on October 31, 2015.

Wagner, M., Newman, L., Cameto, R., Garza, N., & Levine, P. (2005). *After high school: A first look at the post-school experiences of youth with disabilities. A report from the National Longitudinal Transition Study-2 (NLTS-2).* Menlo Park, CA: SRI. Retrieved from http://files.eric.ed.gov/fulltext/ED494935.pdf on October 31, 2015.

Wehmeyer, M. L., Shogren, K. A., Zager, D., Smith, T. E. C., & Simpson, R. (2010). Research-based principles and practices for educating students with autism: Self-determination and social interactions. *Education and Training in Autism and Developmental Disabilities, 45,* 475–486.

White, S. W., Oswald, D., Ollendick, T., & Scahill, L. (2009). Anxiety in children and adolescents with autism spectrum disorders. *Clinical Psychology Review, 29,* 216–229.

CHAPTER 3

Alexander v. Choate, 469 U.S. 287 (1985).

Bartlett v. New York State Board of Law Examiners, 156 F.3d 321 (2d Cir. 1998), vacated and remanded, 119 S. Ct. 2388 (1999), aff'd in part & remanded, 226 F:3d 69 (2d Cir. 2000); 2001 WL 930792 (S.D.N.Y. Aug. 15, 2001).

Burgstahler, S. E. (2008). Universal design in higher education. In S. E. Burgstahler & R. C. Cory (Eds.), *Universal design in higher education: From principles to practice*. Cambridge, MA: Harvard Education Press.

Concepcion v. Puerto Rico, 682 F. Supp. 2d 164 (D.P.R. 2010).

Federal Register, September 17, 2008.

Gonzales v. National Board of Medical Examiners, 225 F. 3d 620 (6th Cir. 2000).

Grossman, P. D. (2014). The greatest change in disability law in 20 years. In M. L. Vance, N. E. Lipsitz, & K. Parks (Eds.), *Beyond the Americans with Disabilities Act*. Washington, DC: NASPA.

Gruttadaro, G., & Crudo, D. (2012). College students speak: A survey on mental health. *National Alliance on Mental Illness (NAMI)*. Retrieved from http://www.nami.org/Content/NavigationMenu/Find_Support/NAMI_on_Campus1/collegereport.pdf on November 14, 2014.

Horn, L., & Nevill, S. (2006). *Profile of undergraduates in U.S. postsecondary education institutions: 2003–04* (NCES 2006-184). Washington, DC: National Center for Education Statistics, U.S. Department of Education.

Lewis, L., & Farris, E. (1999). An institutional perspective on students with disabilities in postsecondary education. *Education Statistics Quarterly, 1*(3). Retrieved from http://nces.ed.gov/programs/quarterly/vol_1/1_3/4-esq13-b.asp on November 14, 2014.

Price v. National Board of Medical Examiners, 966 F. Supp. 419 (S.D. W.Va. 1997).

Raue, K., & Lewis, L. (2011). *Students with disabilities at degree-granting postsecondary institutions* (NCES 2011-018). US Department of Education, National Center for Education Statistics. Washington, DC: US Government Printing Office.

Simon, J. A. (2011). Legal issues in serving students with disabilities in postsecondary education. In M. S. Huger (Ed.), *Fostering the increased integration of students with disabilities*. San Francisco, CA: Jossey-Bass.

Solano Community College, OCR Case No. 09-94-2064-1 (Region IX, 1995).

Sutton v. United Airlines, Inc., 527 U.S. 471, 119. Ct. 1752 (1999).

Toyota Motor Manufacturing v. Williams, 534 U.S. 184, 122 S. Ct. 681 (2002).

Wichita State University, 2 NDLR 154 (OCR Region VII, 1991).

Wong v. Regents of the University of California, 1999 WL 717729 (9th Cir. 1999).

Wong v. Regents of the University of California, 379 F.3d 1097 (9th Cir. 2004).

Wynne v. Tufts University School of Medicine, 932 F.2d 19 (1st Cir 1991) (en banc).

CHAPTER 4

Adams, M. (1992). *Promoting diversity in college classrooms: Innovative responses for the curriculum, faculty, and institutions*. San Francisco, CA: Jossey-Bass.

Ambrose, H., & Ambrose, K. (1995). *A handbook of biological investigation* (5th ed.). Winston-Salem, NC: Hunter Textbooks.

Bowe, F. G. (2000). *Universal design in education: Teaching nontraditional students.* Westport, CT: Bergin and Garvey.

Burgstahler, S. E. (2008). Universal design in higher education. In S. E. Burgstahler & R. C. Cory (Eds.), *Universal design in higher education, from principles to practice.* Cambridge, MA: Harvard Education Press.

Cain, S. (2013). *Quiet, the power of introverts in a world that can't stop talking.* New York: Random House.

Conway, C. M. & Hodgman, T. M. (2009). *Teaching music in higher education.* New York: Oxford University Press.

Darrow, A. A. (2016). Ableism and social justice: Rethinking disability in music education. In C. Benedict, P. Schmidt, G. Spruce, & P. Woodford (Eds.), *The Oxford Companion to Social Justice and Music Education: From conception to practice.* Oxford: Oxford University Press.

Dolan, R. P., Hall, T. E., Banerjee, M., Chun, E., & Strangman, N. (2005). Applying principles of universal design to test delivery: The effect of computer-based read-aloud on test performance of high school students with learning disabilities. *Journal of Technology, Learning, & Assessment, 3*(7).

DO-IT. (2007a) AccessCollege: Systemic change for postsecondary institutions. Seattle: University of Washington. Retrieved from http://www.washington.edu/doit/Brochures/Academics/access_college.html on December 3, 2014.

DO-IT. (2007b). DO-IT admin: A project to help postsecondary campus services administrators work successfully with students who have disabilities. Seattle: University of Washington. Retrieved from http://www.washington.edu/doit/Brochures/Academics/admin.html on December 3, 2014.

Ehrmann, S. C. (1995). Asking the right question. *Change, 29*(2), 20–27.

Felder, R. (1993). Reaching the second tier: Learning and teaching styles in college science education. *Journal of College Science Teaching, 23*(5), 286–290.

Glass, D., Meyer, A., & Rose, D. H. (2013). Universal design for learning and the arts. *Harvard Educational Review, 83*(1), 98–119.

Hackman, H. W., & Rauscher, L. (2004). A pathway to success for all: Exploring the connections between universal instructional design and social justice education. *Equity & Excellence in Education, 37*(2), 114–123.

Higbee, J. L,. & Barajas, H. L. (2007). Building effective places for multicultural learning. *About Campus, 12*(3), 16–22.

Higbee, J. L. (2008). The faculty perspective: Implementation of universal design in a first-year classroom. In S. E. Burgstahler & R. C. Cory (Eds.), *Universal design in higher education, from principles to practice.* Cambridge, MA: Harvard Education Press.

Huba, M. E., & Freed, J. E. (2000). *Learner-centered assessment on college campuses: Shifting the focus from teaching to learning.* Needham Heights, MA: Allyn & Bacon.

Johnson, J. R. (2004). Universal instructional design and critical (communication) pedagogy: Strategies for voice, inclusion, and social justice/change. *Equity & Excellence in Education, 37*(2), 145–153.

Johnson, D. M., & Fox, J. A. (2003). Creating curb cuts in the classroom: Adapting universal design principles to education. In J. L. Higbee (Ed.), *Curriculum transformation and disability: Implementing universal design in higher education* (pp. 7–21). Minneapolis: University of Minnesota, General College, Center for Research on Developmental Education and Urban Literacy. Retrieved from http://www.cehd.umn.edu/CRDEUL/books-ctad.html on December 3, 2014.

Mead, V. H. (1994). *Dalcroze eurythmics in today's music classroom.* New York: Schott Music.

Michalko, R. (2002). *The difference disability makes.* Philadelphia, PA: Temple University.

Putnam, M., Greenen, S., Powers, L., Saxton, M., Finney, S., & Dautel, P. (2003). Health and wellness: People with disabilities discuss barriers and facilitators to well being. *Journal of Rehabilitation, 69*, 37–45.

Rose, D. H., & Meyer, A. (2002). *Teaching every student in the digital age: Universal design for learning.* Alexandria, VA: Association for Curriculum and Development.

Rose, D. H., Harbour, W. S., Johnston, C. S., Daley, S. G., & Abarbanell, L. (2008). Universal design for learning in postsecondary education: Reflections on principles and their application. In S. E. Burgstahler & R. C. Cory (Eds.), *Universal design in higher education, from principles to practice.* Cambridge, MA: Harvard Education Press.

Smart, J. (2009). *Disability, Society, and the Individual.* Austin, TX: Pro-Ed.

The Center for Universal Design in Education. (n.d.). *Resources for student services staff.* Seattle: University of Washington. Retrieved August 16, 2016, from http://www.washington.edu/doit/programs/center-universal-design-education/overview.

Thompson, S. J., Johnstone, C. J., & Thurlow, M. L. (2002). *Universal design applied to large scale assessments* (Synthesis Report 44). Minneapolis: University of Minnesota, National Center on Educational Outcomes. Retrieved from http://www.cehd.umn.edu/NCEO/OnlinePubs/Synthesis44.html on December 2, 2014.

W3C. (2013). Accessibility evaluation resources. Retrieved from http://www.w3.org/WAI/eval/Overview.html on December 2, 2014.

Wiggins, G., & McTighe, J. (2005). Understanding by design professional development workbook. Alexandria, VA: ASCD.

Wright, B. A. (1983). *Physical disability: A psychological approach* (2nd ed.). New York: Harper & Row.

CHAPTER 5

Atterbury, B. W. (1990). *Mainstreaming exceptional learners in music.* Englewood Cliffs, NJ.: Prentice Hall.

Bateman, B. (1965). An educational view of diagnostic approach to learning disorders. In J. Hellmuth (Ed.), *Learning disorders* (pp. 219–239). Seattle, WA: Special Child Publications.

Besson, M., Schon, D., Moreno, S., Santos, A., & Magne, C. (2007). Influence of musical expertise and musical training on pitch processing in music and language. *Restorative Neurology and Neuroscience, 25*, 399–410.

Chung, K. K. H., Ho, C. S. H., Chan, D. W., Tsang, S. M., & Lee, S. H. (2010). Cognitive profiles of Chinese adolescents with dyslexia. *Dyslexia, 16*, 2–23.

Cortiella, C,. & Horowitz, S. H. (2014). *The state of learning disabilities, facts, trends and emerging issues.* New York: National Center for Learning Disabilities.

Goswami, U. (2011). A temporal sampling framework for developmental dyslexia. *Trends in Cognitive Sciences, 15*, 3–10.

Goswami, U. (2012). Entraining the brain: Applications to language research and links to musical entrainment. *Empirical Musicology Review, 7*(1–2), 57–63.

Grossman, P. D. (2014). The greatest change in disability law in 20 years. In M. L. Vance, N. E. Lipsitz, & K. Parks (Eds.), *Beyond the Americans with Disabilities Act*. Washington, DC: NASPA.

Hammel, A. (2013). *Constructive curricula for students with exceptionalities: Creating positive learning environments*. Paper presented at Intersections: Arts and Special Education Conference. Kennedy Center, Washington, DC, August 10, 2013.

Heikkila, E., & Knight, A. (2012). Inclusive music teaching strategies for elementary-age children with developmental dyslexia. *Music Educators Journal, 99*(1), 54–59.

Helland, T. A., & Asbjornsen, A. (2000). Executive functions in dyslexia. *Child Neuropsychology, 6*(1), 37–48.

Huss, M., Verney, J. P., Fosker, T., Mead, N., & Goswami, U. (2011). Music, rhythm, rise time perception and developmental dyslexia: Perception of musical meter predicts reading and phonology. *Cortex, 47*(6), 674–689.

King, W. M., Lombardino, L. J., Crandell, C. C., & Leonard, C. M. (2003). Comorbid auditory processing disorder in developmental dyslexia. *Ear and Hearing, 24*(5), 448–456.

Lam, C. C. C. (2010). *Developmental dyslexia: Neurobiological perspectives*. Hong Kong: Hong Kong Institute of Education.

Lyon, G. R., Shaywitz, S. E., & Shaywitz, B. A. (2003). A definition of dyslexia. *Annals of Dyslexia, 53*, 1–14.

Markow, D., & Pieters, A. (2011). The Metlife survey of the American teacher: Preparing students for college and careers. New York: Metropolitan Life Insurance. Retrieved from http://files.eric.ed.gov/fulltext/ED519278.pd on December 6, 2014.

McCord, K. A. (2004, Winter). Moving beyond "That's all I can do": Encouraging musical creativity in children with learning disabilities. *Bulletin of the Council for Research in Music Education, 159*, 23–32.

McCord, K. (2015). Specific learning disabilities and music education. In D. V. Blair & K. A. McCord (Eds.), *Exceptional music pedagogy for children with exceptionalities: International perspectives*. New York: Oxford University Press.

Nalavany, B. A., Carawan, L. W., & Rennick, R. A. (2011). Psychosocial experiences associated with confirmed and self-identified dyslexia: A participant-driven concept map of adult perspectives. *Journal of Learning Disabilities, 44*(1), 63–79.

Oslund, C. (2014). *Supporting college and university students with invisible disabilities*. Philadelphia: Jessica Kingsley.

Overy, K. (2003). Dyslexia and music: from timing deficits to musical intervention. *The neurosciences and music*. Retrieved from Annals of the New York Academy of Sciences website: http://www3.interscience.wiley.com.libproxy.lib.ilstu.edu/cgi-bin/fulltext /118876638/ HTMLSTART doi:10:1196/annals.1284.060.

Poole, H. (2001). My music and my dyscalculia. In T. R. Miles & J. Westcombe, (Eds.), *Music and dyslexia: Opening new doors* (pp. 53–56). London: Whurr.

Pratt, C. M. (2008). In and around the classroom. In T. R. Miles, J. Westcombe, & D. Ditchfield (Eds.), *Music and dyslexia: A positive approach* (pp. 19–25). West Sussex, England: Wiley.

Ramus, F., Pidgeon, E., & Firth, U. (2003). The relationship between motor control and phonology in dyslexic children. *Journal of Child Psychology and Psychiatry, 44*(5), 712–722.

Register, D., Darrow, A. A., Standley, J., & Swedberg, O. (2007). The use of music to enhance reading skills of second grade students and students with reading disabilities. *Journal of Music Therapy, 44*(1), 23–27.

Reid, G., & Green, S. (2007). *100 ideas for supporting pupils with dyslexia*. London: Continuum.

Seligman, M. (1975). *Helplessness: On depression, development and death*. San Francisco, CA: W. H. Freeman.

Shalev, R. S. (2004). Developmental dyscalculia. *Journal of Child Neurology, 19*, 765–771.

Stainback, S., Stainback, W., Stefanich, G., & Alper, S. (1997). Learning in inclusive classrooms; what about curriculums? In S. Stainback & W. Stainback (Eds.), *Inclusion: A guide for educators* (pp. 209–219). Baltimore, MD: Brookes.

Supporting accommodation requests: Guidance on documentation practices. (2012). *Home | AHEAD: Association on Higher Education and Disability*. Retrieved from http://ahead.org/.

U.S. Office of Education. (1968). *First annual report of the National Advisory Committee on Handicapped Children*. Washington, DC: US Department of Health, Education, and Welfare.

Westcombe, J. (2002). How dyslexia can affect musicians. In T. R. Miles & J. Westcombe (Eds.), *Music and dyslexia: Opening new doors* (pp. 9–18). London: Whurr.

CHAPTER 6

American Speech-Language-Hearing Association. (1993). Definitions of communication disorders and variations. *ASHA, 35*(Suppl. 10), 40–41.

American Speech-Language-Hearing Association. (1997). What is aphasia? Retrieved from http://www.asha.org/public/speech/disorders/Aphasia/ on December 19, 2014.

Benninger, M. (1994). *Vocal arts medicine: The care and prevention of professional voice disorders* (p. 166). New York: Thieme Medical Publishers.

Bernthal, J., Bankson, N., & Flipsen, P. (2009). *Articulation and phonological disorders* (6th ed.). Boston: Allyn and Bacon.

Dovel, J. (2010). Teaching tongue-tied students: Ankyloglossia in the instrumental classroom. *Music Educators Journal, 6*(4), 49–52.

Gargiulo, R. M. (2012). *Special education in contemporary society: An introduction to exceptionality*. Thousand Oaks, CA: Sage.

Hurley, P. K. (n.d.). Introduction to the study of language. Retrieved from http://emedia.leeward.hawaii.edu/hurley/Ling102web/mod3_speaking/3mod3.2_vocalorgans.htm on December 18, 2014.

NIH National Institute on Deafness and Other Communication Disorders. (2010). Statistics on Voice, Speech, and Language. Retrieved from http://www.nidcd.nih.gov/health/statistics/pages/vsl.aspx on December 19, 2014.

Owens, R., Metz, D., & Farinella, K. (2011). *Introduction to communication disorders: A lifespan evidence-based perspective* (4th ed.). Boston: Allyn & Bacon.

Ramig, P., & Shames, G. (2006). Stuttering and other disorders of fluency. In G. Shames & N. Anderson (Eds.), *Human communication disorders: An introduction* (7th ed., pp. 183–221). Boston: Allyn & Bacon.

Ratner, N. (2009). Atypical language development. In J. Gleason & N. Ratner (Eds.), *The development of language* (7th ed., pp. 315–390). Boston: Pearson Education.

CHAPTER 7

ADA Amendments Act of 2008. P.L. 110–325, 29 U.S.C.S. ___ 705.2008.

American Psychiatric Association. (2013). *Diagnostic and statistical manual of mental disorders* (5th ed.). Arlington, VA: Author.

Belch, H. A. (2011). Understanding the experiences of students with psychiatric disabilities: A foundation for creating conditions of support and success. In M. S. Huger (Ed.), *Fostering the increased integration of students with disabilities* (San Francisco, CA: Jossey-Bass.

Blacklock, B., Benson, B., & Johnson, D. (2003). *Needs assessment project: Exploring barriers and opportunities for college students with psychiatric disabilities*. Unpublished manuscript, University of Minnesota.

Brown, K. S. (2002). Antecedents of psychiatric rehabilitation: The road to supported education programs. In C. T. Mowbray, K. S. Brown, K. Furlong-Norman, & A. S. Sullivan-Soydan (Eds.), *Supported education and psychiatric rehabilitation: Models and methods* (pp. 13–21). Linthicum, MD: International Association of Psychiatric Rehabilitation Services.

Center for Collegiate Mental Health. (2015). 2014 Annual Report. (Publication No. STA 15–30).

Collins, K. D. (2000). Coordination of rehabilitation services in higher education for students with psychiatric disabilities. *Journal of Applied Rehabilitation Counseling 31*(4), 36–39.

Collins, M. E., & Mowbray, C. T. (2005). Higher education and psychiatric disabilities on campus: National survey of campus disability support services. *American Journal of Orthopsychiatry, 75*, 304–315.

Davis, R., & DeBarros, A. (2006). In college, first year is by far the riskiest. *USA TODAY,* 11/19

Fisher, S. (2004). American college health association survey shows increase of depression among college students over four-year period. American College Health Association. Retrieved from http://www.acha.org/newsroom/pr ncha_11_17_04.cfm.

Flanagan, S., Zaretsky, H. H., & Moroz, A. (2010). *Medical aspects of disability: A handbook for the rehabilitation professional* (4th ed.). New York: Springer.

Fleming, A. R., & Fairweather, J. S. (2011). The role of postsecondary education in the path from high school to work for youth with disabilities. *Rehabilitation Counseling Bulletin, 55*(22), 71–81.

Gallagher, R. P. (2014). National survey of college counseling centers. Pittsburgh, PA: International Association of Counseling Services. Retrieved from http://www.collegecounseling.org/wp-content/uploads/NCCCS2014_v2.pdf on June 10, 2015.

Gladding, S. T., & Newsome, D. W. (2009). *Clinical mental health counseling in community and agency settings*. Princeton, NJ: Merrill.

Government Accountability Office. (2009). *Higher education and disability: Education needs a coordinated approach to improve its assistance to schools in supporting students*. Washington, DC: Author.

Gruttadaro, D., & Crudo, D. (2012). *College students speak: A survey report on mental health*. Arlington, VA: National Alliance on Mental Illness.

Kaye, W. H., Bulik, C. M., Thornton, L., Barbarich, N., & Masters, K. Price Foundation Collaborative Group. (2004). Comorbidity of anxiety disorders and anorexia and bulimia nervosa. *American Journal of Psychiatry, 161*(12), 2215–2221.

Kupferman, S. I. (2014). Supporting students with psychiatric disabilities in postsecondary education: Important knowledge, skills, and attitudes. *All Graduate Theses and Dissertations.* Paper 2067. http://digitalcommons.usu.edu/etd/etd/2067. Retrieved June 5, 2015.

Leff, S. , & McPartland, J. (1998). Service quality as measured by service fit and employment status among public mental health system service recipients. Facilitating careers for mental health consumers—A vocational rehabilitation research conference. *The UIC National Research and Training Center on Psychiatric Disabilities,* Chicago, IL, April 13–15, 1998.

Leibert, D. T. (2003). Access to higher education for the mentally ill: A review of trends, implications, and future possibilities for the Americans with Disabilities Act and the Rehabilitation Act. *International Journal of Psychosocial Rehabilitation, 7.*

McClelland, G. M., & Teplin, L. A. (2001). Alcohol intoxication and violent crime: Implications for public health policy. *American Journal on Addictions 10* (Suppl.), 70–85.

McEwan, R. C., & Downie, R. (2013). College success of students with psychiatric disabilities: Barriers of access and distraction. *Journal of Postsecondary Education and Disability, 26*(3), 233–248.

Mancuso, L. L. (1990) Reasonable accommodations for workers with psychiatric disabilities. *Psychosocial Rehabilitation Journal, 14*(2), 3–19.

Mowbray, C. T., Collins, M. E., Bellamy, C. D., Megivern, D. A., Bybee, D., & Szilvagyi, S. (2005). Supported education for adults with psychiatric disabilities: An innovation for social work and psychosocial rehabilitation practice. *Social Work, 50,* 7–20.

National Alliance on Mental Illness. (2012). Survey of college students finds many leave due to mental health issues. *Mental Health Week, 22*(42), 1–8.

Oslund, C. (2014). *Supporting college and university students with invisible disabilities: A guide for faculty and staff working with students with autism, AD/HD, language processing disorders, anxiety, and mental illness.* London: Jessica Kingsley.

President's New Freedom Commission on Mental Health. (2003). *Achieving the promise: Transforming mental health care in America.* Washington, DC: Author.

Rickerson, N., Souma, A., & Burgstahler, S. (2004). Psychiatric disabilities in postsecondary education: Universal design, accommodations and supported education. National Capacity Building Institute on issues of transition and postsecondary participation for individuals with hidden disabilities, Waikiki, HI. Retrieved from http://www.ncset.hawaii.edu/institutes/mar2004/papers/txt/Souma_revised.txt on June 3, 2015.

Santosa, C. M., Strong, C. M., Nowakowski, C. N., Wang, P. W., Renicke, C. M., & Ketter, T. A. (2006). Enhanced creativity in bipolar disorder patients: A controlled study. *Journal of Affective Disorders, 100,* 31–39.

Sharpe, M. N., Bruininks, B. D., Blacklock, B. A., Benson, B., & Johnson, D. M. (2004). The emergence of psychiatric disabilities in postsecondary education. *Issue Brief: Examining current challenges in secondary education and transition, 3*(1), 1–5.

Souma, A., Rickerson, N., & Burgstahler, S. (n.d.). Academic accommodations for students with psychiatric disabilities. Retrieved from http://www.washington.edu/doit/academic-accommodations-students-psychiatric-disabilities on June 10, 2015.

Srivastava, S., Childers, M. E., Baek, J. H., Strong, C. M., et al. (2010). Toward interaction of affective and cognitive contributors to creativity in bipolar disorders: A controlled study. *Journal of Affective Disorders, 125,* 27–34.

Unger, K. (1990, Summer). Supported postsecondary education for people with mental illness. *American Rehabilitation,* 10–14. Unger, K. (1992). *Adults with psychiatric disabilities on campus: Supported education for young adults with psychiatric disabilities.* HEATH Resource Center. Washington, DC: National Clearinghouse on Post-Secondary Education for Individuals with Disabilities.

Unger, K. V. (1998). *Handbook on supported education: Service for students with psychiatric disabilities.* Baltimore, MD: Paul H. Brookes.

Unger, K.V. (2007). *Handbook on supported education: Providing services for students with psychiatric disabilities.* Charleston, SC: BookSurge.

Unger, K.V., Pardee, R., & Shafer, M.S. (2000). Outcomes of postsecondary supported education programs for people with psychiatric disabilities. *Journal of Vocational Rehabilitation* 14, 195–199.

United States Secret Service. (2002). Secret service safe school initiative. Retrieved from http://www.secretservice.gov/ntac_ssi.shtml on June 10, 2015.

Whelley, T., Hart, D., & Zafft, C. (2002, July). *Coordination and management of services and supports for individuals with disabilities from postsecondary education and employment* (White Paper). Honolulu, Hawaii: University of Hawaii at Manoa, National Center on Secondary Education and Transition and the National Center for Study of Postsecondary Educational Supports.

Zuckerman, D., Debenham, K., & Moore, K. (1993). The ADA and people with mental illness: A resource manual for employers. Alexandria, VA: National Mental Health Association.

CHAPTER 8

American Psychiatric Association. (2013). *Diagnostic and statistical manual of mental disorders* (5th ed.). Arlington, VA: Author.

Bedrossian, L. E., & Pennamon, R. E. (2007). *College students with Asperger syndrome: Practical strategies for academic and social success.* Horsham, PA: LRP Publications.

Centers for Disease Control and Prevention. (2015). Autism spectrum disorder: Data and statistics. Retrieved from http://www.cdc.gov/ncbddd/autism/data.html on June 21, 2015.

Freedman, S. (2010). *Developing college skills in students with autism and Asperger's syndrome.* Philadelphia, PA: Jessica Kingsley.

Irlen, H. (1998). *The irlen method.* Retrieved from http://irlen.com/the-irlen-method/ on June 22, 2015.

Moore, A.S. (2006). "A dream not denied": Students on the spectrum. *New York Times.* Retrieved from http://www.nytimes.com/2006/11/05/education/edlife/traits.html?_r=0&pagewanted=print on June 21, 2015.

Ockelford, A. (2007). *In the key of genius: The extraordinary life of Derek Paravicini.* London: Arrow Books.

Shattuck, P .T., Narendorf, S. C., Cooper, B., Sterzing, P. R., Wagner, M., & Taylor, J. L. (2012). Postsecondary education and employment among youth with an autism spectrum disorder. *Pediatrics, 129*(6), 1042–1049.

Welsh, M., & Pennington, B. (1988). Assessing frontal lobe functioning in children: Views from developmental psychology. *Developmental Neuropsychology, 4*(3), 199–230.

Wolf, L., Thierfeld Brown, J., & Kukiela Bork, G. R. (2009). *Students with Asperger syndrome: A guide for college personnel.* Shawnee Misson, KS: Autism Asperger Publishing.

CHAPTER 9

American Foundation for the Blind. (2015). Key definitions of statistical terms. Retrieved from http://www.afb.org/info/blindness-statistics/key-definitions-of-statistical-terms/25?mode=print on June 26, 2015.

Gaab, N., Schulze, K., Ozdemir, E., & Schlaug, G. (2006). Neural correlates of absolute pitch differ between blind and sighted musicians. *Neuroreport, 17*(8), 1853–1857.

Hamilton, R. H., Pascual-Leone, A., & Schlaug, G. (2004). Absolute pitch in blind musicians. *Neuroreport 15*(5), 803–806.

Raue, K., & Lewis, L. (2011). *Students with disabilities at degree-granting postsecondary institutions.* Washington, DC: US Government Printing Office.

Schneider, K. (2001). *Students who are blind or visually impaired in postsecondary education.* Retrieved from https://heath.gwu.edu/files/downloads/students_who_are_blind_or_visually_impaired_in_postsecondary_education.pdf on June 26, 2015.

Taesch, R., & McCann, W. (2003). Who's afraid of braille music? Valley Forge, PA: Dancing Dots Braille Music Technology, L.P.

CHAPTER 10

Baloh, R. W. (2009). *Clinical neurophysiology of the vestibular system.* New York: Oxford University Press.

Blanchfield, B. B., Feldman, J. J., Dunbar, J. L., & Gardner, E. N. (2001). The severely to profoundly hearing-impaired population in the United States: Prevalence estimates and demographics. *Journal of the American Academy of Audiology, 12*, 183–189.

Bond, A. (2014). Even beautiful music may pose hearing-loss risk to pros. Retrieved from http://www.reuters.com/article/2014/05/09/us-hearing-loss-musicians-idUSKBN0DP1DB20140509 on June 29, 2015.

Boutin, D. (2008). Persistence in postsecondary environments of students with hearing impairments. *Journal of Rehabilitation, 74*, 25–31.

Cheng, S., & Zhang, L. (2014). Thinking style changes among deaf, hard-of-hearing, and hearing students. *Deaf Studies and Deaf Education, 20*(1), 16–26.

Christiansen, J., & Leigh, I. (2002). *Cochlear implants in children: Ethics and choices.* Washington, DC: Gallaudet University.

ENT and Allergy. (2011). Helping your hearing loss. Retrieved from http://www.entandallergy. com/news/helping_your_hearing_loss on June 30, 2015.

Hands & Voices. (2014). *Beyond high school.* Retrieved from http://handsandvoices.org/articles/education/ed/V13-1_beyondHS.htm on June 30, 2015.

Kuh, G. D., Kinzie, J., Schuh, J. H., & Whitt, E. J. (2010). *Student success in college: Creating conditions that matter.* San Francisco, CA: Jossey-Bass.

Leppo, R., Cawthon, S., & Bond, M. (2013). Including deaf and hard-of-hearing students with co-occurring disabilities in the accommodations discussion. *Journal of Deaf Studies and Deaf Education, 19*(2), 189–202.

Mackelprang, R. (2011). Cultural competence with persons with disabilities. In D. Lum (Ed.), *Culturally competent practice: A framework for understanding diverse culture* (pp. 437–465). Belmont, CA: Brooks/Cole–Cengage Learning.

Marschark, M., Leigh, G., Sapere, P., Burnham, D., Convertino, C., Stinson, M., Knoors, H., Vervloed, M. P. J., & Noble, W. (2006). Benefits of sign language interpreting and text alternatives to classroom learning by deaf students. *Journal of Deaf Studies and Deaf Education, 11*, 421–437.

Marschark, M. (2009). *Raising and educating a deaf child: A comprehensive guide to the choices, controversies, and decisions faced by parents and educators* (2nd ed.) New York: Oxford University Press.

McIllroy, G., & Storbeck, C. (2011). Development of deaf identity: An ethnographic study. *Journal of Deaf Studies and Deaf Education, 16*, 494–511.

National Center on Deafness. (2009). *Guide to working with deaf and hard of hearing students.* Northridge, CA: PEPNet.

National Institute on Deafness and Other Communication Disorders. (n.d.). Quick statistics. Retrieved from http://www.nidcd.nih.gov/health/statistics/pages/quick.aspx on June 29, 2015.

Newman, L., Wagner, M., Knokey, A.-M., Marder, C., Nagle, K., Shaver, D., Wei, X., with Cameto, R., Contreras, E., Ferguson, K., Greene, S., & Schwarting, M. (2011). *The post-high school outcomes of young adults with disabilities up to 8 years after high school. A report from the national longitudinal transition study-2 (NLTS2)* (NCSER 2011-3005). Menlo Park, CA: SRI International.

Northern, J. L., & Downs, M. P. (2002). *Hearing in children.* New York: Lippincott Williams & Wilkins.

Qi, S., & Mitchell, R. E. (2011). Large-scale academic achievement testing of deaf and hard-of-hearing students: Past, present, and future. *Journal of Deaf Studies and Deaf Education, 17*(1), 1–18.

Schaub, A. (2008). *Digital hearing aids.* New York: Thieme Medical Publishers.

Schraer-Joiner, L. E. (2014). *Music for children with hearing loss.* New York: Oxford University Press.

Simon, J. (2010). Steps toward identifying effective practices in video remote interpreting. *National Consortium of Interpreter Education Centers.*

Stinson, M., Scherer, M., & Walter, G. (1987). Factors affecting the persistence of deaf college students. *Research in Higher Education, 27*, 244–258.

Tye-Murray, N. (2004). *Foundations of aural rehabilitation: Children, adults, and their family members.* Clifton Park, NY: Thomson Delmar Learning.

Walter, G. G., Clarcq, J. R., & Thompson, W. S. (2001). Effect of degree attainment on improving the economic status of individuals who are deaf. *JADARA*, *35*(3), 30–46.

CHAPTER 11

Adaptive Gear, Coalition for Disabled Musicians. (1999). Retrieved from http://www.disabled-musicians.org/equip.html on July 4, 2015.

Agree, E. M., Freedman, V. A., Cornman, J. C., Wolf, D. A., & Marcotte, J. E. (2005). Reconsidering substitution in long-term care: When does assistive technology take the place of personal care? *Journal of Gerontology: Social Sciences*, *60B*(5), S272–S280.

Beers, M., Porter, R., Jones, T., Kaplan, J., & Berkwits, M. (2009). *The Merck manual of diagnosis and therapy* (18th ed.). Whitehouse Station, NJ: Merck.

Clark, C., & Chadwick, D. (1980). *Clinically adapted instruments for the multiply handicapped*. St. Louis, MO: Magnamusic-Baton.

Elliott, B., Macks, P., Dea, A., & Matsko, T. (1982). *Guide to the selection of musical instruments with respect to the physical ability and disability*. Philadelphia: LINC Resources.

Gargiulo, R. M., (2012). *Special education in contemporary society: An introduction to exceptionality*. Thousand Oaks, CA: Sage.

Guralnik, J. H. (2006). Aspects of disability across the life span: Risk factors for disability in late life. In M. J. Field, A. M. Jette, & L. Martin (Eds.), *The workshop in America: A new look* (pp. 157–65). Washington, DC: National Academies Press.

Hedrick, B., Pape, T. L., Heinemann, T. L. B., Ruddell, J. L., & Reis, J. (2006). Employment issues and assistive technology use for persons with spinal cord injury. *Journal of Rehabilitation Research & Development*, *43*(2), 185–198.

Heller, K. (2009). Traumatic spinal cord injury and spina bifida. In K. Heller, P. Forney, P. Alberto, S. Best, & Y. M. Schwartzman (Eds.), *Understanding physical, health, and multiple disabilities* (2nd ed., pp. 94–117). Upper Saddle River, NJ: Pearson Education.

Hoenig, H., Taylor, D. H., & Sloan, F. A. (2003). Does assistive technology substitute for personal assistance among the disabled elderly? *American Journal of Public Health*, *93*(2), 330–337.

Iddon, J., Morgan, D., Loveday, C., Sahakian, B., & Pickard, J. (2006). Neurophysical profile of young adults with spina bifida with and without hydrocephalus. *Journal of Neurology, Neurosurgery & Psychiatry*, *75*, 1112–1118.

Kaye, H. S., Chapman, S., Newcomer, R. J., & Harrington, C. (2006). The personal assistance workforce: Trends in supply and demand. *Health Affairs*, *25*(4), 1113–1120.

Kennedy, J., LaPlante, M. P., & Kaye, H. S. (1997). Need for assistance in the activities of daily living. *Disability Statistics Abstract*, *18*, 1–4.

LaPlante, M. P., Kaye, H. S., Kang, T., & Harrington, C. (2004). Unmet need for physical assistance services: Estimating the shortfall in hours of help and adverse consequences. *Journals of Gerontology*, *59B*(2), S98–S108.

Miller, F. (2005). *Cerebral palsy*. New York: Springer.

My Breath, My Music. Retrieved from http://www.mybreathmymusic.com/en/magic_flute.php on July 4, 2015.

Scherer, M. J., & Glueckauf, R. (2005). Assessing the benefits of assistive technologies for activities and participation. *Technology and Disability, 50*(2), 132–141.

Stumbo, N. J., Martin, J. K., & Hedrick, B. N. (2008). Personal assistance for students with severe physical disabilities in post-secondary education: Is it the deal breakers? *Journal of Vocational Rehabilitation, 30,* 11–20.

Targett, P., Wehman, P., West, M., Dillard, C., & Cifu, G. (2013). Promoting transition to adulthood for youth with physical disabilities and health impairments. *Journal of Vocational Rehabilitation 39,* 229–239.

CHAPTER 12

Akinbami, L. J., Moorman, J. E., Bailey, C., Zahran, H. S., King, M., Johnson, C. A., & Liu, X. (2012). Trends in asthma prevalence, health care use, and mortality in the United States, 2001–2010. *NCHS Data Brief, 94,* 1–8.

American Cancer Society. (2013). *Cancer in young adults.* Retrieved from http://www.cancer.org/acs/groups/cid/documents/webcontent/acspc-042002-pdf.pdf on July 8, 2015.

Balfe, M. (2009). Healthcare routines of university students with type 1 diabetes. *Journal of Advanced Nursing, 65*(11), 2367–2375.

Benlysta. (n.d.). About lupus. Retrieved from http://www.benlysta.com/lupus/index.html on August 4, 2015.

Bleyer, A. (2007). Young adult oncology: The patients and their survival challenges. *CA, a cancer journal for clinicians, 57*(4), 242–255.

Body and Mind. (2012). Managing a chronic disease as a college student. Retrieved from http://www.pennlive.com/bodyandmind/index.ssf/2012/08/managing_a_chronic_disease_as.html on August 6, 2015.

Brown, R. T., & Madan-Swain, A. (1993)/ Cognitive, neuropsychological, and academic sequelae in children with leukemia. *Journal of Learning Disabilities, 26,* 74–90.

Centers for Disease Control. (n.d.). What you should know about sickle cell disease: Nine steps to living well with sickle cell disease in college. Retrieved from http://www.cdc.gov/ncbddd/sicklecell/documents/scd-factsheet_9steps.pdf on August 3, 2015.

Centers for Disease Control and Prevention. (2015). HIV among youth. Retrieved from http://www.cdc.gov/hiv/group/age/youth/index.html on August 4, 2015.

Centers for Disease Control and Prevention. (2009). QuickStats: Percentage of young adults aged 18–29 years with selected chronic conditions, by sex. Retrieved from http://www.cdc.gov/mmwr/preview/mmwrhtml/mm5825a3.htm on July 8, 2015.

Charlton, C. (1997). Learning with epilepsy in the classroom. *Australian Journal of Learning Disabilities, 2,* 30–33.

Chronic Action. (2013). 504 plans for college students with chronic illnesses. Retrieved from http://chronicaction.org/schools/504-plans/ on August 6, 2015.

Crohn's and Colitis Foundation of America. (2015). What are Crohn's and colitis? Retrieved from http://www.ccfa.org/what-are-crohns-and-colitis/what-is-crohns-disease/ on August 3, 2015.

DegreeJungle. (2013). Raise your hand for epilepsy. Retrieved from http://epilepsyu.com/blog/preparing-college-epilepsy/ on August 4, 2015.

Edwards, L. (2014). When it comes to chronic illness, college campuses have a lot to learn. Retrieved from http://cognoscenti.wbur.org/2014/03/05/school-and-health-laurie-edwards on August 5, 2015.

Findeison, R., & Barber, W. H. (1997). Childhood leukemia—A look at the past, the present and the future. *BC Journal of Special Education, 21*, 41–51.

Houman, K. M., & Stapley, J. C. (2013). The college experience for students with chronic illness: Implications for academic advising. *NACADA Journal, 33*(1), 61–70.

Lehr, D. H. (1990). Providing education to students with complex health care needs. *Focus on Exceptional Children, 22*, 1–9.

Lemly, D. C., Lawlor, K., Scherer, E. A., Kelemen, S., & Weitzman, E. R. (2014). College health service capacity to support youth with chronic medical conditions. *Pediatrics 134*(5), 885–891.

Maslow, G., Haydon, A. A., McRee, A. L. & Halpern, C. T. (2012). Protective connections and educational attainment among young adults with childhood-onset chronic illness. *Journal of School Health, 82*(8), 364–370.

Mayo Clinic Staff. (2013). Migraine. Retrieved from http://www.mayoclinic.org/diseases-conditions/migraine-headache/basics/definition/con-20026358 on August 5, 2015.

Mayo Clinic Staff. (2015). High blood pressure (hypertension). Retrieved from http://www.mayoclinic.org/diseases-conditions/high-blood-pressure/basics/definition/con-20019580?p=1 on August 6, 2015.

Mayo Foundation for Medical Education and Research. (2015). Fibromyalgia. Retrieved from http://www.mayoclinic.org/diseases-conditions/fibromyalgia/basics/definition/con-20019243?p=1 on August 4, 2015.

Mellinger, D. C. (2003). Preparing students with diabetes for life at college. *Diabetes Care, 26*(9), 2675–2678.

National Heart, Lung, and Blood Institute. (2014). What is asthma? Retrieved from http://www.nhlbi.nih.gov/health/health-topics/topics/asthma on August 4, 2015.

National Institute of Arthritis and Musculoskeletal and Skin Diseases. (2014). Questions and answers about fibromyalgia. Retrieved from http://www.niams.nih.gov/health_info/fibromyalgia/ on August 4, 2015.

National Institute of Neurological Disorders and Stroke. (2015). What is epilepsy? Retrieved from http://www.ninds.nih.gov/disorders/epilepsy/epilepsy.htm on August 4, 2015.

National Multiple Sclerosis Society. (n.d.). Who gets ms? (epidemiology). Retrieved from http://www.nationalmssociety.org/What-is-MS/Who-Gets-MS on August 6, 2015.

O'Brien, B., Goeree, R., & Streiner, D. (1994). Prevalence of migraine headache in Canada: A population-based survey. *International Journal of Epidemiology, 23*(5), 1020–1026.

Reeb, R. N., & Regan, J. M. (1998). Neuropsychological functioning in survivors of childhood leukemia. *Child Study Journal, 28*, 179–200.

Rheumatoid Arthritis. (2014). RA symptoms. Retrieved from https://www.ra.com on August 4, 2015.

Royster, L., & Marshall, O. (2008). The chronic illness initiative: Supporting college students with chronic illness needs at DePaul University. *Journal of Postsecondary Education and Disability, 20*(2), 120–125.

Shiu, S. (2001). Issues in the education of students with chronic illness. *International Journal of Disability, Development and Education, 48*(3), 269–281.

Stewart, K. (2011). Succeeding at school with fibromyalgia. Retrieved from http://www.everyday-health.com/fibromyalgia/succeeding-at-school-with-fibromyalgia.aspx on August 4, 2015.

Thompson, R. J., & Gustafson, K. E. (1996). *Adaptation to chronic childhood illness.* Washington, DC: American Psychological Association.

Way, J. (2014). The perception of HIV among college students. Retrieved from http://www.hivequal.org/hiv-equal-online/the-perception-of-hiv-among-college-students on August 4, 2015.

Wilson, V. (2010). Students' experiences of managing type 1 diabetes. *Pediatric Nursing, 22*(10), 25–28.

CHAPTER 13

American Psychiatric Association. (2013). *Diagnostic and statistical manual of mental disorders* (5th ed.). Arlington, VA: American Psychiatric Association.

Barkley, R. A. (2014). *Attention deficit hyperactivity disorder: A handbook for diagnosis and treatment* (4th ed.). New York: Guilford.

Barkley, R. A., Fischer, M., Smallish, L., & Fletcher, K. (2002). The persistence of attention-deficit/hyperactivity disorder into young adulthood as a function of reporting source and definition of disorder. *Journal of Abnormal Psychology, 111,* 279–289.

Biederman, J. (2005). Attention deficit/hyperactivity disorder: A selective overview. *Biological Psychiatry, 57*(11), 1215–1220.

Buchanan, T., St. Charles, M., Rigler, M., & Hart, C. (2010). Why are older faculty members more accepting of students with attention deficit hyperactivity disorder? A life-course interpretation. *International Journal of Disability, Development and Education, 57,* 34–43.

Carlson, C., Booth, J. E., Shin, M., & Canu, W. H. (2002). Parent-, teacher-, and self-rated motivational styles in ADHD subtypes. *Journal of Learning Disabilities, 35,* 104–113.

Connor, D. J. (2012). Helping students with disabilities transition to college: 21 tips for students with LD and/or ADD/ADHD. *Teaching Exceptional Children, 44*(5), 16–25.

Costello, C. A., & Stone, S. L. M. (2012). Positive psychology and self-efficacy: Potential benefits for college students with attention deficit hyperactivity disorder and learning disabilities. *Journal of Postsecondary Education and Disability, 25*(2), 119–129.

Evans, S. W., Pelham, W. E., & Smith, B. H. (2001). Dose-response effects of methylphenidate on ecologically valid measures of academic performance and classroom behavior on adolescents with ADHD. *Experimental and Clinical Psychopharmacol, 9,* 163–175.

Faraone, S. V., Beiderman, J., & Lehman, B. K. (1993). Intellectual performance and school failure in children with attention deficit disorder and their siblings. *Journal of Abnormal Psychology, 102,* 624–632.

Forness, S. R., Cantwell, D. P., Swanson, J. M., Hanna, G. L., & Youpa, D. (1991). Differential effects of stimulant medication of reading performance of boys with hyperactivity with and without conduct disorder. *Journal of Learning Disabilities, 24,* 304–310.

Forness, S. R., Swanson, J. M., Cantwell, D. P., Youpa, D., & Hanna, G. L. (1992). Stimulant medication and reading performance: Follow-up on sustained dose in ADHD boys with and without conduct disorders. *Journal of Learning Disabilities, 25,* 115–123.

Gable, S., & Haidt, J. (2005). What (and why) is positive psychology? *Review of General Psychology, 9*, 103–110.

Gaddy, S. (2008). Students with ADHD get "ACCESS" to support network. *Disability Compliance for Higher Education, 13*(12), 3.

Gaub, M., & Carlson, C. (1997). Behavioral characteristics of *DSM*-IV ADHD subtypes in school-based population. *Journal of Abnormal Child Psychology, 25*, 103–111.

Glanzman, M., & Sell, N. (2013). In M. L. Batshaw, N. J. Roizen, & G. R. Lotrecchiano (Eds.), Attention deficits and hyperactivity. *Children with disabilities* (7th ed.). Baltimore, MD: Brookes.

Gregg, N. (2009). *Adolescents and adults with learning disabilities and ADHD: Assessment and accommodation*. New York: Guilford.

Griffiths, K., & Campbell, M. (2009). Discovering, applying and integrating: The process of learning in coaching. *International Journal of Evidence Based Coaching and Mentoring, 7*(2), 16–30.

Hamilton, S.S., & Armando, J. (2008). Oppositional defiant disorder. *American Family Physician, 78*(7), 861–866.

Harbour, W. (2004). *The 2004 AHEAD Survey of Higher Education Disability Service Providers*. Waltham, MA: Association on Higher Education and Disability.

Heilingenstein, E., Guenther, G., Levy, A., Savino, F., & Fulwiler, J. (1999). Psychological and academic functioning in college students with attention deficit hyperactivity disorder. *College Health, 47*, 181–185.

Kadesjo, B., & Gillberg, C. (2001). The comorbidity of ADHD in the general population of Swedish school-age children. *Journal of Child Psychology and Psychiatry, 42*(4), 487–492.

Katz, L. J. (1998). Transitioning to college for the student with ADHD. *ADHD Challenge, 12*, 3–4.

Loe, I. M., & Feldman, H. M., (2007). Academic and educational outcomes of children with ADHD. *Journal of Pediatric Psychology, 32*(6), 643–654.

Mannuzza, S., Gittelman-Klein, R., Bessler, A., Malloy, P., & LaPadula, M. (1993). Adult outcomes of hyperactive boys: Educational achievement, occupational rank, psychiatric status. *Archives of General Psychiatry, 50*, 565–576.

Oslund, C. (2014). *Supporting college and university students with invisible disabilities*. Philadelphia: Jessica Kingsley.

Parker, D. R,. & Banerjee, M. (2007). Leveling the digital playing field: Assessing the learning technology needs of college-bound students with LD and/or ADHD. *Assessment for Effective Intervention, 33*(1), 5–14.

Parker, D. R., & Boutelle, K. (2009). Executive function coaching for college students with learning disabilities and ADHD: A new approach for fostering self-determination. *Learning Disabilities Research & Practice, 24*(4), 204–215.

Quinn, P. O., Ratey, N. A., & Maitland, T. L. (2000). *Coaching college students with AD/HD: Issues and answers*. Silver Spring, MD: Advantage Books.

Rapport, M. D., Denney, C., DuPaul, G. J., & Gradner, M. J. (1994). Attention deficit disorder and methylphenidate: Normalization rates, clinical effectiveness, and response prediction in 76 children. *Journal of American Academy of Child and Adolescent Psychiatry, 33*, 882–893.

Reaser, A., Prevatt, F., Petscher, Y., & Proctor, B. (2007). The learning and study strategies of college students with ADHD. *Psychology in the Schools, 44*(6), 627–638.

Swartz, S. L., Prevatt, F., & Proctor, B. E. (2005). A coaching intervention for college students with attention deficit/hyperactivity disorder. *Psychology in the Schools, 43,* 647–656.

Tominey, M. F. (1996). Attributional style as a predictor of academic success for students with learning disabilities and/or attention deficit disorder in postsecondary education. Paper presented at the International Conference on Learning Disabilities Association. Dallas, TX.

Turnbull, A., Turnbull, R., & Wehmeyer, M. L. (2010). *Exceptional lives: Special education in today's schools.* Upper Saddle River, NJ: Merrill.

Upadhyaya, H. P., Rose, K., Wang, W., O'Rourke, K., Sullivan, B., Deas, D., & Brady, K. T. (2005). Attention-deficit/hyperactivity disorder, medication treatment, and substance use patterns among adolescents and adults. *Journal of Child and Adolescent Psychoparmacol, 15,* 799–809.

Vance, T.A., & Weyandt, L. (2008). Professor perceptions of college students with attention deficit hyperactivity disorder. *Journal of American College Health, 57,* 303–308.

Voeller, K. S. (2004). Attention-deficit hyperactivity disorder (ADHD). *Journal of Child Neurology, 19*(10), 798–814.

Wagner, M., Newman, L., Cameto, R., Garza, N., & Levine, P. (2005). *After high school: A first look at the postschool experiences of youth with disabilities. A report from the National Longitudinal Transition Study-2 (NLTS2).* Menlo Park, CA.

Wallace, B. A., Winsler, A., & NeSmith, P. (1999). Factors associated with success for college students with ADHD: Are standard accommodations helping? Paper presented at the American Educational Research Association. Montreal, Quebec.

Wedlake, M. (2002). Cognitive remediation therapy for undergraduates with ADHD. *ADHD Report, 10*(5), 11–13, 16.

Weyandt, L. L., and DuPaul, G. J. (2008). ADHD in college students: Developmental findings. *Developmental Disabilities, 14,* 311–319.

Weyandt, L. L., Iwaszuk, W., Fulton, K., Ollerton, M., Beatty, N., & Fouts, H. (2003). The international restlessness scale: Performance of college students with and without ADHD. *Journal of Learning Disabilities, 36,* 382–389.

Wilens, T. E. (2004). Attention deficit/hyperactivity disorder and the substance use disorders: The nature of the relationship, subtypes at risk, and treatment issues. *Psychiatric Clinics of North America, 27*(2), 283–301.

Whitworth, L., Kimsey-House, K., Kimsey-House, H., & Sandahl, P. (2007). *Co-active coaching: New skills for coaching people toward success in work and life* (2nd ed.). Mountain View, CA: Davies-Black.

Wolf, L. E. (2001). College students with ADHD and other hidden disabilities: Outcomes and interventions. In J. Wasserstein, L. E. Wolf, & F. F. LeFever (Eds.), *Adults attention deficit disorder: Brain mechanisms and life outcomes* (pp. 385–395). New York: New York Academy of Sciences.

CHAPTER 14

Bawden, H. N., Stokes, A., Camfield, C. S., Camfield, P. R., & Salisbury, S. (1998). Peer relationship problems in children with Tourette's disorder or diabetes mellitus. *Journal of Child Psychology and Psychiatry, 39,* 663–668.

Berardelli, A., Curra, A., Fabbrini, G., Gilio, F., & Manfredi, M. (2003). Pathophysiology of tics and Tourette syndrome. *Journal of Neurology, 250*(7), 781–787.

Bodeck, S., Lappe, C, & Evers, S. (2015). Tic-reducing effects of music in patients with Tourette's syndrome: Self-reported and objective analysis. *Journal of Neurological Sciences, 352,* 41–47.

Boudjouk, P. J., Woods, D. W., Miltenberger, R. G., & Long, E. S. (2000). Negative peer evaluation in adolescents: Effects of tic disorders and trichotillomania. *Child and Family Behavior Therapy, 22,* 17–28.

Caurin, B., Serrano, M., Fernandez-Alvarez, E., Campistol, J., & Perez-Duenas, B. (2014). Environmental circumstances influencing tic expression in children. *European Journal of Paediatric Neurology, 18*(2), 157–162.

Chudley, A., Kilgour, A., Cranston, M., & Edwards, M. (2007). Challenges of diagnosis in fetal alcohol syndrome and fetal alcohol disorder in the adult. *American Journal of Medical Genetics, Part C, Seminars in Genetics, 145*(3), 261–272.

Duquette, C., & Orders, S. (2013). Postsecondary experiences of adults with fetal alcohol spectrum disorder. *International Journal of Special Education, 28*(3), 68–81.

Eapen, V., Fox-Hixley, P., Banerjee, S., & Robertson, M. (2004). Clinical features and associated psychopathology in a Tourette syndrome cohort. *Acta Neurologica Scandinavica, 109*(4), 255–260.

Eddy, C. M., Cavanna, A. E., Gulisano, M. Agodi, A., Barchitta, M., & Cali, P. (2011). Clinical correlates of quality of life in Tourette syndrome. *Movement Disorders, 26,* 735–738.

Friedrich, S., Morgan, S.B., & Devine, C. (1996). Children's attitudes and behavioral intentions toward a peer with Tourette Syndrome. *Journal of Pediatric Psychology, 21,* 307–319.

Gould, H. N., Bakalov, V. K., Tankersley, C., & Bondy, C. A. (2013). High levels of education and employment among women with Turner syndrome. *Journal of Women's Health, 22*(3), 230–235.

Howlin, P., Davies, M., & Udwin, O. (1998). Cognitive functioning in adults with Williams syndrome. *Journal of Child Psychology and Psychiatry, and Allied Disciplines, 39,* 183–189.

Kerns, K. A., Don, A., Mateer, C. A., & Streissguth, A. P. (1997). Cognitive deficits in nonretarded adults with fetal alcohol syndrome. *Journal of Learning Disabilities, 30,* 685–693.

Lees, A. J., Robertson, M., Trimble, M. R., & Murray, N. M. F. (1984). A clinical study of Gilles de la Tourette's syndrome in the United Kingdom. *Journal of Neurology, Neurosurgery & Psychiatry, 47,* 1–8.

Levitan, D. J., Cole, K., Lincoln, A., & Bellugi, U. (2005). Aversion, awareness, and attraction: Investigating claims of hyperacusis in the Williams syndrome phenotype. *Journal of Child Psychology and Psychiatry, 46,* 514–523.

Maher, B. (2001). Music, the brain, and Williams syndrome. *The Scientist Magazine.*

Nigam, A., & Samuel, P. R. (1994). Hyperacusis and Williams syndrome. *Journal of Laryngology & Otology, 108,* 494–496.

Nussey, C., Pistrang, N., & Murphy, T. (2014). Does it help to talk about tics? An evaluation of a classroom presentation about Tourette syndrome. *Child and Adolescent Mental Health, 19*(1), 31–38.

O'Connor, K. P., Gareau, D., & Blowers, G. H. (1994). Personal constructs associated with tics. *British Journal of Clinical Psychology, 33*(2), 151–158.

Robertson, M. M. (2015). Series: A personal 35-year perspective on Gilles de la Tourette syndrome: Assessment, investigations, and management. *Lancet Psychiatry 2*(1), 88–104.

Robertson, M. M., & Cavanna, A. (2008). *Tourette syndrome* (2nd ed.). Oxford: Oxford University Press.

Robertson, M. M., Banerjee, S., Eapen, V., & Hixley, P. (2002). Obsessive-compulsive behavior and depressive symptoms in young people with Tourette syndrome: A controlled study. *European Child and Adolescent Psychiatry, 11*(6), 261–265.

Roessner, V. Banascheswki, T., & Rothenberger, A. (2004). Therapie der Tic-Storungen. *Zeitschrift fur Kinder—und Jugenpsychiatrie und Psychotherapie, 32,* 245–263.

Sacks, O. (1995). *An anthropologist on Mars: Seven paradoxical tales.* London: Picador.

Sacks, O. (1998). *The man who mistook his wife for a hat.* New York: Touchstone.

Sacks, O. (2006). The power of music. *Brain, 129*(10), 2528–2532.

Sacks, O. (2007). *Musicophilia. Tales of music and the brain.* New York: Alfred A. Knopf.

Simpson, K. L. (2013). Syndromes and inborn errors of metabolism. In M. L. Batshaw, N. J. Roizen, & G. R. Lotrecchiano (Eds.), *Children with Disabilities* (7th ed.). Baltimore, MD: Brookes.

State, M. (2011). The genetics of Tourette disorder. *Current Opinion in Genetics & Development, 21*(3), 302–309.

Steinhausen, H. C., Willms, J., & Spohr, H. L. (1993). Long-term psychopathological and cognitive outcome of children with fetal alcohol syndrome. *Journal of the Academy of Child and Adolescent Psychiatry, 32*(5), 990–994.

Stokes, A., Bawden, H. N., Camfield, P. R., Backman, J. E., & Dooley, J. M. (1991). Peer problems in Tourette's disorder. *Pediatrics, 87,* 936–942.

Storch, E. A., Merlo, L. J., Lack, C., Milsom, V. A., Geffken, G. R., Goodman, W. K., & Murphy, T. K. (2007). Quality of life in youth with Tourette's syndrome and chronic tic disorder. *Journal of Clinical Child and Adolescent Psychology, 36,* 217–227.

Streissguth, A.P. & O'Malley, K. (2000). Neuropsychiatric implications and long-term consequences of fetal alcohol spectrum disorders. *Seminars in Clinical Neiropsychiatry, 5*(3), 177–190.

Udwin, O., Yule, W., & Martin, N. (1987). Cognitive abilities and behavioural characteristics of children with idiopathic infantile hypercalcaemia. *Journal of Child Psychology and Psychiatry, and Allied Disciplines, 28,* 297–309.

CHAPTER 15

Baum, S., Ma, J., & Payea, K. (2010). *Education pays, 2010: The benefits of higher education for individuals and their society.* College Board Advocacy & Policy Center. Retrieved from https://trends.collegeboard.org/sites/default/files/education-pays-2010-full-report.pdf on August 10, 2015.

Carnevale, A. P., & Derochers, D. M. (2003). Preparing students for the knowledge economy: What school counselors need to know. *Professional School Counseling, 6*(4), 228–236.

Casale-Giannola, D., & Wilson Kamens, M. (2006). Inclusion at a university: Experiences of a young woman with Down syndrome. *Mental Retardation, 44*(5), 344–352.

Council for Exceptional Children. (2015). *Disability Terms and Definitions.* Retrieved from https://www.cec.sped.org/Special-Ed-Topics/Who-Are-Exceptional-Learners on August 13, 2015.

Flannery, K. B., Yovanoff, P., Benz, M. R., & Kato, M. M. (2008). Improving employment outcomes of individuals with disabilities through short-term postsecondary training. *Career Development and Transition for Exceptional Individuals, 31*(1), 26–36.

Grigal, M., & Hart, D. (2010). *Think college! Postsecondary education options for students with intellectual disabilities.* Baltimore, MD: Brookes.

Grigal, M., Dwyre, A., & Davis, H. (2006). Transition services for students aged 18–21 with intellectual disabilities in college and community settings: Models and implications for success. National Center on Secondary Education and Transition. *Information Brief: Addressing Trends and Developments in Secondary Education and Transition, 5*(5).

Grigal, M., Hart, D., & Migliore, A. (2011). Comparing the transition planning, postsecondary education, and employment outcomes of students with intellectual and other disabilities. *Career Development and Transition for Exceptional Individuals, 34*(1), 4–17.

Grigal, M., Neubert, D. A., & Moon, M.S. (2001). Public school programs for students with significant disabilities in postsecondary settings. *Education and Training in Mental Retardation and Developmental Disabilities, 36,* 244–254.

Hall, M., Kleinert, H. L., & Kearns, J. F. (2000). Going to college! Postsecondary programs for students with moderate to severe disabilities. *Teaching Exceptional Children 32,* 58–65.

Hamill, L. B. (2003). Going to college: The experiences of a young woman with Down syndrome. *Mental Retardation, 41*(5), 340–353.

Hart, D., Zafft, C., & Zimbrich, K. (2001). Creating access to college for all students. *Journal for Vocational Special Needs Education, 23*(2), 19–31.

Hart, D., Zimbrich, K., & Parker, D. R. (2005). Dual enrollment as a postsecondary education option for students with intellectual disabilities. In E. E. Getzel & P. Wehman (Eds.), *Going to college: Expanding opportunities for people with disabilities.* Baltimore, MD: Paul H. Brookes.

Hendrickson, J.M., Carson, R., Woods-Groves, S., Mendenhall, J., & Scheidecker, B. (2013). UI REACH: A postsecondary program serving students with autism and intellectual disabilities. *Education and Treatment of Children, 36*(4), 169–194.

Karp, M. M., Calcagno, J. C., Hughes, K. L., Jeong, D. W., & Bailey, T. (2007). *The postsecondary achievement of participants in dual enrollment: An analysis of student outcomes in two states.* St. Paul: University of Minnesota.

Lee, S. (2009). Overview of the federal Higher Education Opportunities Act reauthorization. Think College Policy Brief No. 1 Boston: Institute for Community Inclusion, University of Massachusetts, Boston.

Marcotte, D. E., Bailey, T., Borkoski, C., & Kienzl, G.S. (2005). The returns of a community college education: Evidence from the national education longitudinal survey. *Educational Evaluation and Policy Analysis, 27*(2), 157–175.

Martinez, D. C., & Queener, J. (2010). Postsecondary education for students with intellectual disabilities. *George Washington HEATH Resource Center.* Winter.

Newman, L., Wagner, M., Knokey, A. M., Marder, C., Nagle, K., Shaver, D., & Schwarting, M. (2011). *The post-high school outcomes of young adults with disabilities up to 8 years after high school.* A report from the national longitudinal transition study-2 (NLTS2). Menlo Park, CA: SRI International. Retrieved from www.nlts2.org/reports/ on August 11, 2015.

Rammler, L., & Wood, R. (1999). *College lifestyle for all!* Middlefield, CT: Rammler & Wood Consultants.

Resonaari Music Centre. (2015). Retrieved from http://www.resonaari.fi/?sid=31 on August 13, 2015.

Think College. (2016). *Think college program database*. Retrieved from http://www.thinkcollege.net/college-search?view=programsdatabase on June 24, 2016.

CHAPTER 16

Abramo, J. M. (2015). Gifted students with disabilities: "Twice exceptionality" in the music classroom. *Music Educators Journal, 101*(4), 62–69.

Al-Hroub, A. (2014). Identification of dual-exceptional learners. In the International Conference on Educational Sciences (5th ed.) *Procedia—Social and Behavioral Sciences, 21*(116), 63–73.

Assouline, S. G., Foley Nicpon, M., & Whiteman, C. (2010). Cognitive and psychosocial characteristics of gifted students with specific learning disabilities. *Gifted Child Quarterly, 54*, 102–115.

Baum, S. M. (1984). Meeting the needs of learning disabled gifted students. *Roeper Review, 7*, 16–19.

Baum, S. M., & Owen, S. V. (1988). High ability/learning disabled students: How are they different? *Gifted Child Quarterly, 32*, 321–326.

Brody, L. E., & Mills, C. J. (1997). Gifted children with learning disabilities: A review of the issues. *Journal of Learning Disabilities, 30*, 282–297.

Campanelli, J., & Ericson, C. (2007). *Twice exceptional guide: Preparing Ohio schools to close the achievement gap for gifted students with disabilities*. Columbus: Ohio Department of Education.

Cash, A. B. (1999). A profile of individuals with autism: The twice-exceptional learner. *Roeper Review, 22*, 22–27.

Chae, P. K., Ji-Hye, K., & Kyung-Sun, N. (2003). Diagnosis of ADHD among gifted children in relation to KEDI-WISC and T.O.V.A. performance. *Gifted Child Quarterly, 47*, 192–202.

Cramond, B. (1995). *The coincidence of attention deficit hyperactivity disorder and creativity*. Storrs: University of Connecticut, National Research Center on the Gifted and Talented.

Foley Nicpon, M., Allmon, A., Sieck, B., & Stinson, R. D. (2011). Empirical investigation of twice-exceptionality: Where have we been and where are we going? *Gifted Child Quarterly, 55*(1), 3–17.

Gallagher, S. A., & Gallagher, J. J. (2002). Giftedness and Asperger's syndrome: A new agenda for education. *Understanding Our Gifted, 14*, 1–9.

Harnett, D. N., Nelson, J. M., & Rinn, A. N. (2004). Gifted or ADHD? The possibility of misdiagnosis. *Roeper Review, 26*, 73–76.

Higgins, D., Baldwin, L., & Pereles, D. (2000). *Comparison of students with and without disabilities*. Unpublished manuscript.

Klin, A., Volkmar, F. R., & Sparrow, S. (2000). *Asperger syndrome*. New York: Guilford.

McCoach, D. B., Kehle, T. J., Bray, M. A., & Siegle, D. (2001). Best practices in the identification of gifted students with learning disabilities. *Psychology in the Schools, 38*(5), 403–411.

Neihart, M. (2008). Identifying and providing services to twice exceptional children. In S. I. Pfeiffer (Ed.), *Handbook of giftedness in children: Psychoeducational theory, research, and best practices* (pp. 115–137). New York: Springer.

Nielsen, M. E. (2002). Gifted students with learning disabilities: Recommendations for identification and programming. *Exceptionality, 10*, 93–111.

Reis, S. M., & McCoach, D. B. (2002). Underachievement in gifted and talented students with special needs. *Exceptionality, 10*, 113–125.

Webb, J. T., & Latimer, D. (1993). ADHD and children who are gifted. *Exceptional children, 60*, 183–184.

Weinfeld, R., Barnes-Robinson, L., Jeweler, S., & Shevitz, B. R. (2006). *Smart kids with learning difficulties: Overcoming obstacles and realizing potential.* Waco, TX: Prufrock Press.

CHAPTER 17

Bryant, D. P. & Bryant, B. R. (2012). *Assistive technology for people with disabilities* (2nd ed.). Boston: Allyn and Bacon.

Edyburn, D. L. (2013). Critical issues in advancing the special education technology evidence base. *Exceptional Children, 80*(1), 7–24.

Individuals with Disabilities Education Improvement Act of 2004, 20 U.S.C. ss 1401, 1481.

King-Sears, M. E., & Evmenova, A. S. (2007). Premises, principles, and processes for integrating technology into instruction. *Teaching Exceptional Children, 40*(1), 6–14.

Scherer, M. J., & Craddock, G. (2002). Matching person & technology (MPT) assessment process. *Technology and Disability, 14*, 125–131.

Simon, J. A. (2011). Legal issues in serving students with disabilities in postsecondary education. In M. S. Huger (Ed.), *Fostering the increased integration of students with disabilities* (pp. 95–107). San Francisco, CA: Jossey-Bass.

Touch Autism. (2014). Autism Apps. Retrieved from http://touchautism.com/app/autism-apps/ on December 4, 2014.

US Congress (1988). US Congress, Public Law 100–406, Technology-Related Assistance for Individuals with Disabilities Act of 1988.

Zabala, J., Bowser, G., & Jorsten, J. (2005). SETT and ReSETT: Concepts for AT implementation. *Closing the Gap, 23*(5), 1–4.

Index